Crawling over a tree trunk, Simon in his exhaustion miscalculated and lost his footing. Swearing, he groped for the big flashlight. He found it, and thankfully, was able to switch it back on, only to find himself staring into a slack-jawed human skull. In his fall he had crushed the rib cage of a skeleton.

Simon flung himself off the corpse, scuttling backward until he hit the wall of the mine, his flashlight trained on the corpse.

He found himself gripping the flashlight as if it were a weapon, with his injured hand pressed to his pounding heart. He raked the skeleton with the light. Whoever it was had been dead a long time. Dust hovered over its rib cage, where Simon had crushed it in his fall. So much for avoiding corpses.

★

"...there's much to admire, from insights into ginseng harvesting to explanations of Indian-trail trees, from multi-casserole southern family dinners to devious plotting."

—Kirkus Reviews

THE FUGITIVE
KING

SARAH R. SHABER

W🌐RLDWIDE®

TORONTO • NEW YORK • LONDON
AMSTERDAM • PARIS • SYDNEY • HAMBURG
STOCKHOLM • ATHENS • TOKYO • MILAN
MADRID • WARSAW • BUDAPEST • AUCKLAND

In memory of
Lynette Glazener Spencer
1953-2000

"Fare thee well, brave heart."
—Shakespeare

THE FUGITIVE KING

A Worldwide Mystery/March 2004

First published by St. Martin's Press LLC.

ISBN 0-373-26485-2

Printed in U.S.A.

Acknowledgments

I want to thank Captain Paula Townsend, chief deputy of the Watauga County Sheriff's Office, for her invaluable help and assistance; Debra Rezelli, for drawing the map of the Shaw homeplace; Charles Wilcox, for giving me a tour of his beautiful Christmas-tree farm, *Appalachian Evergreens,* and for talking about his legendary family business, the Wilcox Drug Company; and the staff of the Appalachian Room at Appalachian State University Library.

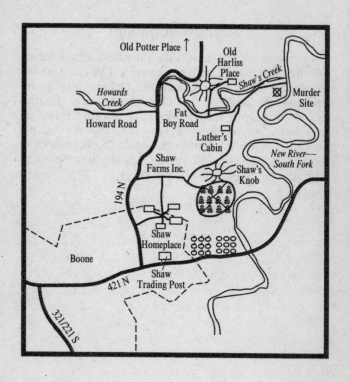

Old Potter Place ↑

Old Harliss Place

Shaw's Creek

Murder Site

Howards Creek

Fat Boy Road

Howard Road

Luther's Cabin

New River— South Fork

Shaw Farms Inc.

Shaw's Knob

194 N

Shaw Homeplace

Boone

Shaw Trading Post

421 N

321/221 S

PROLOGUE

A THICK rhododendron branch whipped back, smacking the face of the older of the two men forcing their way through dense vegetation near the base of the Blue Ridge Parkway.

"Damn it," the man said. "That hurt!" He rubbed the red weal on his cheek, then stooped over to retrieve his sunglasses and his black baseball cap, both knocked off by the swinging branch. He jammed the cap back on his head and wiped sweat from his face with the tail of his black polo shirt. Both cap and shirt bore the logo of the North Carolina Alcohol Law Enforcement Agency. The ALE agent wore a gun holstered on one side of his belt and a hatchet and a cell phone on the other. "I swear the jungles in Vietnam weren't any thicker than this," he said. "Where the hell are we?"

The younger man wore the khaki uniform of a U.S. Park Ranger. He shifted his heavy belt, hung with a sidearm, a satellite telephone, and a machete, and realigned it on his waist. He was still uncomfortable. Most days he didn't tote around this much stuff; just a can of Mace for subduing unruly tourists. The ranger shaded his eyes and looked up, where he could barely make out the curve of the scenic highway cut into the side of a mountain ridge about ten miles from Boone, North Carolina.

"I'd guess we're about four hundred and some feet below Milepost Two-forty and maybe fifty feet from the base of the mountain," he said.

"Are we inside or outside the parkway?" the ALE agent asked. In some places the Blue Ridge Parkway, a national park, was only two hundred feet wide; crimes committed inside its boundaries were under federal jurisdiction.

The day before a Watauga County helicopter on a routine scan for marijuana fields spotted something suspicious partly obscured in the dense forest at the foot of the parkway. When the sheriff brought a photo to the U.S. Park Service office, "still" leapt into the minds of everyone who saw it. The object was about the right size, shape, and color to be a big one. The rangers on duty that morning drew straws, and Ranger Gwyn got the job of guiding a North Carolina ALE agent to the site.

Breathing heavily, the ALE agent glared at the Catawba rhododendron, big as a school bus, blocking his path. The rhododendron hung heavy with plate-sized white blossoms, each with a couple of bees dancing attendance. "What I wouldn't give for a little Agent Orange right now," he said. He pulled out his hatchet and hacked at the bush, sending blossoms and branches flying.

"Here," the park ranger said quickly, unstrapping the machete from his belt, "let me do that."

Clearing a narrow path ahead of himself and the agent, the ranger made quick progress toward their goal.

"Almost there," he said. Instinctively the two men rested a hand on their sidearms.

Then, as he pushed carefully through the feathery,

drooping limbs of a hemlock tree, the ALE agent puffing along behind him, the ranger saw it.

Overgrown with vines and completely rusted-out, the old truck lay with its front bumper half-buried in the dirt. A dogwood tree, thick with emerald green leaves and scarlet berries, grew right up through the roof of the cab. The short truck bed rested almost vertically on the slope of the mountain. The ranger noted the pickup's round fenders and thick radiator grille, wide as a giant's smile.

"What is it?" the ALE agent asked.

"It's a Ford pickup," the ranger said. "Old, maybe early fifties."

"What's it doing here?"

"Don't know. Let's take a look at it."

"Be my guest," the agent said. "It's on parkway property." The agent sat heavily on the ground and slumped against a tree. He chugged half the fluid from his water bottle. The crisp mountain air was deceiving— you could still get overheated and dehydrated from climbing up and down these steep slopes.

The ranger circled the truck, inspecting it carefully, then climbed up the slope behind it. He disappeared behind the truck bed, pushing aside vines and branches as he tried to get a look at the license plate.

The ALE agent was restless and tired. He wanted to get back to his office. What the hell was the ranger looking for? It was obvious to him that the old truck had been abandoned, pushed off the edge of the parkway to get rid of it. Showed some ingenuity on the owner's part. Most of these hillbillies sat their worn-out vehicles up on cinder blocks in the backyard. It was no wonder the truck had been mistaken for a still from the air—the size was about right, and the rust color suggested copper.

The ranger slid down the slope, dusting off his hands when he reached the bottom.

"Truck's been here since 1958," the ranger said, "that's the date on the license plate." He peered through the driver's side window, rubbing at the dirt caked thick. Then he drenched his handkerchief with water from his bottle and scrubbed at the window.

"Let's go," the ALE agent said. "This is a waste of time."

"Not really," the park ranger said. "Someone's still inside."

ONE

"NO ONE OUR AGE sneaks out of bed and slips away in the middle of the night anymore," Simon said.

"I'm just not comfortable staying here all night," Julia said. "Chalk it up it to a traditional Southern upbringing, honey, and take me home. I've got to be in court at nine in the morning."

"I thought it was men who couldn't commit," Simon said.

Still grumbling under his breath, Simon pressed the accelerator with his bare foot, backing slowly down his driveway and into the street. He set his windshield wipers to their slowest speed to deal with the gentle rain, almost a mist, that had been falling all evening. The rain was a blessing; Raleigh had sweltered all day and into the early evening. He and Julia had abandoned his screened porch to eat dinner inside, where his antique air conditioner labored to cool his house down into the high seventies. If July was this hot, what would August be like?

It wasn't far from Simon's home in the old 1920s neighborhood of Cameron Park to Julia's new townhouse near the Governor's Mansion. They lived "inside the beltline," in Raleigh parlance, where pre-war neighborhoods, state capitol buildings, museums, and colleges clustered. Simon taught at Kenan College, a tiny school

compared with that red-and-white behemoth, North Carolina State University, which sprawled a few blocks
away down Hillsborough Street. Two other prestigious
institutions, Duke University and the University of North
Carolina at Chapel Hill, were nearby. But Simon preferred teaching at Kenan, despite the Pulitzer Prize that
could have been his ticket to the Ivy League. Julia was
a bit of an underachiever, too, although she wasn't as
comfortable with it as Simon was. She was legal counsel
to the Raleigh Police Department. She grumbled about
the low pay and constant on-call status, but made no real
effort to leave the job.

As Simon turned onto Jones Street, he slowed, startled
by the sight of a rack of rotating red-and-blue lights,
blurry in the rain. A Capitol Police car was parked at a
slant across the road, leaving just one lane for traffic.
Simon saw the policeman inside speaking into his radio,
and could hear the crackling static of a reply. A block
further along Simon came upon a State Highway Patrol
car. Two officers were inside, their Smokey-the-Bear
hats bent over a dashboard computer screen.

"I wonder what's going on?" Julia asked.

"I have no idea, but it must be big, if both the Capitol
Police and the Highway Patrol are involved. I wonder
where your colleagues are?"

He found out at the intersection of Peace and Blount
Streets, where a Raleigh policeman, wearing a bright
yellow rain slicker, directed him to go left, instead of
straight toward the Governor's Mansion and the row of
townhouses where Julia lived. Simon flicked on his turn
signal to indicate a right turn, and pointed right. The
policeman shook his head, and forcefully signaled to
Simon's left with the two flashlights he held in his

hands. The bright beams formed tunnels of light in the rain.

"Hope the governor's okay," Julia said.

As Simon turned the wheel to follow the policeman's directions, Julia took his arm to restrain him.

"Pull over," she said. "I want to find out what's going on."

Simon obediently did so. Julia stuck her arm out her window, waving her ID at the policeman who approached them.

"Hey there, Ms. McGloughlin," he said, touching the tip of his hat to her. Without a pause he nodded to Simon. "Hello, Dr. Shaw."

"What's up?" Julia asked.

"Escaped convict," the policeman said.

"Someone broke out of Central Prison?" Simon said. The new prison was supposed to be impregnable, a good thing considering its proximity to downtown.

"Nah, that place is escape-proof," the policeman said. "This guy was incarcerated at Wake Correctional Center. He's been working the evening shift at the Governor's Mansion for years. Tonight he assaulted a guard, took his shotgun, and was out the back door and over the wall before anyone could sound the alarm."

"He can't be dangerous," Julia said, "if he's been working at the Mansion."

The soft rain was falling a little harder, and the policeman scrunched up inside his rainsuit.

"What was he in for?" Simon asked.

"Murder."

"Uh, oh," Julia said.

"It was a domestic thing. He pled guilty."

"I didn't know you could serve a life sentence for murder in minimum security," Simon said.

"You can if you earn enough points for good behavior," Julia said.

"This guy's had no infractions during the forty years he's been in prison," the policeman said. "But he's considered armed and dangerous now, so keep your doors locked tonight, Ms. McGloughlin."

A FEW MINUTES LATER Simon parked in front of Julia's place.

"See?" Simon said. "That policeman recognized me. Everyone knows we're a couple."

"Get over it," Julia said. "It's not as if you want to stay here overnight."

"All those down pillows you've got make me sneeze," Simon said.

Julia collected her oversized bag from the floor of the car. Simon leaned over and surprised her with a tender kiss. She hated it when he did that. She preferred to know in advance when intimacy was likely, so she could feel in control of herself. She didn't want to like Simon any more than she already did. When the two of them started dating, she told herself that it was just until she found Mr. Right, who was taller, richer, and more ambitious than Simon.

"Let me walk you to the door," Simon said.

"Not necessary," Julia said. "I'm packing heat, remember?" She tipped her open handbag toward him so that he could see her handgun. Simon harrumphed.

"Don't scoff," she said. "You never know when you might need one of these babies." She patted the revolver affectionately before closing her handbag.

Simon and Julia differed on the issue of civilian handgun ownership. Simon opposed a new North Carolina state law making it legal for almost anyone to carry a concealed weapon, for "protection." Of course Julia was practically a policewoman, and frequented the Raleigh Police Department shooting range to practice.

ONCE INSIDE his own home Simon locked his front door but didn't bother to turn on the lights. Glare from the streetlights outside his windows lit his way around the first floor of his Craftsman-style bungalow.

He picked up a hair elastic off the floor, all Julia had left behind. She kept nothing permanently at his house, not even a toothbrush. Simon tried not to think what that meant about their relationship. He hooked the elastic over a doorknob, where Julia could find it the next time she was over.

He wasn't really hungry, but he opened his refrigerator door out of habit. He tore a wing and a thigh off the chicken they had for dinner. He munched on the thigh and broke the wing into sections, putting them in his cats' bowls. Where were his cats, anyway? They should be rubbing up against his legs and whining.

"Ladies?" he called out. There was no response.

Worried, Simon opened the back door and called them. Still no cats. Then he heard a scuffling noise behind him. He looked under his kitchen table, and, sure enough, there they were, Maybelline, who couldn't be true, and her daughter Ruby, who took her love to town, hunkered down and scrunched up against the back wall of the kitchen.

"What's wrong with you?" he asked. "There's roast chicken out here. Teriyaki, your favorite. Come on out."

The cats didn't move. Maybe they were frightened by the heat lighting flashing outside. Or maybe they weren't hungry. They'd had plenty of scraps while he and Julia fixed dinner.

Simon got a Coke out of the refrigerator and walked into the living room on his way upstairs to bed.

Just as he stepped on the bottom tread of his staircase, he realized why his cats were cowering in the kitchen. He sensed, rather than saw, that a stranger was in his house. He turned quickly, looking for something to use to defend himself, wishing his baseball bat was within reach instead of upstairs under his bed.

"Don't do it, Professor Shaw," a voice said.

The man sat in the living room next to the fireplace in Simon's favorite chair, the Mission armchair upholstered in cracked brown leather that he'd inherited from his parents. The intruder was dressed in a tuxedo with the top shirt button undone and his tie loosened. A shotgun lay across his lap, casually pointed toward Simon, right at his lower body.

"Don't move," the man said. "I haven't shot a gun in years, but believe me, I haven't forgotten how."

"What do you want?" Simon asked. "I've got a little cash on me, and…"

"Sit down, Professor Shaw," the man said, waving Simon into the living room with his shotgun. Simon did the obvious. He went to sit on his sofa opposite the intruder. He felt fairly calm, except for the little tic that fluttered over his right eye. When his adrenaline stopped flowing, whenever that was, he'd probably get a migraine.

"I know who you are," Simon said. "The cops are all over downtown. You're the prisoner who escaped from the Governor's Mansion tonight. You assaulted the guard."

"Assaulted? They said that?" the man laughed. "The guard was eating leftover appetizers with both hands. His shotgun was leaning up against the wall ten feet away. I just picked it up and locked him in the pantry. He promised to give me fifteen minutes' head start before he started hollering if I said he'd put up a fight.''

"So," Simon said, trying to sound conversational. "You know my name?"

"I read about you in the newspaper. I don't want to hurt you," the man continued, slightly raising the shotgun off his lap and then lowering it to his knee again. "I just want to talk to you about something, okay?"

"Talk away," Simon said.

"I've messed up what there is left of my life by coming here. After I get caught, which I'm not deluded enough to think won't happen, I'll get sent to Central Prison, maximum security. No more working at the mansion, no television, no money to spend at the canteen, no one to play checkers with. If I don't have your full attention, I might get a little frustrated. And I'm a good shot, at least I used to be. I won't hesitate to blow off your kneecap if you don't listen to me. I got nothing to lose."

"I'm listening, I'm listening."

Simon's captor was clean-shaven, with salt-and-pepper hair cut very short, small square hands, a thick body, black eyes, and an olive complexion. His face suggested something familiar to Simon, something not personal, but ethnic, but he couldn't place it. He was probably taller than Simon, but that wasn't saying much. Simon guessed he was around five-six or seven. He wasn't overweight, but he carried some fat around his middle. It was hard to say how old he was. His face was smooth and unlined, but then he'd spent most of his life indoors, in prison, hadn't he?

"You're a hard man to get in touch with," the man said.

"You could have written," Simon said, "or called. You didn't have to break into my house."

"I wrote and called several times. Your secretary put me off."

Of course she did. Ever since he had solved that World War II-era murder at Pearlie Beach, Simon had been fending off requests for his services. The term "forensic historian" had been bandied about by the local newspaper and TV stations. *The North Carolina Historical Review* printed an extra two thousand copies of the issue that contained his article on Carl Chavis's murder. He'd been the *News and Observer*'s Tar Heel of the week and appeared on public television's *N. C. People*. Simon enjoyed all the attention, to a revolting degree, according to his friends, but not enough to consciously continue his sleuthing. Solving Chavis's murder had opened decades-old wounds and impacted so many innocent lives, it had exhausted him emotionally. So he got a new, unlisted, home phone number, and his secretary informed all who inquired after him that he was not for hire.

"My name is Roy Freedman, I'm sixty-three years old, and I've spent the last forty-odd years in prison for murder. I didn't do it."

"No, not really," Simon said, and instantly regretted his sarcasm.

But Freedman just grinned.

"Yeah," he said. "There are no guilty people in prison. Furthermore, I pled guilty. I had to. Otherwise any jury raised in Watauga County would have sent me to the gas chamber. But I digress."

Freedman made sure that his shotgun stayed aimed right at Simon's knee as he dug into his pocket. He retrieved two folded newspaper clippings, which he shook open with his free hand. He dropped one in his lap and handed one to Simon.

"This was in the newspaper a few weeks ago," he said. "Did you see it?"

"Yeah," Simon said, scanning the account of a mountain car wreck. He hadn't read the story through. It reminded him too much of his parents' fatal accident. A tractor trailer with locked brakes forced them off U.S. 421 going down the Blue Ridge Mountains. Their car crashed through a guardrail and landed in a pine tree three hundred feet below, killing them both instantly.

"Read it," Freedman said.

Simon read it.

PARKWAY GIVES UP MORE OF ITS DEAD

The U.S. Park Service announced today that the skeleton of a young woman was discovered inside a truck beneath the Blue Ridge Parkway on Friday. According to a spokesman for the Park Service, the remains were found in a Ford pickup bearing a 1958 license plate. The medical examiner's preliminary report described the remains as those of a young female whose corpse had most likely been at the scene since that time. The skeleton has been sent to the North Carolina medical examiner's office in Chapel Hill for autopsy. The sheriff's office, is searching its records for missing persons reports filed in 1958.

The state division of motor vehicles expects to identify the owner of the pickup from its license registration within twenty-four hours, a DMV spokesman said earlier today.

Ranger Gary Gwyn, who with an unidentified ALE agent discovered the remains, speculated that the victim had a single car accident, plunging 450 feet off the parkway into dense vegetation where the vehicle lay undiscovered until now.

This accident is not the first of its kind. The parkway is filled with brushy, overgrown areas that can conceal wreckage. Unwitnessed wrecks can be lost for days or weeks, and now, it seems, even for years. Ranger Gwyn cited speeding, driving while impaired, and driving while sleepy as the chief causes of accidents.

"The parkway is just a very unforgiving road. It was designed as a scenic route, not as a commuter road. You have to be alert and attentive. It requires your full attention."

When Simon looked up from the first clipping, Freedman handed him the second.

PARKWAY SKELETON IDENTIFIED
AS MURDER VICTIM

The Watauga Sheriff's Office today announced that the skeleton found in a Ford pickup below the parkway is the corpse of Eva Potter, who was murdered forty years ago.

Deputy Sheriff George Lyall, whose uncle by marriage, Micah Guy, was sheriff of Watauga County at that time, said that Potter's sister alerted the office to the possibility that the corpse was Eva as soon as it was discovered.

Eva Potter disappeared in the summer of 1958. A blanket soaked with blood, a bloody knife, and the remains of a picnic lunch were discovered at a local lover's lane. Potter's corpse was never found. Her suitor, Roy Freedman, confessed to her murder and is currently serving a life sentence in Wake Correctional Institute in Raleigh.

According to *Watauga Democrat* news files, Freedman admitted that he had killed Potter when she refused to marry him. He insisted, however, that he had not moved her body.

"I think Freedman disposed of the body by pushing Potter and his truck off the parkway. I reckon he felt he couldn't get the death penalty without a corpse," Lyall said.

"That's quite a story," Simon said.

"That's nothin'," Freedman said. "It's what the paper left out that's interesting. It'll take me a while to tell it to you. You got any beer? I eat good at the Mansion, but I haven't had a beer in forty years."

Simon went into the kitchen, followed close behind by Freedman carrying his shotgun in the crook of one arm. Simon took two beers out of the refrigerator, and handed one to Freedman. Freedman tipped it back and drained it, without taking his eyes off Simon.

"God, that's good," he said, smacking his lips. Simon handed him the second.

"Don't think I'm going to get drunk," he said, motioning Simon back into the living room. "I'm going to stay in control, believe me."

They settled back down in the living room, looking like old friends about to have a friendly chat, except for the shotgun. Freedman put one foot up on the coffee table and sipped on his second beer.

"Comfortable?" Simon asked. "Can I get you a pillow?"

"You know," Freedman said, "I knew your father."

"Really?" Simon said, taken aback.

"Yeah. I was a student at Appalachian State Teachers College when all this happened. I had my life planned out. I was the first person in my family to go to college. I was going to teach history in high school back in Kentucky, coach football, get married, have a bunch of kids, and hunt and fish with my sons for the rest of my life."

Simon placed Freedman in the chronology of his own life. Appalachian State Teachers College had become Appalachian State University in 1967, a couple of years before his parents had met. Simon was born in 1970, twelve years after Freedman had been sent to prison for life without parole. In 1958 his father would have just started teaching in Boone.

"Your daddy taught me Greek and Roman history. I thought I was going to hate it, but it sure was interesting. He talked about Athens and Rome like they were just down the road, and about Cicero and Aristotle like they were his old friends."

"That was him, all right," Simon said.

"And you know what? Sometimes he would start talking in Latin! We'd have to stop him and remind him that we were just country boys at teachers' college, and we didn't understand a word he said. There was this one thing he used to say to us all the time. Ipsa science something."

"Ipsa scientia, potestas est."

"That's it! 'Knowledge is power.' I forget who said it."

"Francis Bacon."

Freedman leaned forward, studying Simon's face in the dim light.

"You don't look much like him," Freedman said.

"I know," Simon said. "My mother was from Queens. I take after her." Rachel Simon Shaw was a petite woman with black curly hair and dark brown eyes. She was a public-health nurse, moved by the television pictures of poor, dirty, and hungry Appalachian mountain folk that Lyndon Johnson plastered all over the news to pressure Congress to back his War on Poverty. Rachel found plenty to do while on staff at the Public Health Department in Boone, and later as its director. Her family in New York never stopped begging her to come home, but she fell in love with the mountains, and Simon's father, in that order, as Simon's dad used to say.

"Please," Simon said, "finish your story. I'm eager for you to put that shotgun down."

"I can understand that. Well, the summer after my sophomore year I decided to stay in Boone to work. Folks were making good money foraging for herbs and selling them to Wilcox Drug Company. They would buy all the catnip, witch hazel, and ginger you could bring them. And ginseng, of course, it was worth a fortune even back then."

"Green gold," Simon said. "My cousin and I dug it up wherever we could find it, too."

"You couldn't harvest it but every seven years," Freedman said. "And for some reason the wild stuff was better than any you could grow. Anyhow, there was a guy living in the boarding house with me who foraged for a living. His name was Earl Barefoot. His daddy died, and Earl left Boone to go back home to Tennessee before Eva died, but before he left he taught me to forage and showed me his favorite spots.

"I boarded with the Potters. They had two daughters, Eva and June, who were both real pretty. It started out to be a good summer. I worked hard and made money. I fell in love with Eva, and we courted when we could, but her parents watched us like hawks. We sneaked out to go on that picnic, and I did ask her to marry me. She said she wouldn't because I was a Melungeon, and she didn't want to have Melungeon kids. She said if she did, her family would disown her.''

Simon's impression of the man's ethnicity clicked. Melungeons were what anthropologists called a "tri-racial isolate." Descended from whites, African-Americans, and Native Americans in the Appalachians, they intermarried in isolation until they developed a racial identity and a culture all their own. In a time when any person who wasn't obviously white was a "free person of color" and could be assigned to segregated schools and otherwise discriminated against, Melungeons insisted that they were descended from Spanish and Portuguese explorers who searched the Appalachians for gold and silver in the seventeenth century, or from the Welsh prince Medoc, who left Wales in the twelfth century and never returned.

Since the sixties, Melungeons, like other American minorities, had come out of the closet. Anthropologists wrote books and articles about them. Melungeons formed societies to preserve their culture and study their origins. Melungeon researchers claimed that Elvis, Abe Lincoln, and Ava Gardner were Melungeon. In 1958, would a white Appalachian family have wanted a daughter to marry a Melungeon? Definitely not. Would a jury have been biased against one? Simon wasn't sure.

''When Eva said we couldn't get married, I was that upset that I just walked away from her and kept going. I wandered around the woods for hours. When I got back to the house it was late, and the sheriff was there. I didn't touch her, I swear.''

''But you admitted you were guilty.''

"Eva's daddy and the sheriff made me confess. They beat me and threatened to lynch me. They had the rope hung over the tree in the backyard and were dragging out a kitchen stool for me to stand on when I confessed. What kind of chance would I have had in front of a jury? Me being Melungeon and all."

Simon shook his head.

"What? You think you wouldn't admit to a murder you didn't commit to save your own life?"

"I don't know."

"Trust me, you would have. Anyway, my lawyer told me I wouldn't have a chance in court. No jury would take my word about the confession against that of the sheriff and Mr. Potter. I'd already admitted that Eva and I were on that picnic together that day. When she didn't come home, her sister told their daddy where we'd gone. When he got to the place, he found blood soaked into the blanket, and blood was all over the knife she had brought to cut the pie. There was no sign of Eva or my truck. Days went by while I sat in jail and waited. Search parties combed those mountains and never found her. My lawyer worked a deal so I could plead guilty to first-degree murder and get life without parole. You don't think you would have done that? Well, I did. And I got used to the idea I was going to die in prison. There wouldn't be any point in getting out anyway. Eva's daddy would just kill me himself the second he could get at me. Part of me felt like I deserved to go to prison for leaving her alone, and part of me has been praying all these years that something, somehow, would happen to reopen the case."

"Couldn't you petition the authorities, or something?" Simon said. "Say there was new evidence?"

"Did you know that a prison inmate can't get a free

lawyer unless he's on Death Row? I can't raise ten thousand dollars for a deposit for a lawyer to file the right motions for me. Besides, the guys in prison who know a lot of law, they say that finding Eva's body alone means nothing. To get a new trial, new evidence has to prove that I didn't do it. Finding her body just shows I got rid of her corpse to avoid the gas chamber, like everyone said in the first place."

"I'm not trying to be negative about this," Simon said, with an eye on Freedman's shotgun, "but I don't know what I can do. I don't see that finding her body means much, either."

"It stirs things up. People start to remember. Go up there. I read about how you solved those old crimes, lots older than this one. And you grew up in Boone. You know people. Ask questions. Help me out. The difference between 1958 and now is it ain't shameful to be Melungeon anymore, and I got no other hope."

Before Simon could answer, Freedman suddenly swung his arm in anger and knocked over a stack of books on the table next to his chair. Then he jabbed toward Simon with his shotgun.

"What the hell. Of course you'd say yes. Then after I gave myself up and went quietly back to prison, you'd back out."

"No," Simon said. "That's not true."

Simon's grandfather clock struck two in the morning, and both men started. Freedman stroked the stubble on his chin, thinking.

"You and I could start driving now and be a long way away before anyone missed you," Freedman said. "What kind of car you got?"

This was not a good development, thought Simon. If Freedman forced him on the run with him, his odds of surviving were greatly diminished. Simon had office hours in the morning, but no one would really miss him until it was time to proctor the afternoon exam for North Carolina History. By then he and Freedman would be hundreds of miles away.

"Look," Simon said. "I'll promise you one thing. I'll look into this for you, and if I think I can help, I'll go on up to Boone. I swear I'll do it, okay? If you leave this house with me, God knows what will happen, to both of us."

"Let me think," Freedman said.

"You think about the consequences of first-degree kidnapping, I've got to use the bathroom."

The barrel of Freedman's shotgun followed Simon to the bathroom, but his eyes focused on the ceiling. He was probably calculating the driving time from Raleigh to Canada. Or maybe Mexico. Simon's cordless telephone rested in a niche in the short hall between the living room and the bathroom. With his back to Freedman, Simon smoothly and silently removed the phone from its carriage and, holding it up against his body to conceal it, took it with him into the bathroom. There he did his business and flushed the toilet, hoping the noise would drown out the sound of him dialing 911. It didn't. The bathroom door slammed open, crashing against the outside wall. Simon stood with the phone in his hand. He could hear the 911 dispatcher on the other end of the line, but he couldn't understand what she was saying. For the first time that evening, he felt real fear nibbling at the edges of his composure. He prayed that Freedman would just take his car and run for it.

"Oh, what the hell," Freedman said. He handed the shotgun to Simon, stock first, and reached for the phone. "Give me that. It'll look better if I turn myself in."

TWO

DETECTIVE SERGEANT Otis Gates's huge hand squeezed Simon's shoulder.

"Pleased to see you alive," Gates said. "You okay?"

"Sure, fine." Simon had been up all night. His eyelids felt like sandpaper.

Gates put down a Styrofoam cup of steaming liquid and a Krispy Kreme bag on the battered metal table in front of Simon.

"The coffee's just the way you like it," Gates said, "way too much milk and sugar. The doughnuts are hot."

"Bless you," Simon said. He slurped the coffee and opened the bag, inhaling the energizing odor of hot sugar and fat.

The two glazed doughnuts had to be breakfast. Simon needed to be in his office by eight o'clock. The final exam for North Carolina History was scheduled for one that afternoon, and he'd promised his students he'd hold office hours all morning. Then he had to proctor the exam, grade thirty-odd term papers, and correct the exams, all so he could turn in the session's grades to the Student Records Office tomorrow morning. Oh, and then there were the fifteen papers from his Topics in Southern History seminar that he'd intended to mark last night, when he was taken hostage instead. He would just have to catch up on last night's sleep tonight, or was it already tomorrow?

Otis Gates, a senior member of the Major Crimes Division, Raleigh Police Department, pulled up a chair and sat down next to Simon in the interview room at the police station. The single barred window was closed tight. A floor fan rotated slowly, moving warm air around the room. Gates noticed a vulgar expression etched onto the table surface, and set his briefcase carefully over it. He took a packet of cigarettes out of his pocket, and withdrew the first of the three he allowed himself a day.

"Mind?" he asked.

"No," Simon said. "I'm considering taking it up myself."

"Alcohol is better for your health," Gates said, "but unfortunately my employer frowns on drinking at work." He did keep a bottle of Jack Daniels in his bottom desk drawer, Simon knew, having partaken of it once. At that time, Otis had gone down the hall and punched out before returning to his office, closing the door, and pouring three fingers for each of them.

"I'm supposed to read this statement and sign it if it's okay and correct it if it's not," Simon said. "But I can't concentrate. I keep losing my place about halfway through." He put the statement down on the table and massaged his temples with his fingertips. "By the way, how did you know I was here?"

"Heard all about it at the shift briefing this morning," Gates said. "All the guys were wondering how a quiet, scholarly history professor such as yourself managed to get taken hostage by an escaped murderer. Didn't surprise me, though. I know you."

Simon and Gates met when Gates consulted Simon

about an unsolved murder dating to 1926. During the ensuing investigation, which relied heavily on Simon's historian's skills, they became close friends. Gates was an African-American ex-football player, almost six-and-a-half-feet tall, carrying the bulk to match his height. His nose had been broken several times, but his impeccable dress—this morning a blue seersucker suit with a white-and-blue-striped bow tie—grizzled hair cut short, and tortoiseshell reading glasses hanging from a chain around his neck, softened his appearance.

"Freedman had a shotgun aimed at me while he told me his story, and he actually expected me to help him prove he's innocent," Simon said.

"Let me read that while you eat," Gates said, reaching for Simon's statement. When he had finished, he handed it back to Simon.

"It looks fine," he said, "go ahead and sign it. It's not like there's any question about what happened. Freedman has admitted everything."

"I told you you needed a gun," Julia said, entering the room behind them. Before Simon had a chance to turn around in his chair, Julia had wrapped her arms around him from behind. "And don't ever sign anything just because he says so," she said, nodding toward Gates. Simon held onto her arms for a minute, then released her so she could sit down next to him. She rubbed his cheek affectionately.

"Normally I find morning-stubble sexy," she said, "but you look awful."

"I was up all night placating a convicted murderer. I'm tired." Simon leaned toward her to kiss her, but she stopped him.

"Not here," she said. "This is my workplace, after all."

Julia had put on a few pounds since she had been dating Simon. Simon, who weighed one hundred and thirty pounds wet, after dinner, thought she looked wonderful. He didn't know what annoyed Julia the most, the pounds, or the fact that he preferred her a size ten rather than an eight. Of course she had many other delightful physical attributes, among them long auburn hair, hazel eyes, fair skin, and great legs. Oh, and she was smart and competent, Simon added, hastily, to himself. That was important, too. This morning Julia concealed her charms well. She wore a boxy gray suit, white tailored shirt, with a gray-and-maroon scarf knotted at her throat, and no makeup. Her beautiful hair was tied back in a knot. Simon thought it was a pity that a good-looking woman like Julia felt she had to dress like a man at work. In his opinion it was a terrible waste of the female figure, but Julia insisted that she had to look "professional."

Julia noticed the greasy Krispy Kreme bag scrunched up in a ball on the table.

"You didn't eat any of those things, did you?"

"Two of them, and I wish I had more."

"Let me buy you a decent lunch later."

"I can't. I've got to stay at work all day."

"Dinner, then. You've got to eat."

"Sounds good, but it'll have to be fast. I've got to get my grades in by tomorrow morning, and I'm way behind."

"I'll meet you at your place after work. But right now, as Sam Rayburn would say, I have to go strike a blow for justice."

Despite her earlier concern about propriety in the workplace, she bent over and kissed him on the cheek.

"I'm so glad you're okay," she said.

A RALEIGH POLICEMAN delivered Simon to his front door, where he was greeted by his cats, who twined around his legs and meowed for breakfast.

"Don't try to make it up to me," Simon said to them. "You were completely useless last night. I've a mind to get a dog."

Thanks to dissolving a couple of Goody's powders in a cold Coke before going to the police station that morning, Simon had prevented his predictable migraine from reaching its full force. Now he popped a prescription pill and pressed an ice bag to his temple as he sat on the shower floor and let hot water stream over him. He reflected on the previous night's experience. He was impressed by the risks that Freedman had taken to get to him and tell him his story. It made him wonder if it was true. And that made him wonder what it would be like to be imprisoned for years for a crime that he didn't commit. If Freedman wasn't telling the truth, why bother to take such a chance, one that would result in the loss of what privileges he had? For the first time, and not the last, Simon wondered if Freedman was innocent. He shoved the thought into the back of his mind for the moment. He had to go to work.

Simon dressed in blue jeans, polo shirt, and athletic shoes. He often walked to the Kenan College campus, just a few blocks away, but he was tired and late. He got into his black Thunderbird, unhooked his sunglasses from the visor, and drove to campus. He had time to listen to just one song from Paul Simon's new CD, but it was enough to put him in a better mood.

Kenan College occupied a block near downtown Raleigh. Once the home of the Bloodworth family, the Bloodworths had donated the grounds and orchards, and later their eighteenth-century mansion, to Kenan in 1832.

The college evolved from a "women's institute" into one of the finest small liberal arts colleges in the South.

Simon was pleased that Kenan didn't have a graduate school. He wanted to teach undergraduates while they were still intellectually curious and uncorrupted by academic politics and scholarly nit-picking. Too many academic historians were pedants instead of scholars, writing stuffy books and articles on such narrow subjects only Ph.D. candidates read them, caring more about assignments to faculty committees, conference panels, and journal boards than educating their students. Only by avoiding the academic fast track and accepting a position with Kenan had Simon escaped that fate himself. It didn't hurt that Simon's first, and only book so far, *The South Between the World Wars,* had won the Pulitzer Prize. He received tenure years before he might have otherwise, which meant he could do anything he wanted to as long as he taught his classes and didn't hit on the women students. Simon knew that his colleagues who went on to more prestigious institutions thought he had consigned himself to a backwater, but Simon was grateful every day that he had made the decision he did.

Despite the July heat, Raleigh had enough rain to nourish the college's beautiful grounds. "Torch Glow" bougainvillea, red poppies, magenta petunias, and cardinal flowers bloomed in the sun. Red coleus, impatiens, and Indian pinks clustered in the shade of the great oak trees. The profusion of red blossoms set against the intense green of the lawns gave the campus a perverse Christmasy look.

Simon's parking space adjoined Bloodworth House's kitchen garden. The garden was meant to be authentic, planted with heirloom vegetables and herbs. Simon had helped choose the plants from the Monticello seed catalog.

An acrid, fetid odor permeated the garden. Kenan's gardeners tended the vegetables just as Jefferson's slaves did—they fertilized with horse manure, which in this case came from the NCSU vet-school barn, and mulched the growing plants with wet tobacco leaves.

Simon picked a tarragon leaf. He crushed it between his fingers, inhaling the odor. He wasn't crazy about its mild licorice flavor himself, but Jefferson had loved it, soaking handfuls of it in wine vinegar to use as salad dressing. Jefferson made a lot of wine vinegar. His wines weren't much good for drinking.

Checking his watch, Simon hurried through the rose garden that grew on the large island in the middle of the traffic circle in front of the college. A few white Albas, descended from the White Rose of York, were scattered amongst the reds. Simon had donated a Rosa Mundi— an heirloom white striped with pink or red, one of Jefferson's favorites. He stopped briefly to inhale its odor. Only historic roses still had a wonderful smell.

The old college building that housed the history department was built in 1834 from stone left over from construction of the North Carolina Capitol Building. Like the Capitol, it had the dome and pedimented portico characteristic of Greek Revival architecture. Eight-foot-high windows allowed natural light to stream into the building. In spring and fall the windows were often thrown wide open so that the breezes brought the odors of honeysuckle and someone barbecuing on a dorm balcony wafting in. Dark, hand-carved woodwork and staircase balustrades framed the wide halls, classrooms, and offices. Biscuit-colored walls in the entryway displayed oil portraits of every chair of the history department since it was founded in 1857. The portrait of the current chair, Walker Jones, painted by Raleigh artist Andrea Gomez, hung over the fireplace centered in the reception area outside the department's administrative offices. The building was quiet, almost deserted. The history department offered just two courses and one seminar in each summer session, and often only the faculty teaching them were in residence. Simon had seen Walker Jones around a few times, and Judy Smith, the departmental secretary, kept her regular hours.

Simon walked down the long center hall of the first floor to the faculty lounge, which was once the library of the original college. It was lined with age-darkened pine bookshelves that still contained some of Kenan's collection, old but not valuable books on subjects ranging from domestic science to Chaucer. A coffeepot on a stand and a refrigerator stood in a corner behind a wicker screen studded with notices and announcements.

Professor Marcus Clegg, who sat at a long wooden table grading papers, was alone in the room. Marcus was a few years older than Simon, and cultivated a sixties image. He wore Birkenstock sandals year-round, John Lennon eyeglasses, and a blue oxford shirt frayed at the neck and cuffs. His brown hair hung to his shoulders. He was teaching the other course offered this summer session, History of Science.

Marcus scrawled a C in big red letters on a paper he was grading, then threw it onto a small stack to his left. Then he selected another from a much taller stack to his right, slamming it down in front of himself with an impatient noise.

"Remind me never to assign a term paper during a summer school session again," Marcus said. "The results are always miserable."

"Then we'll have to stop teaching history during the summer," Simon said. "There's no way to learn how to think about the past without writing about it. Writing requires thought, and thought is what we're looking for. Anyone can look up facts."

"Well, this guy wrote, but he certainly didn't think," Marcus said, putting his big C- on the paper before tossing it aside.

"You didn't read it," Simon said.

"One paragraph is enough," Marcus said. "If I finished it, I might have to flunk him."

Marcus had two Ph.D.s, one in history and one in psychology. Until recently he had divided his time between the two departments, teaching the history of science and behavioral psychology. Then just before the NASDAQ crashed, the owner of a successful Internet company out at the Research Triangle Park endowed a chair at Kenan in the history of science and technology. Marcus gave up his dual appointment to assume the new chair. Kenan was lucky to be able to keep him. The reviews of Marcus's first book, *The Recantation of Galileo,* glowed, and Simon expected Marcus's book to be short-listed for the National Book Award. Simon didn't envy Marcus professionally, but he was jealous of Marcus private life: his wife, his four daughters, and his busy home on four acres outside of town.

Simon sat his bulging briefcase on the table and went to the coffee machine, finding it empty. He groaned, and moved to the refrigerator, where he grabbed a Coke from a twelve-pack with his name written on it in large letters. He sat down at the table with Marcus.

"You have that look of a man who spent the whole night grading mediocre test papers," Marcus said, "like you've been nibbled half to death by butterflies."

"I was up all night, but not grading papers," Simon said, and told him his story.

"What are you going to do?" Marcus asked. "Do you think Freedman was telling the truth?"

"I don't know. I'd dismiss the whole idea except for one thing I can't get out of my mind. If he's guilty, why would he risk giving up what freedom he had to get to me? He had a job at the Governor's Mansion, and now he's back in maximum security at Central Prison, locked down in his cell twenty-three hours a day."

"He never tried to escape?"

"He talked about it for just a minute or two," Simon said. "Then he gave it up. I had nine-one-one on the line, but he could have still made a break for it. Besides, he could have stolen my car hours before. Instead he tried to convince me he was innocent. He'll be charged with kidnapping, second-degree, since he did turn himself in and didn't injure me."

"How can you be kidnapped in your own living room?"

"Kidnapping," Simon said, "is holding a person against his will. You don't actually have to take the victim, in this case me, anywhere. I doubt that Freedman will ever leave Central Prison."

Distantly, a bell rang.

"I need to get to my office," Simon said.

To Simon's surprise there were no desperate-looking students lined up outside his office door. Maybe they were all resigned to their fate, cramming for Simon's latest fifty-short-answer-and-two-essay final. They didn't have much choice but to study if they wanted to do well in his class. Simon never asked the same question on a test twice. He had a photographic memory, and knew exactly which tests and papers were on file in the student dormitories, and what could be purchased on the Internet. While some students felt it was impossible to fail a social sciences class, he didn't agree, and often proved it.

Simon settled behind the deep mahogany partner's desk in his office. It dwarfed him, but he didn't mind because it gave him room to spread out. He had furnished the rest of the room himself, too. A jewel-toned Oriental rug covered the floor, and two Audubon prints hung on the wall opposite his chair. Dozens of books were shoved every which way into dark wood bookcases. The bookcases, which had belonged to Simon's father, were labeled neatly with little white cards in tiny metal frames, but when you got closer you could see the labels had nothing to do with the books actually resting on the shelves. They were printed, in Simon's father's neat hand, in Latin. Several file boxes were stacked next to two wooden file cabinets. One box was labeled *N.C. COASTAL HISTORY* and another *CIVIL WAR HERESIES,* evidence of Simon's current research interests. Simon pulled a pile of term papers toward him, and punched the play button of his CD player. The sweet sounds of Andrea Bocelli's tenor filled the room.

A tentative knock sounded at his door. Simon sighed, turned the term paper over so the author's name couldn't be seen, and turned down the CD player.

"Come in," he said.

Todd Spetz poked his head around the edge of the door. *Hot damn,* Simon thought, *gotcha!*

"Can I come in, Dr. Shaw?"

"Of course, Todd. What's up?"

Todd sat in an armchair facing Simon across his desk. He crossed one khaki-covered leg over the other.

"It's about my term paper," Todd said. "You might have noticed that I haven't turned it in."

"I hadn't, yet," Simon said. "What's the problem?"

"Well," Todd said, "it's not done, I mean, not finished."

"I'm sorry to hear that, Todd, I really am. But you can turn it in tomorrow morning before eight and still pass."

Todd squirmed in his seat.

"Well, you see, I've had this cold, **a sinus infection** really, and, you know, Jack Gill was using the same books I needed, and, well, I don't think it can be ready tomorrow."

Simon raised his eyebrows and started to tap his pen on his desk. Todd shifted his weight in the chair nervously.

"I was wondering, if you could like, give me an Incomplete, and I could finish it like, over the weekend. I just need to pass, Dr. Shaw. That's all."

"I see," Simon said. "FedEx didn't deliver it today, so you can't meet the deadline."

Todd went white. His mouth formed a few words before sound actually came out.

"What? I don't know what you're talking about, Dr. Shaw."

"Who's been writing your papers for you? Your mom? Your dad?"

"Wait just a minute! You're accusing me of cheating!" Todd was on the edge of his seat now, with his legs crossed at the ankles and wedged under the bottom rung of his chair.

"FedEx doesn't deliver to student mailboxes because they just have post office box numbers. This building has a street address. You received two FedEx boxes here last semester, right before the two essays were due in Vera Thayer's class. What do you think we are, unconscious? Vera said the papers were damn good, too good, considering you were asleep in class half the time and absent the other half.''

Todd collected himself.

"That's just not true! My mom is always sending me like, you know, newspaper clippings, and magazines, and snacks, and vitamins—stupid stuff mothers send, you know."

"Then I'm sure you can show me your notes for this paper. If you can, I'll let you have the Incomplete."

Todd's mouth dropped open again.

"Don't add lying to your problem, Todd. I can't prove you've cheated, but I can flunk your butt for not turning this paper in. From now on every faculty member in this college will be watching you like hawks tracking a mouse, and if I were you I'd start hitting the books if you don't want to be expelled for cheating."

There was another knock at Simon's office door, and Todd took this chance to leave without saying another word. He opened Simon's office door and slipped past Kim Jewell, who had just raised her hand to knock again. She moved aside to let Todd pass.

"Dr. Shaw," Kim said, hovering in the doorway. "Can I talk to you?"

"Of course," Simon said. Kim closed the door behind her.

"Open the door, please, Kim," Simon said.

Kim left the door ajar a couple of inches and sat down in the armchair Todd had just left. Kim was a very pretty girl. She wore a short denim skirt, pink tank top with spaghetti straps, and high-heeled sandals enclosing pink-polished toenails. Her long blonde hair hung to her shoulders. Her makeup was perfect.

"Dr. Shaw," Kim said, "I was wondering if you'd read my paper yet?"

"I have, Kim. You got a C," Simon said.

She frowned, creases forming above her eyes.

"Is that good enough to pass?" she asked.

"No, not quite. You flunked both quizzes. You'll still need a C on the exam," Simon said.

"Well," Kim said, crossing and uncrossing her legs "I've had this cold, you know. Like, really a sinus infection."

"You're wasting my time, and yours," Simon said. "You should be in the library right now."

"Oh, I have been. I'm just on a break. But I was wondering, could I do something for extra credit, over the weekend?"

"We don't make posters in college, Kim."

"Dr. Shaw, you know, I do much better in discussion classes. Lectures sort of inhibit my creativity."

"This was an introductory course, Kim. To paraphrase Rabbi David Small, how can you discuss something you don't know anything about?"

"Huh?"

"Never mind."

Kim glanced over at the door. Simon's office was on the second floor, at the end of the hall. His door hinged so that, even if opened fairly wide, no one could see into his office. Kim got up and walked over to Simon, hitching herself up onto his desk.

"I really need to pass this course," she said. "I can't enroll this fall if I flunk. My parents will make me get a job. I'll do anything you say to pass."

Simon looked up at her. Her hair fell forward as she bent over him. She wasn't wearing a bra.

"Anything?" he said.

"Yes, anything," she said.

"Well," Simon said. "Let's talk about that."

She smiled at him, crossing her legs so that her skirt rode even further up her thigh.

"What did you have in mind?" she asked.

"Make a suggestion," Simon said.

"Oh, no, you tell me."

"Remember, you said you'd do anything," Simon said.

"I meant it," she said, smiling at him.

"Would you study?"

She jerked upright.

"What!" she said.

Simon looked at his watch.

"You've got three hours before the exam," Simon said.

Red splotches broke out on Kim's neck and arms.

"You jerk," she said, "you led me on!"

"It's time for you to leave," Simon said. "If we need to talk about your work again, we'll meet in the front room downstairs."

Without another word, she stormed out, slamming the heavy door behind her so hard it trembled, then popped open again.

Simon went back to grading papers. He was breathing a mite quickly. He was human, after all.

BY TWELVE O'CLOCK Simon had graded half the term papers. Most of them were competent, but one was outstanding. It was written by a quiet, prematurely bald premed major who proved to Simon's complete satisfaction that Union doctors understood sterile operating procedures and used them during the Civil War. The paper was well-written, too, well enough that Simon concluded his comments on the paper by suggesting that the student come see him about possible publication. A published article would look good on his medical school applications.

Stomach growling, Simon went to the lounge looking for something to eat. Marcus was still there, working. He raised the flat of his hand toward Simon in a gesture requesting silence. Simon surveyed the contents of the refrigerator and found a two-day-old fast-food bag that he thought was his. Inside was most of a cheeseburger. He warmed it up in the microwave, got another Coke, and went over to sit down at the table. Marcus wrote an A in big letters, with a flourish, on his last term paper.

"Yes, thank you, Lord," Marcus said, stretching his arms over his head. "Thank goodness I could give one A. Otherwise I would have had to admit that I was too hard on these guys, and go back and regrade everything."

"I had a good one, too," Simon said. "It does give you hope."

"Are you going to eat that? Throw it away and we'll go out to lunch."

Simon shook his head.

"I've got more term papers to grade, and I can't do them while I'm proctoring my exam. Wondering if I'm reading their paper distracts the students."

Simon would be grading papers and exams far into the night, without any sleep the night before. It tired him just to think about it. Maybe he should cancel dinner with Julia so he could work.

"You need some sleep," Marcus said. "Why don't you let me proctor?"

"I can't ask you to do that," Simon said.

"Nonsense," Marcus said. "I can grade my exams at the same time." Simon looked longingly at the battered couch in a corner of the lounge. Three hours sleep sounded awfully good to him.

"Okay," he said. "Room Two-oh-two. I've got the exams here in my briefcase."

When Simon woke up, sunlight angled in low through the windows, stretching across the floor of the lounge. He looked at his watch. It was five o'clock. Marcus was back in his spot at the table, but he was packing up his briefcase. He saw that Simon was awake, and patted a stack of blue books at his side.

"These are all yours," he said.

"Thanks," Simon said, sitting up and rubbing his eyes. "Any problems?"

"None. Oh, but there was this girl. She seemed very disappointed that you weren't there. Slammed her pen and papers around a lot before she settled down."

"Long blonde hair, long legs, short skirt, no bra?"

"That's her. She certainly was dressed for extra credit."

THREE

SIMON COULD BARELY breathe in the baking-hot interior of his car. The air conditioner wouldn't make a dent in the heat during the short drive to his house, so he didn't bother to turn it on. The hot air that blew in through the open car windows sucked up all the moisture from his face and rustled papers in the backseat.

Once inside, Simon stripped off his damp shirt and splashed cold water over his face. His cats whined at the back door. He let them in, and they ran straight to the cool tile floor under the kitchen table and lay down on their backs, with their feet in the air.

"I know just how you feel," Simon said, stripping off the rest of his clothes on the way to the shower. He didn't touch the hot-water control, and decided to stay wet, in his boxers, until it was time to change for dinner with Julia.

He passed his blinking answering machine several times, postponing checking his messages, for fear he'd hear something that would make him feel more beat up than he already did. He almost erased them, but then, thinking one might be from Julia, he lifted the receiver.

"This is Chaplain Harry Mitchell at Central Prison," a deep, drawling voice said. "I'd appreciate it if you'd call me. It's about Roy Freedman." Mitchell left a number and an extension. Annoyed, Simon jotted down the numbers. He wondered why on earth the chaplain had called him. He did not want to think about Freedman just now. In fact, there was no law that he had to ever have anything to do with Freedman again. In spite of everything, though, his curiosity was piqued. Suddenly he thought, what if Freedman had committed suicide? That worry prompted him to return the call immediately. Chaplain Mitchell was gone for the day, but the chaplain on duty assured him that Freedman was alive and well. Simon hung up. Of course Freedman hadn't committed suicide. Maximum security was too well-monitored for that to happen. He'd call the chaplain tomorrow, after he'd had a decent night's sleep.

Simon didn't teach in the second summer session, which gave him over a month off before he needed to prepare for the fall semester. He was not, he told himself sternly, not, going to spend it dealing with Roy Freedman's problem. He was going to Pearlie Beach, staying in Marcus's beach house, for several glorious weeks of sun and water, where he would toy with the idea of writing a coastal history of North Carolina.

Simon changed into khakis, an Alexander Julian sport shirt, and deck shoes. Julia had been giving him a hard time about his blue jeans and catalog knit shirts, so he had spent some time finding more fashionable clothes in his size. He didn't think it was worth the effort, but it made Julia happy, so he did it.

Julia called him a minute later on her car phone.

"I've changed, and I'm on my way to your place," she said. "Where should we go? Someplace new?"

"You know if we don't go to the Irregardless Cafe we'll regret it. Those new trendy places just don't measure up. But don't let me drink any wine, or I'll wind up facedown in my plate, snoring."

JULIA LOOKED WONDERFUL in a mint green linen sheath and flat silver sandals. Her auburn hair just grazed her shoulders, the way Simon loved it, but before long, complaining that her neck was hot, she twisted it into a knot on top of her head, securing it with a dangerous-looking spike she took out of her handbag.

Once at the Irregardless Simon and Julia sat at their favorite rear table under the oil painting of God anointing chef and owner Arthur Gordon. None of his devoted customers, which included anyone who ever set foot in the place, considered it heretical. Simon and Julia ordered crab quesadillas to start, and studied the menu, which changed depending on the season and the chef's latest interests.

Although founded years ago as a vegetarian restaurant, the Irregardless now grilled the best steak in town. Simon ordered the ribeye with mushroom sauce, garlic mashed potatoes, and steamed baby vegetables bought fresh at the Farmer's Market that morning. Julia had grilled salmon and shrimp with perfect jasmine rice, a fresh spinach salad, and a half bottle of chardonnay. She kept the bottle on her side of the table, and Simon had the waiter remove his wine glass.

"I know I'm going to regret asking this," Simon said, pausing halfway through his meal, "but why can't Roy Freedman get his case reopened?"

"Why would you regret asking?"

"Because when you answer my legal questions, it's always more information than I really want. I wind up with a two-page memo and a copy of the statute."

"I will try to dumb down my response."

"I appreciate that."

"The courts consider a guilty plea to be the equivalent of a fair trial, constitutionally speaking. If there's no constitutional error in the 'trial,' then there's no reason to reopen a case. You can't just ask for a new trial because you don't like the verdict forty years later.''

"But Freedman says that the sheriff and the girl's father threatened to lynch him if he didn't confess. That's a constitutional issue, isn't it? Didn't they violate his rights?''

"Are you sure that happened? Why hasn't he brought this up before? He's been tucked away safe and sound in prison for forty years, where no one can touch him. Where are the sheriff and the girl's father now? Dead or alive, they haven't been able to threaten him in years.''

"What about the discovery of the girl's corpse? Isn't that considered new evidence?''

"Sure, but it's no basis for a new trial unless it might prove his innocence, which it doesn't,'' Julia said. "I suspect Mr. Freedman's gotten tired of prison and wants out. He couldn't afford a lawyer, so he tried to get you interested in helping him.''

"Think about this, though. If Freedman is guilty, what evidence could he hope that I could find to prove him innocent? It doesn't make sense.''

"It's called grasping at straws, babe.''

The waiter cleared their dishes. Julia wanted to stay for coffee, but Simon was worried about getting his work done. It was a sacrifice passing up the triple chocolate brownie with vanilla ice cream for dessert, but it had to be done.

"The pitiful thing is,'' Julia said in the car on their way home, "in 1958 Roy Freedman pled guilty to first-degree murder in exchange for a life sentence without parole. These days, considering that the murder was a crime of passion and the corpse was missing, he'd get second-degree murder, or maybe manslaughter one, and he'd be out of prison by now. For years he's been watching guys who did crimes like his come and go from prison while he rots there.''

''That hardly seems just.''

''It's not, but it's the law. The two don't always coincide.''

JULIA, GOD BLESS HER, stayed at Simon's house for a couple of hours and graded the short-answer section of his exam papers. She tried to leave around eight thirty, but their good-night kiss evolved into a more extended experience. Before she met Simon, Julia would never have believed that bending over to kiss a man could be sexy. Was she ever wrong. Simon held her close to him, nuzzling her neck, kissing her lips, moving to the indented spot just at her breastbone, and then lower. His hands caressed the curve of her body from waist to hips. Julia felt Simon's heartbeat intensify, and hers raced to catch up with his. His touch made her want to close her eyes and sink down on something soft and convenient, like the sofa.

''I've been thinking,'' Simon said. ''I believe we could both use a little nap.''

''No, you'll fall asleep, and you won't get your work done.''

She pulled away from him, opening the door with one hand while holding the other flat against his chest, to stop him from kissing her again.

''Be strong,'' she said.

''Please don't go. I might die before tomorrow. Then how would you feel?''

She patted him on the cheek.

''Tomorrow night,'' she said.

"I've just remembered. I've got tenure. They can't fire me."

"I'm going," she said, stepping out onto the front porch. "Good night!"

"Bring a bag tomorrow, spend the weekend here," Simon said. "We'll have fun."

"I'll think about it," she said.

"If you stay, I promise not to read too much into it."

THE HOUSE ECHOED with the sound of Julia's car pulling out of the driveway, then went silent. There was nothing left for Simon to do but to get a cold Coke and a box of chocolate-chip cookies and go upstairs to his study to finish his work. There he stacked some CDs into his stereo and turned the bass up as far as it would go. As he sat down to work, the first guitar chords of Clapton's "After Midnight" pulsed through the room.

Simon was interrupted an hour later by a reporter from the Raleigh *News and Observer* asking for details of the Freedman incident. Simon told him everything. He saw no point in trying to keep anything from the press. If Simon didn't talk to the reporter, he'd just piece the story together from other sources, and whatever appeared in the paper would be full of mistakes. Besides, Simon wasn't unaware of the publicity value of his exploits to Kenan. It wasn't like they had an ACC athletic team to keep them in the news. Still, Simon hung up hoping that tomorrow was a big news day and that the editor would bury any story about him on a back page.

At three o'clock Friday morning Simon was finished. He entered his faculty password and code on Kenan's secure student records Web site and registered his final grades. Then he typed up and e-mailed a grade list to

Judy Smith, to post on his office door. There was no way he was going to show up at the office tomorrow.

Simon was so tired that he drifted a little to the right on the way out of his study and hit the door jamb. Rubbing his forehead, he went downstairs and put plenty of food in his cats' bowls so they wouldn't wake him up in the morning. He locked his front and back doors carefully, then spent fifteen minutes looking for a bottle of household oil to grease the locks on his windows so he could secure them, too. Feeling fairly safe from another kidnapping, he went back upstairs and crawled onto his bed, fully dressed. It was hot despite the labored efforts of his air conditioner and ceiling fan to cool his bedroom. He considered moving downstairs to the sofa, but decided he didn't have the strength. The last thing he did before falling asleep was turn off the ringer on his telephone.

THE FULL FORCE of the Carolina noonday sun made Simon's eyes water when he opened his front door the next day. When he picked up his newspaper, he saw that the story about his kidnapping was below the fold on the front page, accompanied by a file photo of him leaning up against the bookcases in his office looking professorial. He glanced around his street. Good thing it wasn't a weekend, or his neighbors would be queueing up to razz him.

Back inside he noticed that more messages had accumulated on his answering machine. Fame could be so intrusive. He ignored the machine's blinking light and fixed breakfast—three scrambled eggs, bacon, and an English muffin heaped with homemade apple butter from the fruits of his aunt's orchard outside of Boone. He felt almost human when he finished eating. For the first time in weeks no pressing deadlines loomed over him, and Julia might actually spend the weekend at his house. If she was even thinking about it, he considered that progress in their relationship. Then Simon remembered the chaplain's phone call.

"ROY FREEDMAN ASKED me to ask you if you were going to keep your promise," Chaplain Mitchell said. The chaplain had a deep, smoker's voice, thick with tar and phlegm.

"Hold on," Simon said. "What promise?"

"You promised to help him," Mitchell said. "Didn't you? He says you did."

"Wait just a minute," Simon said. "I'd have promised him season tickets to Tar Heel basketball if that would have made him happy. I hardly think I can be held to a commitment I made at the point of a gun."

"Don't pop a blood vessel. I'm just the messenger," Mitchell said.

"Do you think he's innocent?"

"I don't know. I don't try to figure out if these guys are telling the truth or not. It's not my job. Spiritual comfort is my job."

"And relaying messages."

"Yeah, I guess so."

"Can he have visitors? I'd be willing to talk to him, I suppose, if there were enough bars between us."

"Not just now," Mitchell said. "He has no privileges at all. That will change eventually, but I don't know when. So, what should I tell him?"

Simon could not bring himself to deny all hope to the man, not just yet.

"Oh, hell. Tell him I'll think about it some more."

Simon slammed the receiver down. Imagine, trying to

make him feel guilty. Freedman had taken Simon hostage and threatened to shoot him. He's the one who should feel guilty.

But what if Freedman was innocent? Simon didn't see how he could be. The man would have done something about it before now.

Simon didn't have the energy for this. He resolved to put the convict out of his mind. He'd wait a decent interval, then call Chaplain Mitchell and tell him that he wouldn't investigate Freedman's story, and that would be the end of it.

Simon listened to the rest of his phone messages while skimming the newspaper, with his bare feet up on his coffee table, ignoring the story about himself. Judy Smith said she had received Simon's E-mail and would post his grades on his office door. Kim Jewell complained that some of the course material on reserve at the library was missing, and that's why she didn't do well on the exam. She didn't—she got a D. He wondered what kind of job her parents would make her get. Probably answering the telephone at her daddy's office.

Then he heard a voice he hadn't heard in over a year, and the shock kept him from absorbing the message. He hit the save button, then played it again. It was Tess, his ex-wife. She wanted him to call her.

Simon had taken his divorce hard. When Tess had left him, declaring that she had never been so bored in her life as during their marriage, he was taken completely by surprise. He'd had no clue that she was unhappy. He didn't know what depressed him the most, the divorce, or realizing that he'd been living with a stranger for five years.

Thinking about the morning she left still made him wince. She had packed her Mustang with only her personal belongings, assuring Simon that she wanted no part of their joint property.

But one tiny possession escaped. Maybelline was Tess's cat, but she refused to leave, hiding under the sofa when she saw Tess with the cat carrier. After Simon moved the sofa, Maybelline zoomed through Tess's legs into the dining room, leapt from the floor to a chair, then to the dining table, and from there scrambled to the top of a curio cabinet. A hellish hour followed while both Simon and Tess chased the cat, Tess screaming at him and Simon placating her. Finally Simon lured Maybelline out of hiding with an open can of tuna fish. She fought like a bobcat when Tess tried to stuff her into the carrier, scratching Tess's face and beating it to the backyard, where she climbed so far up into a maple tree they couldn't have gotten her down without the fire department. Tess screamed at Simon some more, then threw the cat carrier at him. She unloaded the cat bed, water bowl, and bag of cat food from her car and threw them at him too, one item at a time. The neighbors considerately stayed inside while all this was going on, but Simon knew they could hear, and see, if they wanted to, everything that went on.

Simon and Tess were separated for a year, as required by North Carolina law, then divorced. They had only spoken a few times since she left. Simon couldn't imagine what she wanted now.

He paced the floor a few times, then decided to call her back. If he didn't return her call, wondering what she wanted would eat away at him. He might as well get past it. She was probably at work, but he could leave her a message. Thank God for answering machines, everyone's escape from real conversation. As he dialed,

Simon noted the exchange of Tess's phone number—
Manhattan. She must have moved.

Her phone rang. To his surprise, Tess answered.

"I've got a new apartment," she said. "I took a couple of days off to settle in."

When he heard her voice, Simon could see her as if she was sitting next to him, barefoot on a hot summer day, wearing shorts and a tank top, with her legs tucked up under her. She used to paint her toenails bright red, and drank Earl Grey tea instead of coffee. She was petite and pretty, with curly strawberry-blonde hair, blue eyes, and frown lines just beginning to form. Those frown lines should have clued him in.

"Oh," Simon said, "good."

"It's a great location."

Simon didn't think anywhere more than a couple of floors up and not within walking distance of a good barbecue sandwich was a great location, but he didn't say anything.

"That's nice."

"You're wondering why I called."

"Yeah. What's up?"

"I've got a great new job—casting director for *Young Bloods*."

"What's that?"

"Only the number-one soap opera on television this season."

"Well, that's great. Congratulations."

He heard her take a deep breath.

"I want you to give me some money, Simon."

"Excuse me? You want what?"

"I need some money."

Simon recalled the nasty remarks Tess made when they divorced, about how she wanted to take nothing at all from their marriage to remind her of how she had wasted five years of her youth, his money would be tainted by bad memories, and so forth.

"We're divorced, Tess, remember? All that financial stuff is settled."

"You don't understand," she said. "I want you to give it to me. I need to furnish this place, and I want to buy new clothes. I've got to upgrade my image. And I don't want all that much, just ten thousand dollars."

"Ten thousand dollars! What planet are you living on? You want me to send you ten thousand dollars? What for, old time's sake?"

"Out of the goodness of your heart and sense of fairness." Tess didn't sound as if she had one ounce of concern that he'd refuse.

"Oh, hell, Tess. I don't have that kind of money lying around."

"You can get it. Please, Simon, I really need it, and I realize now that it was stupid of me not to accept a financial settlement. We were married for five years, you know, that should count for something."

Simon felt sick.

"I'll think about it," he said.

"Thank you, sweetie. Let me give you my new address." She read it out to him and he dutifully copied it down.

He hung up, not believing what he had just heard. The woman had the gall, after breaking his heart, to ask him for money. He had no illusions about her—she was taking advantage of whatever affection he had left for her without caring a fig about him. If he were dying of thirst she wouldn't go an inch out of her way to give him a drink of water.

Simon went upstairs to his study and went over his

bank statements. He could just about swing it, if he wanted to. Interest had accumulated in the small trust fund his parents had left him, and he was due a lease payment on property he owned in Boone.

Simon sensed depression hovering, looking for a suitable landing spot free of the defenses he had built over the past couple of years. He refused to grant it permission to land—not without a fight, at least. Half the people in the country were divorced, and he was going to be one of those who got past it. A closet Freudian, Simon believed that repression was the best weapon any psyche possessed against neurosis. Through experience he'd found that the best way to survive unhappy times was to distract himself intellectually, to get his brain wrapped around a complex problem until his feelings were under control. Sprawling in a lounge chair and reading a Rex Stout mystery with a bottle of cold beer in his hand wouldn't do the job. The solution was obvious. He'd check out Freedman's story. He would have done it eventually, anyway. Then, fortified by his research, he'd call the chaplain Monday and assure him that Freedman was guilty. He'd call Tess back then, too, and refuse to send her any money. If she had such a good job that she could afford to move to Manhattan, she could max out her credit cards for clothes and furniture like everyone else. Once all these decisions were made, he could relax and enjoy the weekend.

Simon's first phone call was to the office of the state medical examiner, at the University of North Carolina Medical Center in Chapel Hill, where the Boone newspaper article said Eva Potter's corpse, or what was left of it, had been sent for autopsy. Coincidentally, he was put through to the only pathologist he knew, Dr. Philip Boyette.

Simon didn't like Boyette, though he couldn't have explained why in any logical way. He had first met the doctor rooting around old human remains in an unmarked grave, picking at the corpse's quilted shroud with forceps. The sight revolted Simon, but Boyette was unmoved. Of course, he would be, pathologists couldn't be bothered by dead people, or they wouldn't be in their line of work. Maybe it was Boyette's looks and behavior that repelled Simon—his pencil-thin moustache, his thin, soft body, his obsessive neatness.

Boyette was delighted to hear from Simon. He loved to talk about the gory details of his work, and relished finding his name in Simon's article about his first case, the murder of Anne Bloodworth. He kept a stack of reprints in his office that he handed out to all his visitors. Boyette told Simon that the "Report of Investigation" on the remains of Eva Potter was a public document, but he couldn't fax it to Simon until the chief medical examiner initialed it, which wouldn't be until Monday. If Simon wanted to, he could drive over to Chapel Hill and meet Boyette in his office and look over the preliminary report. Boyette had a slow afternoon, and he would be happy to talk to Simon about Eva Potter's autopsy.

It must have been a slow afternoon at the Watauga County District Attorney's Office in Boone, too, because the clerk Simon spoke to offered to fax a copy of their file on Eva Potter's murder to him that afternoon. The file was still on his desk, the clerk said, since the sheriff's office had just returned it to the file library. Simon gave him the history department's fax number. He'd collect it after his trip to Chapel Hill and dispense with the entire question of Freedman's guilt by evening.

AFTER CIRCLING THE UNC Medical Center campus for half an hour looking for somewhere to park, Simon got out of his car and removed a large orange traffic cone from the middle of a parking spot and pulled his car into the space. He had no idea why the cone was there, and he had a Ph.D. He placed the cone under a maple tree scarred by ugly gashes about the right size to have been made by the bulldozer parked nearby.

This part of the UNC campus was under constant construction. The noise of jackhammers, generators, and earth-moving vehicles was incessant. Mountains of red earth, orange fencing, piles of construction debris, and fleets of heavy equipment created an obstacle course for patients, visitors, and students. The oppressive summer heat made the ordeal of getting around even more difficult.

Simon had read in the newspaper recently that undergraduate students living in residence halls nearby were suing the university because of the stress. It made sense to him.

The chief medical examiner's office occupied the tenth-floor of a tall, beige-colored building behind the Health Sciences Library. The receptionist directed him to Boyette's office. Boyette, wearing spotless, and yes, ironed and creased scrubs, was typing at a computer keyboard when Simon tapped on his door frame, but he waved Simon into the office and pointed at a chair. A few seconds later he shut down his computer and leaned over the desk to shake Simon's hand.

"Good to see you," Boyette said.

"You too," Simon lied.

"On another case?"

"Not exactly. Just looking into something for a guy at Central Prison."

"Eva Potter's murderer?"

"He says he didn't do it."

"Not my job. But here's the report."

Boyette tossed the file across his desk to Simon. He opened it—it contained just two pages.

"This is it?"

"What's to say? The remains were skeletonized. The bones came to us in a bag. When we reconstructed the skeleton, its height, age, gender, build, all matched Eva Potter's description. We verified that she'd never been pregnant, never broken a bone. Her jaw was missing some teeth, but otherwise its dentition matched Eva's dental records."

"It doesn't mention the cause of death here."

"It wasn't obvious from the remains. I understand from the sheriff's report that she was stabbed. Any number of mortal stabbing injuries wouldn't mark the skeleton."

"I thought you guys could look at a femur and tell what the victim's last meal was, what she did for a living, and whether she voted Republican or Democrat."

"Sometimes," Boyette laughed. "But not this time."

"Can I have a copy of the report?"

"I'll fax one to you just as soon as the chief's okayed it."

Fortunately Boyette had an appointment, so Simon was able to leave sooner than might otherwise have been polite. He paused outside the entrance to the medical center. Hot asphalt sucked at his shoes. He shaded his eyes from the glare reflecting off hundreds of parked cars. What next? Simon wanted copies of the newspaper clippings that Freedman had showed him. The Kenan Library didn't have microfilm of the *Watauga Democrat,* so while he was in Chapel Hill, he might as well go over to the Carolina Collection and make copies. While he was there he would browse all the 1958 issues of the newspaper for contemporary reports of Eva's murder.

The university library was just a few blocks away, but the temperature was in the high-nineties and the heat index even higher, so he decided to drive. He managed to park in a narrow spot between a gaping hole in the ground surrounded by orange plastic fencing and a posthold digger chained to a Dumpster.

A flight of steep stone steps climbed up to the imposing neo-classical facade of the university library. He remembered that he had met Tess on these steps. He had finished the oral exams for his Ph.D., and had the time and inclination to think about romance. Tess had arrived on campus to start a master's degree in education. He saw her sitting on the steps of the library, looking at a campus map. He asked if he could help her, then walked her over to the education department, securing a date before they got there. It was only nine years ago, but it no longer felt real to Simon. He remembered it as if it was a scene from a movie he saw long ago, or as if it had happened to a lovelorn friend who told him about it at lunch one day. He supposed that someday he'd be completely unaffected by a phone call from Tess like the one he'd received this morning. He didn't know whether to feel happy or sad about that.

The library was dark and cool. He felt calm and relaxed as soon as he entered. Simon knew exactly how the library worked, and how to pry information out of it. He was in control here.

Simon showed his Kenan faculty ID and UNC library pass to the student manning the desk inside the front door of the library. She nodded at him, and he walked across the granite floor of the lobby. He passed by the elevators, preferring to walk the four flights of stairs

down to the newspaper reading room. There he located
the most recent reel of the *Watauga Democrat,* wound
it onto the reader, found the articles on the discovery of
Eva Potter's corpse in Freedman's truck, and photocopied them. Then he fetched the 1958 reel. The white noise
of a dozen microfilm readers whirring and the buzz of
the fluorescent lights masked all other distractions, and
Simon settled down to learn about Boone, North Carolina, in 1958.

Ah, the fifties. What a fascinating age. Sociologically
speaking, the fifties lasted longer than a decade, born
when Chuck Yeager broke the sound barrier in 1947 and
dying when President John F. Kennedy was assassinated
in 1963.

So much that Americans accepted today as part of
their culture didn't exist until the fifties. Rock and roll
was born, and *American Bandstand* aired daily coast-to-
coast. In 1956 Elvis Presley scored his first number-one
hit, "Heartbreak Hotel," and for twenty-five of the next
twenty-seven weeks Elvis stood on the pinnacle of the
charts with no less than seven single million-seller hits.

The Russians launched Sputnik, the United States re-
sponded with the American space program, and now the
world took it for granted that there were always astro-
nauts floating around somewhere in outer space.

Americans learned to eat packaged foods like Swan-
son TV dinners, Minute Rice, Redi-Whip, and Kool-Aid.
The birth rate reached its highest level in U.S. history,
giving rise to the "baby boom." Tailfins decorated cars,
freeways began to link the country, the McDonald brothers opened their first hamburger stand, Buddy Tupper
introduced Tupperware, Jonas Salk discovered a polio
vaccine, and Dwight D. Eisenhower added the phrase

"under God" to the Pledge of Allegiance at his inauguration.

In 1958, the year Roy Freedman went to prison, Elvis was drafted, the sack dress became the fashion rage, Truman Capote wrote *Breakfast at Tiffany's,* and Liz Taylor appeared with Paul Newman in *Cat on a Hot Tin Roof.* Coca-Cola tested an experimental plastic soft drink bottle.

Valium was introduced less than a month after President Kennedy's death, just in time for the nervewracking sixties and seventies.

After a couple of hours of reading the *Watauga Democrat,* it was clear to Simon that Boone, North Carolina, wasn't much different from any other small American town in the fifties. Watauga County High School and a handful of churches centered the community. Football games, band competitions, church socials and bazaars, advertising, and the comics occupied most of the newspaper's pages.

Occasionally, though, a stray article betrayed Boone's rural, mountain soul. One front page story described sheriff's deputies dynamiting two moonshine stills each capable of producing sixty to seventy cases of "white lightnin'" a day. The picture that accompanied the story showed the huge, copper contraptions surrounded by grinning lawmen with a box of dynamite at their feet.

That winter Boone suffered a heavy snowstorm, massive even by Blue Ridge Mountain standards. In the wake of the blizzard, schools closed and roads were impassable. A deep freeze followed, pipes froze, the electricity went out, and the mail stopped. On the editorial page one commentator suggested folks were better off in the "old days," before they got dependent on cars, grocery stores, electricity, and indoor plumbing. Not so long ago, hams, pork shoulders, and side meat hung in the family smokehouse, thirty cords of wood filled the wood house, the well never froze, and fireplaces and cast-iron cooking stoves glowed hot, radiating warmth throughout small homes. Home-canned food, wrapped in newspapers for insulation, filled every shelf in the pantry. Potatoes dug out of the root cellar roasted in the hot coals of the fire every night. Families slept together for warmth, tucked under down comforters and homemade quilts.

Oh, and Mrs. Ed Ray won first prize in the Betty Crocker cake baking contest, winning a 1958 Oldsmobile 88, which she planned to drive to Florida "straight away" to get away from the cold for a week or so.

The snow finally melted and summer came. On June 21 Vice President Richard Nixon spoke at the twelfth Annual Rhododendron Festival, then broke ground for a hospital in Banner Elk.

In July, when Eva Potter died and Roy Freedman was arrested, the Sky-Vu drive-in theater screened *The Virginian*, starring Joel McCrea. Maxwell House coffee was on sale for sixty-nine cents a pound at the Winn-Dixie.

Simon was disappointed by the newspaper's coverage of Eva Potter's murder and Roy Freedman's arrest and trial. He longed for tabloid details—gory descriptions and tear-jerking interviews—but instead the paper printed just three terse articles, accompanied each time by Eva Potter's senior high school picture. It was an unbecoming photograph. Eva posed in an artificial position, head slightly cocked, chin resting in her hands, too self-conscious to smile. She was plump by today's standards, and her long dark hair was pulled back in a ponytail. She wore a white blouse with a shiny pin displayed on the neat Peter Pan collar. Simon recognized the pin—it was a church perfect-attendance pin, which teenagers wore with pride even when Simon was growing up. Not he, though. His mother was Jewish and his father was a profoundly lapsed Baptist. Simon went to church for the weddings, funerals, and baptisms (dunkings, his Dad called it) of his relatives and friends. He remembered the food at these occasions best. He daydreamed briefly about perfect fried chicken—crispy on the outside and moist on the inside, greens cooked with ham hocks, butterbeans, scalloped tomatoes, hot buttered biscuits, and banana pudding.

The *Watauga Democrat* described Freedman as an Appalachian State Teachers College student, "a Melungeon man from Kentucky," who boarded in the Potter home. Freedman had taken a romantic interest in Eva, but was forbidden by her parents to court her because of his race.

According to the story, when Eva's father got home from work at five thirty in the afternoon and found Eva missing, he questioned June, Eva's sister, who admitted that Eva had gone on a picnic with Freedman. Angry and worried, Mr. Potter went to the picnic spot, where to his horror, he found a blood-soaked blanket, a blood-caked knife, and the remains of a picnic lunch. He immediately notified Sheriff Micah Guy, who formed a search party which combed the area. After dark fell, Potter and Guy returned to the Potter home, where Roy Freedman had just arrived. Freedman was "in a highly emotional state, near hysteria," according to the sheriff. Under questioning Freedman confessed to murdering Eva in a blind rage after she refused to marry him.

Freedman couldn't account for her missing corpse, his missing truck, or for the hours that had elapsed between the picnic and nightfall. He'd only say he'd been wandering around the woods on foot, grief-stricken, for hours.

The second news article briefly recapped the facts of the case, then stated that no progress had been made on the case. Eva Potter's corpse and Freedman's truck were still missing. Freedman was in jail, and a court date had been set for his murder trial. The newspaper mentioned again that Freedman was "a Melungeon from Kentucky" who had been forbidden to court Eva by her father.

A final short paragraph announced that Freedman had been sentenced to life in prison without parole. He was spared execution because of his confession and because Eva's corpse was never found. That was the end of that.

Simon folded up photocopies of the three articles and stuffed them in his back pocket. He lingered in the chair, tilted back, rubbing his eyes. Eva and Roy's story was so timeless, so human, and so tragic it was practically Shakespearean. It would make a great country song.

Shaking himself out of his reverie, Simon went out to his car. He cushioned his hand with the tail of his shirt to open the blazing hot car-door handle. The interior of the car was unbearably stuffy. He started the engine and cranked up the air conditioner to its highest setting. He waited outside, in the shade of an oak, for the car to cool off, listening to the car radio and chugging an ice cold Coke, thinking about Roy Freedman. He admitted to himself that he was interested in the man's case. He hoped that the fax from Watauga County would be waiting for him when he got back to Raleigh.

TO SIMON'S SURPRISE, the history department was locked up tight. Judy must have taken advantage of the end of the summer session to go home early. He turned on the lights in the main office and checked his mailbox, a slot in an old-fashioned bank of wooden cubbyholes. A sheaf of papers protruded from it. When he opened them, he saw the letterhead of the Watauga County District Attorney's Office. Judy must have retrieved them from the fax machine and placed them in Simon's box before she left.

It was quiet and peaceful in Simon's office without the noise and clatter of students on their way to class. He sat down at his desk and began to read the file.

Law enforcement was simpler in 1958, eight years before *Miranda v. Arizona*. Still, he could hardly believe the minimal work that had been done on the Potter case. The blood that soaked the blanket and spattered the knife hadn't been typed, nor was the knife dusted for fingerprints. It seemed that the sheriff's office had no interest in corroborating Freedman's confession.

Sheriff Guy's big, loopy handwriting documented the events much as Simon already knew them, adding a few new details. According to June Potter, Eva had spent the morning baking an apple pie and frying chicken for the picnic, while Freedman was out foraging for herbs. June and her mother, who was a "granny woman," a self-taught midwife and lay physician, were called out to deliver a baby and didn't get home until late afternoon. Supposedly, Freedman picked Eva up in his Ford truck after delivering his morning's collection of herbs to Wilcox Drug Company, and they went on their picnic. When the family reassembled that evening, Eva was missing. Once June had explained the picnic plans to her father, Mr. Potter and the sheriff searched the picnic site. They found the bloody blanket and knife, but no Eva, no Roy, and no truck. Freedman showed up, on foot, at the Potter home that night and "confessed" to her murder.

Sheriff Guy assumed that Freedman had disposed of the body and the truck. And why shouldn't he? What were the other possibilities? If another person murdered Eva and stole Freedman's truck, why did Roy confess? If he was forced to confess, why didn't he change his story as soon as he was safe and sound in prison? Wouldn't he want the law to find Eva's real murderer?

Sheriff Guy did speculate that it was possible that a bear had carried off Eva's corpse and Roy's truck had been stolen by some unknown person. From the tone of the report, Guy didn't think that was likely. Neither did Simon. In the mountains the exploits of bears were greatly exaggerated—Simon had grown up there, and the only bear he ever saw was in the zoo on Grandfather Mountain. Say Roy killed the girl and wandered off in shock—was it possible that someone just happened to be sauntering around an isolated picnic spot, discovered Roy's truck, and stole it, ignoring the corpse, or if a bear had already dragged it away, the bloody evidence of the murder? It was patently ridiculous.

Simon understood clearly now why finding Eva's body and Roy's truck didn't constitute new evidence that favored reopening Roy's case. The discovery actually "proved" that Roy had disposed of the body as Sheriff Guy had guessed that he had all those years ago.

The only other documents in the file were a signed copy of Freedman's confession, just a few lines long, and a copy of the judge's order sentencing Freedman to life in prison.

None of the evidence made any sense unless Freedman was guilty, which conclusion took Simon right back where he started, with the same niggling question. If Freedman was guilty, why on earth did the man give up minimum security and a cushy job at the governor's mansion to get to Simon and tell him his story? It seemed he wasn't going to resolve Freedman's problem in just one afternoon. He wasn't sure exactly what he was going to do next.

The Bloodworth House cast a long shadow over Simon's car in its parking spot next to the kitchen garden. The sprinklers had come on, and Simon walked deliberately through the cool mist on the fringes of the spraying water.

When Simon arrived home he noticed that his small front lawn had been newly mown and assumed that Danny, the teenager next door, had done it when he was mowing his own yard. He could hear the sound of the lawn mower behind Danny's house, so he wandered around back, sorting his mail as he went. He found the teenager steering his mower carefully around his mother's herb garden. Simon raised his hand when the boy turned his way, and Danny stopped and idled the engine.

"Hey," Simon said.

"Hey yourself," Danny answered. He was very thin and fair, with dark hair and dark blue eyes, and a hint of a moustache growing above his lip.

"Thanks for mowing my yard," Simon said.

"You're welcome," Danny said. The boy stretched so that his navel showed above his boxers, which stuck an inch out of his jeans. The blue boundary of a tattoo poked out of the boxers. "Boy, I sure would like a beer."

"There's a law against that—contributing to the delinquency of a minor. Not that you aren't already well on your way to a misspent youth. What with that tattoo, and all."

"You're just jealous—you're too old to get one."

"Nuts," Simon said, "that's not it. I'd worry that other people who have tattoos might like me."

"By the way," Danny said, "you missed your girl-friend."

"What?" Simon said.

"She sat on your front porch for an hour. Boy, did she look pissed when she left."

"Oh, my God!" Simon said, looking at his watch. It was seven thirty.

"Dude, you stood her up?"

Simon sat down, hard, on a wrought-iron chair.

"I don't believe it."

"She had a suitcase with her. Were you guys going somewhere?"

FOUR

WHAT COULD SIMON possibly say to Julia that would compensate for leaving her cooling her heels on his front porch the evening she had decided to spend a weekend with him? That he'd lost track of the time? That he'd gotten so involved in the murder of a complete stranger that he'd forgotten her? That he hadn't bothered to check his watch? That he was so distracted he didn't realize that when he had to unlock the history department to get into his office that meant it was after five o'clock?

Simon thought about his approach. No way was he going to admit he had forgotten her. He was just running a little late. He decided that the best approach was to be apologetic, but at the same time indicate that he expected to be promptly forgiven. It didn't work.

"I'm so sorry," Simon said, when Julia answered the phone. "You must be furious with me. I didn't realize what time it was. Let me make it up to you. We'll go out to dinner somewhere."

"No," Julia said. "I don't want to see you just now."

Her tone of voice was one he hadn't heard before. Simon pictured icicles hanging from her words.

"Listen, babe, I…"

"I haven't been stood up since the eighth grade."

"I didn't stand you up. I told you, I didn't realize what time it was."

"Then you can't exactly have been waiting with bated breath for my arrival."

"Please, let me come over so we can talk about this."

"You don't understand. I'm really, really angry. I don't want to see you."

"When can we talk?"

"I don't know. Maybe around Christmas."

She hung up. Simon didn't blame her. What had he been thinking? He didn't want to overanalyze his behavior, but he wondered if Tess's phone call had rattled him enough to make him unconsciously sabotage his relationship with Julia. Simon slumped back and rolled his neck around the hard edge of the sofa to release the muscle tension. It didn't help much.

This was no time for pride. First he called the florist and ordered a dozen red roses sent to Julia's house, and a dozen to her office on Monday, with "I'm sorry" written on the attached notes. Not that he thought for one minute that Julia would be swayed by flowers. He just wanted to cover all the bases, do all the things a contrite lover was supposed to do. If Julia didn't forgive him for his, yes, really stupid and inconsiderate behavior, he was going to be an unhappy man.

Suddenly the rest of a long, very hot summer stretched before him. To make matters worse, his closest bachelor friend, state archeologist David Morgan, was out of town. A few days earlier a farmer in Pasquotank County clearing a fallow pasture had found the remains of an eighteenth-century homestead. The site wouldn't be available for long, so every professional and amateur archeologist who could get free converged on the farm to mount a salvage operation. David packed his tools, his lawn chair, his charcoal grill, and his two Labrador retrievers into his camper and headed out of town. On the way to the grocery store to stock up on beer and hamburger, he stopped by Simon's house to ask him to keep an eye on his house. With David gone Simon had no one to drink beer and watch bad television with.

Not that David would be sympathetic to Simon's problems. He was an old-fashioned confirmed bachelor. He wasn't gay, he wasn't pining over a long-lost love, he just didn't think girlfriends and wives were worth the trouble and expense it took to get and keep them.

Simon went into his kitchen and opened his refrigerator door. He had planned to go to the market and stock up on groceries for his weekend with Julia, but of course he had forgotten to do that, too. He did have lots of beer. He was able to pick enough meat off the carcass of the roast chicken he and Julia had had for dinner—it seemed like months ago—to make himself a chicken sandwich. He twisted the cap off a bottle of beer, and went out on his back porch to brood.

A few hours later, he had finished a six-pack. It was pitch dark on his porch except for the tiny glow of the strands of Christmas lights strung around the porch ceiling. Drinking so much had emptied his mind of everything except awareness of the sounds of a summer night—the whoosh of the ceiling fan, the bursts of static that signaled the random electrocution of bugs attracted to his neighbor's bug zapper, the bass beat of Danny's guitar pulsing through the walls of his bedroom in the house next door, and the voices of his neighbors walking their dogs in the alley behind the house.

Simon became aware that it was late, he was tired, hot, and drunk. He went upstairs to bed, where in a final piece of bad luck, he found his air conditioner making a metallic, grinding noise. The thermostat registered ninety-two degrees, and the air was so hot it was hard to breathe. His vintage air conditioner was busted again. Simon turned it off to silence the noise and went downstairs to sleep on the living room sofa.

To cap off the evening, he saw that a crack in the outside wall of his kitchen had widened since the last time he had noticed it. The house was seventy-five years old. A large beam in the basement already supplemented the foundation. He prayed that the crack was just old plaster, not evidence of imminent collapse.

Early the next morning Simon woke up with a crick in his neck, sticky with sweat, and logy from a beer hangover, complete with pounding headache. On his way to the kitchen he passed his reflection in the mirror. He was unshaven, red-eyed, and his damp hair was plastered to his head. He looked as if he'd spent the night on the streets.

"You look like the loser you are," he said to himself, and meant it. He dissolved two Goody's powders into an ice cold Coke and carried the can into the shower with him, alternating pressing the cold can to his temples and drinking from it. After a while he felt a little better. Still damp from the shower, he lay back down on the sofa with an ice pack resting on his forehead, and went back to sleep.

When he awoke, the worst of his hangover, and his self-pity, had passed. He knew he had to do something constructive with his time. He mustn't spend day after day like this until the fall semester. He couldn't afford it emotionally or psychologically. He had spent a year of his life being depressed after his breakup with Tess and he wasn't going to do that again.

THE PHONE RANG three times before Simon's cousin, Luther Coffey, picked it up.

"Hey, stranger," Luther said. "How the hell are you?"

"Hot. Bored. I was just wondering, what's the temperature up there?"

"Warm down east, is it? Let me check the gauge." Luther put the phone down, and Simon could hear his heavy footsteps recede and the screen door slam as he went out onto the front porch of his cabin. Luther cheerfully whistled a few bars of "Cripple Creek" on his way back to the telephone.

"We're having a heat wave," Luther said. "It's seventy-nine degrees."

"Oh, man. It's been close to a hundred here every day for a week."

"Why don't you come on up? You're off now, aren't you? I got plenty of room. I don't get my boys until August."

"I just might do that. I'll have to stay at your momma's first, though."

"I bet you a case of that imported beer you bought last time you were here against a first-class detail job that you don't last there more than two days."

Simon laughed. "Forget it," he said, "that's a fool's wager if I ever heard one."

Simon called his aunt, Rae Coffey. She answered from a house extension out at her store. Simon could hear the sound of the cash register ringing up apple butter, cider, and peach preserves.

"Sugar, I am so glad to hear your voice!" his aunt said. "Do you know how long it's been since we laid eyes on you?"

"Don't say it."

"Two years."

"Not true. I was up there when you and Mel had your forty-fifth."

"That's what I said, two years ago."

"Well, I'm planning to come up. Would next week be okay?"

"Honey, tonight would be just fine. How long can you stay?"

"I don't know yet. Maybe a while. I've got this research project I'm working on."

"You have to have a reason to come up here, other than seeing your people who love you?"

"It's not that."

"Why don't you bring your girlfriend? We'd all like to meet her."

Simon dithered for a minute, thinking up an excuse.

"She's too busy at work right now, but I'll come Monday, if you're sure that's all right."

"I can't wait to hug your neck. Get here by dinner. I'll fix one of your favorites."

"Aunt Rae?"

"Yes?"

"Do you remember a murder that happened up there in 1958? A girl named Eva Potter…"

"Lord, yes! And they just found her body! Right off the parkway, not ten miles from here!"

"You remember when it happened?"

"Of course I do. How could I forget? Nobody talked about anything else for weeks."

"There wasn't much in the newspaper."

"Everyone in town knew all the details before it could even get printed. The whole town shut down to go to the trial. 'Course, there wasn't a trial after all. The murderer pleaded guilty. He was a Melungeon man, I remember. My mother used to tell me the bogeyman was

Melungeon, the silly woman. I hear the murderer's still alive, in prison in Raleigh.''

''Were you in the courtroom yourself?''

''I can't talk now, I've got a store full of customers. I'll see you Monday.''

Simon decided to spend the rest of the day in the Kenan College Library boning up on Melungeon history. He often went to the library when he was unhappy, because he felt in charge of his life there. He loved research, he loved teaching, and he was very good at both. No matter how chaotic his personal life, he focused completely while working. When he was successful finding an answer to whatever question plagued him, he got an endorphin rush, similar to the elation a professional athlete experiences after winning a race or a game.

Kenan Library was almost empty because of the break between the two summer sessions. Simon even had to turn on some lights on the way to his carrel. He opened the door with his keycard and set his laptop on his desk. He liked to do his Internet research here, rather than at home or in his departmental office, because of the quiet. No one disturbed faculty in their carrels. Simon turned on the desk and floor lamps he had brought in. He hated fluorescent lights. Pushing a jumble of books and papers aside, all of which dealt with his current research interests, he went through the library's holdings online. Then he went out to the library stacks looking for books, and into the periodical room for articles. He came back to his carrel with an armful of materials. He didn't have to check them out. Since he was a full professor, a nice librarian would come by Monday and do that for him. He could keep whatever he wanted in the carrel indefinitely, unless someone else needed it.

Much of the material Simon skimmed, because he was

somewhat familiar with the fascinating story of the Melungeon people.

The Melungeons were a mysterious, secretive ethnic group that settled in remote parts of the Appalachians during the eighteenth century. They lived by farming and "distilling spirits."

A North Carolina Historical Society report of 1912 said that the Melungeons appeared to be Mediterranean. They were swarthy, heavyset, and had black eyes and straight black hair.

The Melungeons clung to their own territory, repelling visitors, sometimes violently. They had a fierce, deadly reputation. When anyone trespassed on what the Melungeons considered their territory, they swept down from the hills, burning houses and livestock. It was not until 1885 that Melungeon territory was considered safe for outsiders. Over time they became less of a menace, becoming famous for their whiskey and fine brandy.

The Melungeons were the first non-Native Americans to penetrate Kentucky's Cumberland County. For centuries their origins were unknown. The Melungeons themselves claimed to be Portuguese, insisting their ancestors chartered a ship around 1768, landed in North Carolina, then pushed on into Kentucky.

For generations in Appalachia, the word "Melungeon" was an epithet, and worse. Melungeons were classed as non-whites, pushed off fertile land, barred from schools, prohibited from voting. It's no wonder they retreated into their own communities.

For many years anthropologists thought the Melungeons were a mixture of Portuguese explorers, Native Americans, and African-Americans, who became so isolated that they developed into a racial and ethnic subgroup. That notion was consistent with the pattern of

Portuguese exploration. The Portuguese were the first Europeans to travel the world. Their king encouraged them to marry native women wherever they went, so their descendants couldn't be displaced.

The Melungeons themselves insisted that they had no African or Native American ancestry. Before the 1950s, most researchers dismissed this as the common desire of most Americans to be white, to avoid racial stereotyping and discrimination.

Historians now knew that the Melungeons came to America from Barbados, a Portuguese colony, first settling in South Carolina in the late 1600s and 1700s, then moving into the mountains. They assumed English surnames to better blend into their new environment.

Since Simon had last studied the Melungeon mystery, modern research methods, including work on their oral traditions, cultural evidence, linguistics, physical phenotypes, and disease patterns, had solved much of their mysterious origins. Researchers even analyzed DNA samples of modern Melungeon volunteers.

When Simon read the DNA studies, the results gave him goose bumps. Melungeons were descended from some Portuguese, African, and Barbados Indian people, as was expected, but the largest part of their genetic heritage was Middle Eastern. They shared their ancestors with modern Turks, Arabs, and Jews. These results stunned everyone, but the scientific evidence was conclusive.

How had a Semitic race arrived in the Appalachian Mountains in the seventeenth century? The answer wasn't difficult. They were fleeing the Spanish Inquisition. Many of the Portuguese who colonized Barbados in the sixteenth century were "conversos," ethnic Jews and Arabs who converted to Roman Catholicism to escape the Inquisition. When the time came to leave Barbados, the group simply moved north, first into South Carolina, then into the Appalachians, where they were safe from persecution. Even the mystery of the word Melungeon had been solved. The Arabic words "Melun jinn" meant "cursed soul," an apt description of a Muslim or a Jew who was forced into Christianity and then shipped halfway around the world. They didn't belong anywhere in Europe, so they journeyed, as so many other outcasts did, to the American frontier. Over time, Melungeon descendants forgot almost everything about their own origins, except that they were olive-skinned because they were Portuguese.

The Melungeons remained isolated and were considered legally non-white by many Southerners until the 1950s. During the Civil Rights era they began to integrate American society, along with other minority groups. Ray Freedman was one of those who left the security of his community and went away to college. Not only that, he fell in love with an Anglo-Scots girl. It followed that when the girl was murdered, he instantly fell under suspicion.

Of course, Roy Freedman really might have murdered Eva Potter. Now Simon's innate curiosity kicked into high gear. He wanted to know if Freedman was a murderer, or a convenient scapegoat. If he was a scapegoat, who did murder Eva, and why? Simon wasn't sure he could answer those questions, but he wanted to try. Going to Boone would kill several birds with one stone. He would investigate Freedman's story, visit his family, and put some breathing space between himself and Julia. He hoped that space would amount to no more than a week.

Another advantage to this case, Simon told himself, was that he didn't have to examine some moldering old corpse. He hated that.

ON SUNDAY Simon packed and arranged for Danny to look after his cats and take care of his mail and newspapers, in return for the use of his fast Internet connection, after Danny swore on his learner's permit not to surf any Web sites originating in Amsterdam.

He called Julia three times, without success. Finally he left her a message, apologizing again, and inviting her to Boone for the following weekend, dangling cooler weather and a Pinchas Zuckerman concert at Appalachian State University as bait. He suggested she call him at his aunt's Monday night, and tried to sound confident that she would.

Simon doubted that Julia could be swayed to forgive him so soon—he hadn't suffered enough—but he wanted her to know he was thinking about her.

Sunday evening, after a take-out Chinese dinner, Simon walked next door to his neighbors, the Lysachts. Chuck and Greer sat outside on their back porch. Chuck opened the screen door for him. He was a tall, lean, blond man who looked much younger than his years. His wife, Greer, an athletic woman with a pixie haircut, offered him lemonade, which Simon accepted. She went inside for a glass full of ice, then came back out and poured lemonade from a silver pitcher into his glass. The glass frosted and instantly condensed water drops that rolled down its sides and soaked his napkin. The ceiling fan, set on high, spun hot air around the porch, sounding like an airplane engine. Simon mentioned that he was going out of town, and asked Greer if he could leave a key with her, and if she could let the air-conditioning repairman into his house. Danny had a summer job and couldn't be there during the day.

"Certainly," Greer said, "on one condition." Simon knew what was coming. "You set a date to speak to my book club. You promised ages ago."

"September," Simon said. "After the fall semester starts."

"Second Wednesday," she said.

"I'm there. And I have another favor. The crack in my back kitchen wall is bigger."

Chuck grinned at him.

"Want an estimate?" he asked.

"No," Simon said. "Just tell me if the house is going to fall down soon. If I need a new foundation, I need some time to fortify myself before hearing how much it will cost."

MONDAY MORNING Simon stopped by the history department to leave various Boone telephone numbers in case someone needed him, as if there were ever emergencies in the history business.

His footsteps echoed in the empty hallway. Judy sat at her desk, knitting.

"I'm leaving town for a few days," Simon said.

"I wish I was. I hate the time between sessions. It's so quiet and boring around here."

Simon checked his mailbox for the last time, and then gave Judy his list of telephone numbers—cell, Aunt Rae's, and Luther's.

"What do you think might happen here while you're gone?" Judy asked him. "Someone might steal a footnote?"

Simon collected a copy of the medical examiner's report that Dr. Boyette faxed him from his office in Chapel

Hill, and stuffed it in a file folder with the rest of the notes he'd gathered concerning Eva Potter's murder. The bulging folder gave him a sense of purpose, a Sherlockian feeling that the game was afoot.

History, and detection, was all about documents and their interpretation. Notes, reports, case files, and interviews were the primary sources of a murder investigation, comparable to the primary sources he used to solve an historical problem—newspapers, letters, diaries, and other records from the past. He used the same analytical and interpretive skills for one as he did for the other. So far he'd solved two old murders. Embarking on his third, he wondered if he was developing an avocation. He'd hooted when newspapers called him a forensic historian, but maybe he shouldn't. Other academic professions had forensic divisions. There were forensic psychologists, forensic pathologists, and forensic entomologists, so why not forensic historians?

Simon stopped by his office to make sure his door was locked. Judy had thumbtacked his list of final grades on his door. Simon never consciously graded on the curve, but this group of grades fell into a predictable pattern; four As, seven Bs, seven Cs, and two Fs. Next to his anonymous student ID number and the F beside it, Todd Spetz had written, in red felt-tip marker, "Screw you, you dwarf." Simon surmised that Todd wouldn't be matriculating at Kenan next semester.

The last thing Simon did on the way out of Raleigh was stop off at his bank, transfer some funds into his checking account, and mail a check for ten thousand dollars to Tess. Simon was well aware that most of his friends, all right, all of them, would tell him he was a spineless wimp. He didn't care. He'd thought it over, and he felt it was a fair request, so he did it.

FIVE

SIMON PULLED OFF at a lookout on NC Highway 421 North a few miles outside of Boone. Into the distance stretched the familiar but no less spectacular view of the Blue Ridge Mountains, part of the Appalachian Mountain chain that stretched from Maine to Georgia. Everywhere he looked, trees stretched toward the horizon, rising and falling in waves over hills and valleys, until in the far distance, the mountains appeared blue, circled at their rims with clouds like haloes. Bright sun bathed the mountaintops in light, while the valleys and hollers below lingered in darkness.

Like all tourists, the big family that had pulled off the highway at the lookout tumbled out of their minivan and, ignoring the printed warning sign, stood on the stone retaining wall, exclaiming at the view. Simon obligingly took their picture with the camera they pressed into his hand.

After the family left the lookout, Simon turned away from the view, hitching himself up on the wall, and faced the cut where the road sliced through the mountainside. The layered sediments represented millions and millions of years of geologic time.

The Appalachian mountains were among the oldest rock formations in the world, belonging to the Archean and Cambrian geological ages. About 225 million years ago rocks that were a billion to a billion and a half years old were squeezed, faulted, folded, and twisted when Africa rammed North Carolina, then pulled away again. It was a remarkable mountain-building event, when the Appalachians surged to heights once equal to the Andes.

In the road cuts you could see the Archean progress into the Cambrian and then into the modern age. Simon wasn't a geologist, but he could identify most of the layers of rock. Embedded in these rocks, formed by cataclysmic geological events humans had never experienced, were deposits of gold, silver, copper, many other minerals and metals, and precious and semiprecious stones.

Today the Appalachians were quiet, mellowed into a range of round mountains and fertile valleys layered deep and rich with soil and humus. For millions of years now, much of the surface had eroded away, uncovering the ancient rocks that had built the mountains.

Erosion also revealed the minerals and gems that Native Americans, and later European settlers, discovered and mined. These deposits were so rich that until the California Gold Rush, North Carolina was the only domestic source of gold in the United States. For over a hundred and fifty years, miners found everything from emeralds to borax in these mountains. Even Appalachian clay was valuable—Wedgwood bought it by the railroad-car load.

Driving along the stretch of NC 421 named after Doc and Merle Watson, Simon passed under the Blue Ridge Parkway at the Continental Divide, and drove down and around the hills toward Boone, fighting traffic and road construction all the way. What with students, tourists, and summer people, Watauga County was getting a mite crowded.

Just before the turnoff to his family's farm was the store where his aunt and her family sold produce, cider, homemade apple butter, and applesauce from their apple orchard and vegetable garden. The store was only about ten years old, but was built to look like a trading post, with a broad front porch lined with rocking chairs, a red tin roof, and a big sign bordered and lettered in red that read SHAW TRADING POST with the second ''S'' turned backward. The sight made him cringe, but who was he to judge how his relatives made a living? The store was a cash cow. Even now the parking lot was full of RVs, campers, and minivans, like it would be all summer and well into the autumn leaf-viewing season.

Simon turned right onto NC Highway 194 North, which the locals knew as Jefferson Road, pulling off the asphalt onto the shoulder to collect himself before going on to Shaw's Knob, his family's homeplace.

There was a famous book written by Thomas Wolfe, a native of Asheville, called *You Can't Go Home Again*. Simon thought the title might better be *You Can't Go Home Again Without Getting Weird Feelings in Your Gut*.

He inhaled deeply a couple of times to calm his nerves, drove on, and turned into the complex of graveled and dirt roads that crisscrossed Shaw's Knob. Simon and his aunt owned undivided halves of the property. God knew what chaos would ensue if they ever had to divide it. The property included five homes, the store, a warehouse, a Christmas-tree farm, a truck garden, an apple orchard stocked with heirloom trees, and a significant amount of valuable highway frontage. A Shaw ancestor bought the three-hundred-acre farm in 1843. Only less than half of the property, the south side, and the southern slopes of the knob, got enough sun to be arable.

After Simon's grandparents died, Simon's aunt, Rae Shaw Coffey, built the store and developed a thriving Christmas-tree business. Simon had inherited from his father his half of the land. He leased it to his aunt Rae, his father's only sibling. Simon's cousin, Luther, Rae and Mel Coffey's only son, who owned an automobile detailing business in Boone, lived in a cabin that he'd fixed up on the northern side of the knob. A private road, christened Fat Boy Road after the first Shaw's rotund son, intersected Jefferson Road on the west, ran alongside Shaw's Creek, and dead-ended about where the creek met the south fork of the New River. As children, Simon and Luther explored the woods, built forts amongst the brush, and waded in the creek. They netted jars full of minnows and crawfish, caught a few nice brook trout, and panned the creek for gold, finding enough glittering specks to be exciting. As he grew up, Simon learned to ride a bicycle and then to drive a car on the road. Now, with the family's permission, hikers, fishermen, trail bikers, and student biologists used the road, although Luther called the sheriff on motorcyclists and go-carters.

Another holding lay across the creek to the north. It was rocky and undeveloped except for one old bridge across the creek from Luther's cabin and a footpath up to a decrepit shack. Simon's family owned the road, although they would certainly have permitted access to anyone who lived there. No one had lived on the place as long as Simon could remember.

Simon drove up the short graveled driveway and parked in front of the white-painted clapboard farmhouse where Aunt Rae lived. Tara it wasn't. The squat, two-storied, gabled bungalow sat on a concrete block foundation under tall pine trees. Big flowerpots that crowded the steps up to the porch were filled with red geraniums, and the wide front porch lined with rocking chairs and the Christmas-red front door welcomed him home.

Simon got out of his car and looked around. No one was in sight. His aunt and cousin Debra were most likely still at the store; Debra's husband Hank, who managed the farm, could be anywhere on the property. Simon was glad to be alone for a few minutes. It gave him a chance to get his emotional bearings.

Simon and his parents had lived in Boone in a modern stone-and-glass ranch, sold soon after their deaths, but he had spent a lot of time on the farm during his childhood. He and Luther were the same age, and, in a culture where one's closest friends were your relatives, they were close pals, though otherwise they had little in common.

Although Simon's immediate family rarely went to church, or temple either, they came to Sunday dinner at the farm almost every week. Simon's grandparents hosted it first, then Aunt Rae took over the tradition.

To the left of Aunt Rae's house, across the road that led to the warehouse, was a four-vehicle garage with an apartment over it. If Luther and his mother could have gotten along living so close to each other, Luther would have been living there, but instead it was rented to ASU students. To the right of the farmhouse, and across another dirt road that led up to the Christmas-tree acreage, was Debra and Hank Van Pala's brick split-level, where they lived with their kids, Tammy and Henry. A renovated tenant house sat at the driveway entrance to the road. A Hispanic family, the Lorenzos, who were the only full-time hired help around the place, lived there now. Simon's other cousin, Gail, and her husband, Boyd

Love, and their children lived on their own place, an organic farm near Asheville.

It was a sign of the times that only one of Rae and Mel's three children lived and worked on the homeplace. Simon's father had started the trend, going to college and then to graduate school. When Simon's grandparents were alive, they lived in the big house and Rae and her family lived in the ranch. When they died, Rae moved to the big farmhouse and her children were supposed to take their place in its orbit. That Luther and Gail had left to run their own businesses was a constant source of sorrow to Rae.

The Christmas-tree farm shipped Frasier firs wholesale and retail all over the country. Hank and Aunt Rae managed it from a big corrugated metal warehouse north of the living complex at the end of another graveled road. The Christmas-tree farm went all the way up the cleared southern slopes and to the top of the knob, trees growing in graduated sizes from seedlings with six short branches to eight-footers due to be harvested this winter. An elaborate irrigation system pumped water from the New River to irrigate the crops, although an automatic sprinkler and fertilizer system coddled the tiniest seedlings in a separate fenced bed. These days migrant workers did most of the labor around the place, but in his youth Simon made spending money transplanting seedlings in the summer. Sunburns, blisters, and an aching back helped convince him to follow his father into academics.

The silence broke when the door to Debra and Hank's place burst open, and Tammy and Henry ran screaming across the road to him. He met them halfway, and they almost knocked him down running into his arms. Their father, Hank, a big, quiet man, followed them.

"We're so glad we got to see you before we left," Henry said, hanging onto Simon as he struggled to stay on his feet.

"We're going to band camp for a week," Tammy announced, smoothing her thick, dark curly hair away from her face. "Will you still be here when we get back?"

"Probably," Simon said. "Sure, of course." Seeing the kids he realized just how long he'd been gone. Henry was going to be stocky like his dad. Tammy had always been bright and eager, and now it was obvious she was going to be very pretty, too.

Hank put a hand on Simon's shoulder.

"I'll be right back," he said. "I've got to get these kids to the high school. They're riding to camp with some other band members in the activity bus. You all come on," he said to the kids, who were still hanging on Simon, "help me with this stuff." Tammy and Henry picked up their instruments, a flute and a saxophone by the look of the cases, and Hank shouldered two duffel bags. They got into a Jeep Cherokee wagon and headed out the driveway. Tammy poked her head out of the window and shouted back to him.

"You'd better be here when we get back," she said, "or else!"

As Hank drove away, Rae's old wood-paneled station wagon pulled into the driveway. Debra was in the driver's seat. She parked next to Simon's Thunderbird and Aunt Rae got out of the passenger side, a little stiffly, steadying herself with the car door. Once upright, Aunt Rae moved quickly toward Simon, throwing both arms around him and hugging him, hard. While pressed next to her ample bosom he smelled the Gold Bond medicated powder she'd liberally dusted herself with for years. Simon's grandmother had doused herself with the same stuff. Then, just as roughly, Rae pushed Simon away and held him at arm's length, looking him over critically.

"You look more like your mother every day," she said. "But you're a sight. Don't you ever eat? And you need a haircut."

Aunt Rae never changed. Short and chunky, her dyed red hair showed half an inch of gray at the roots. A sheen of perspiration coated her upper lip. She wore a lime green polyester pantsuit and big eyeglasses with pink frames. She released Simon from her hug, but still held tight onto one hand, so that Debra, small and energetic, with dark chestnut hair like her daughter's, could hug him, too.

"I'm so glad to see you," Debra said.

"It's good to have you home," Aunt Rae said.

"I'm happy to be here, too," Simon said.

And he was.

"DON'T COOK DINNER, please," Simon said, following his aunt into her house. "You've been working all day. Let me take you out."

"Don't be ridiculous," she said. "We're not going out to some restaurant on your first night here, nor ever, if I have anything to say about it. It's a waste of good money, you might as well eat a hundred dollar bill. I'm fixing chicken-fried steak, it's still your favorite, isn't it?" She didn't sit down or even pause, taking her pantsuit jacket off on the way to the kitchen. Debra had gone back to her house, but she and Hank would be back for dinner.

"Let me help," Simon said.

"Stay out of my kitchen," she said. "You go on and

get settled and then come talk to me. You're in Luther's old room.''

The house hadn't changed much since Simon's last visit. The original log cabin, built in 1843, was incorporated into the two front rooms of the modern house so completely that only the wide wood floors hinted at its construction. Though varnished and waxed many times, the floors still showed original axe marks and pegs.

Over many years the house evolved into a traditional antebellum farmhouse, with four rooms downstairs—dining room, kitchen, front and back parlors, and a screened porch. Upstairs were four bedrooms and a sleeping porch.

Between the World Wars a big bathroom and storage closet eliminated the sleeping porch, and a few years later a powder room was squeezed in downstairs under the staircase. The kitchen was last modernized in the seventies, although Aunt Rae had a new double-oven gas range and refrigerator.

The family had always left the living room floor bare, the better to proudly display a large, black burn mark on the old wood planks where a Union Army squad under General Stoneman, a disciple of Sherman's ''destroy but don't fight'' philosophy, shot out an oil lamp during an attack on the house and set it on fire. Of course, the Yankees were valiantly beaten back by Caleb Shaw, Simon's fifth great-grandfather. Simon could never verify that this colorful bit of family oral history actually happened, but it made a good story. In high school while writing a paper on the Civil War in Watauga County, he found Caleb Shaw's name in a document that listed Union sympathizers. This wasn't surprising—Watauga County was pretty evenly split between Unionists and

Confederates. There weren't any slaves or plantations to defend here. To this day the county had few African-American residents, and Simon had few opportunities to indulge in one of his favorite hobbies, protesting the display of the Confederate flag.

Even if Caleb were a Unionist, it wouldn't have stopped Yankees from attacking his farm, since they assumed that any homestead with a scrap of food left on it was available for looting.

Another good family story his grandparents often repeated was the sad tale about how Caleb buried the extensive collection of family silverware, gold and silver coins, and jewelry, then caught pneumonia and died without telling anyone where it was. Simon and Luther crisscrossed the farm with a metal detector when they were teens, looking for the so-called family riches. They never found anything except buttons, nails, horseshoes, and bullets.

The Shaw homeplace wasn't the only place where wealth was supposed to be hidden in the North Carolina mountains. Simon and Luther spent the best part of two summers looking for the fortunes rumored to be buried in Watauga County. Simon's Dad said for years that a metal detector was the best gift he had ever given Simon, since it kept him and Luther out of trouble for two whole years. The boys were too young to drive a car, but in the country kids were expected to operate farm equipment, so they just drove everywhere on their grandfather's tractor, very slowly, searching for lost Cherokee gold and silver mines, buried Confederate treasure, caches of DeSoto's and Pardo's Mexican loot, and yes, the treasure cave of outlaw Jack Vance.

A Confederate deserter who spent some time with Vance wrote a description of his cavern hideout. It was lit, the chronicler said, by dozens of stolen silver candelabra. Chests of jewelry and cases of sterling silverware stood everywhere, and Vance and his men slept on pallets made of looted fine linens and wore silk and wool clothing. There were lots of caves in Watauga County. Every one Simon and Luther explored was empty.

As Simon grew up, he realized that it was just as likely that Caleb knocked over the lamp himself after imbibing a crock of white lightnin', and that his family probably owned a couple of cast-iron cookpots, stoneware, and a dozen pewter knives and forks, at best. Caleb Shaw's wife might have had a silver wedding ring, but that would be the extent of her jewelry collection. Still, the Civil War stories would be defended to the death by his grandparents and Aunt Rae, so he kept his mouth shut. One thing Simon had learned as a history teacher was that it was almost impossible to unteach a myth.

Simon looked around the living room again. Something seemed to be missing, but he couldn't place it. The Victorian living room suite, covered in chintz, the Hummel figurines on the mantel, his great-grandmother's framed samplers, were all in their accustomed places.

Aunt Rae used the back parlor as her office now. The door was closed, so Simon didn't go inside. Instead he opened the door to the back porch. Freshly-painted green rocking chairs moved slightly in the breeze. Ferns hung from the tin porch ceiling in big baskets. A dozen birdhouses and bird feeders stood outside in the yard.

Something about wandering around the house and finding few changes made Simon feel secure. The executors of his parents' will sold their house to add funds to Simon's trust fund, so Aunt Rae's place seemed like home to him now.

Simon went back inside and climbed the staircase and went into the back bedroom to the right, Luther's old room. The same red-and-blue quilts covered twin iron beds. The battered armoire, necessary since the room didn't have a closet, stood in the same spot against the wall. Luther's old dresser, the kind with a towel rack instead of a mirror, had been dressed up with a lacy runner and an antique china bowl-and-pitcher set. Lace curtains hung in the open windows, blowing out into the room.

Just for old times' sake Simon lifted the mattress on the bed Luther always used. His cache of *Playboy* and *Car and Driver* magazines was long gone.

Simon unpacked, washed up, and went on downstairs to the kitchen where Aunt Rae was up to her elbows cooking his welcome-home dinner. Peeled potatoes boiled on the stove. Quart-sized Mason jars that had held homemade applesauce and green beans sat empty on the counter, their contents simmering away on back burners. Rae wrapped biscuits up in foil, sliding the packet into the warm oven. Then she started chopping fresh tomatoes, onions, and cucumbers from the garden. She scraped those into a china bowl and stirred in mayonnaise, salt, and pepper. When the tea-water boiled on the stove, she poured it into a metal pitcher full of tea bags. Then she scooped in the sugar. More dissolved when the water was really hot. You weren't a Southerner unless you liked sweet iced tea. Before they were ready to eat, she'd fill up the rest of the pitcher with ice cubes. It was pointless to ask her for lemon—it was only good for lemon meringue pie.

The radio on the windowsill played softly, tuned to the local Christian radio station. Simon would have loved a beer, but knew better than to mention it. Aunt

Rae was a Baptist of the teetotaler persuasion. Simon's grandmother was even stricter. She'd turn off the television if a beer commercial came on. Watching a football game was a complicated exercise when Grandma was around.

"Where's dessert?" Simon asked.

"Debra's bringing over a peach pie," his aunt said.

"I was joking," Simon said.

"I know you were," she said. "Now stop sassing me and tell me what's going on in your life."

Simon told her a version of the last few weeks, one that left out any hint of danger to himself. While he talked, Simon watched her cook the chicken-fried steak.

She salted and peppered five thick cube steaks. Then she crushed a sleeve of saltine crackers, and beat together milk and eggs. She dredged the steaks in cracker crumbs, dipped them in the milk mixture, and dredged them in the crumbs again. She heated up Crisco oil in a cast-iron skillet, and fried the steaks until they were golden brown. The aroma was wonderful. She placed the steaks in the oven to keep warm while she made the gravy. Leaving the drippings in the skillet, she mixed in a quarter cup of flour, a little salt and pepper, and four cups of milk.

"Here," she said to Simon, "you can do this. Keep stirring while I mash the potatoes."

Simon stirred with a heavy iron whisk that looked like it might have been around since Caleb Shaw's day.

The screen door slammed, hard.

"Don't slam the door, son," Aunt Rae called out.

Simon's cousin Luther Coffey came into the kitchen. He kissed his mother and slapped Simon on the back.

"Good to see you, man," he said to Simon.

"You, too," Simon said.

"I didn't see you in church yesterday," Aunt Rae said to Luther. "Where were you?"

"Working," Luther said.

"If you're going to keep that place open on Sunday, you should at least wait to open until after dinner, like we do the store," Aunt Rae said.

"I got child support to pay," Luther said. "And you know I get to church Wednesday nights."

Luther's hand stayed on Simon's shoulder a second before it dropped. Luther was the same age to the month as Simon, and looked like his mother. His red hair had faded to dirty auburn, and where she was heavy, he was all muscle. As children Luther and Simon were inseparable. They had stayed close, though they had little in common. Simon was a born scholar, while Luther was wild in the best Southern redneck tradition. He drove like a maniac, dropped out of school, and learned to drink and smoke early. A wise country judge gave Luther a choice when he was arrested a second time for drag racing on the highway. Go to jail, or join the army.

Luther grew up safely in the army, returned home, got his GED and went to work on the farm. That was a disaster. Aunt Rae just could not adapt to Luther being a grown man, and a trustworthy one, at that. When Simon's father died, he left Luther a little money, which Luther invested in an automobile detail shop. He now owned the shop outright.

Debra and Hank came in, carrying a peach pie and a bowl of steaming butter beans. They all sat down at the loaded dining room table, held hands, and bowed their heads.

"Bless this food to our use, and us to thy loving service, and keep us ever mindful of the needs of others, Amen," Hank said.

Simon ladled cream gravy over his meat and mashed potatoes. The first forkful melted in his mouth.

"I can't even describe how good this tastes," Simon said. His aunt beamed at him. Suddenly Simon realized someone was missing.

"Where's Uncle Mel?" he asked.

Hank quickly took a long drink of his tea. Debra took a big bite of tomatoes. Luther concentrated on coating every inch of his hot biscuit with butter. Aunt Rae helped herself to another spoonful of butter beans.

"These are pretty good," she said to Debra. "But I like mine without onions." She turned to Simon.

"Melvin and I are getting divorced," she said.

Simon couldn't have been rendered more speechless if an alien spacecraft had landed in the front yard.

"You better shut your mouth," she said to him, "or a june bug might fly in and choke you."

"What did you say?" Simon said. Aging, rural, Baptist, farm people just didn't get divorced. Shoot each other maybe, but not divorce.

"We're getting a divorce."

"Why?" Simon said.

"Irreconcilable differences," his aunt said.

"No one tells me anything," Simon said.

"You haven't been exactly staying in close touch," Luther said.

"Melvin wanted to retire," Aunt Rae said. "Stop working. Spend our savings on one of them RVs and go to Disney World and the Grand Canyon. Have you ever heard of such a thing? Working people like us can't retire. Social Security and Medicare are likely to go broke any day, thanks to those fools in Washington and Raleigh, and then where would we be?"

"Where is he?"

"He's living at the Balm of Gilead Rest Home," Luther said.

"A rest home? Uncle Mel in a rest home? Is he sick, too?"

"It's okay," Luther said. "It's more like a retirement home, although the lady that owns it is a nurse. It's all men Daddy's age, widowed or single. He's got his own room that opens out to the porch, his own furniture, a big TV, and of course he still drives his truck everywhere he wants to go."

"It's shameful, an able-bodied man lying around watching TV or playing checkers when he should be working," Aunt Rae said. "He wasn't good for working more than half a day anymore, anyway. After lunch he'd fall asleep in his recliner."

That was what was missing from the living room. Uncle Mel's recliner.

"He's seventy-four years old," Debra said.

"Time for dessert," Aunt Rae said.

Aunt Rae and Debra brought everyone warm peach pie topped with vanilla ice cream. Simon had two pieces.

After dinner they carried their plates into the kitchen. Simon went to load the dishwasher.

"You get out of here," Aunt Rae said. "The kitchen's no place for a man."

"I'll help, Momma," Debra said.

"You don't rinse the plates well enough," Aunt Rae said.

"There's not much point having a dishwasher if you wash the dishes by hand first," Debra said.

"It don't get them clean enough," Aunt Rae said.

"Maybe you should get a new dishwasher that works," Luther said. "That one's fifteen years old."

"It works just fine," Aunt Rae said.

"Come on over to the house for a few minutes," Hank said to Luther and Simon. "I want to show you the Web site for the Christmas-tree farm."

Hank, standing behind his mother-in-law, rolled his eyes in the direction of his house.

"Go on over, boys," Aunt Rae said. "You ought to know something about this business in case Hank and Debra and I get hit by a logging truck someday."

The four of them scooted like guilty children across the lawn to Hank and Debra's house.

They sagged into lounge chairs on the back deck. Hank brought Simon and Luther beers.

"What is all this about Uncle Mel?" he said.

"He just got fed up and left," Debra said. "He wants to retire. Momma would die if she stopped working. It's as simple as that."

"Is it permanent?"

"I don't think they'll really get divorced," Luther said, "but I don't think that Daddy will ever come back here. They just have to agree on alimony."

"He's got to pay her alimony?"

"Of course not," Debra said. "Momma's got to pay him. He was working here for Granddaddy before they got married, and she never put his name on anything, the land, the businesses, checking accounts, nothing."

"She come to find out from the lawyer that he deserves a big share of the assets," Hank said.

"Do you know what the discovery showed?" Luther said.

"Hush," Debra said. "It's not any of our business. Daddy shouldn't have told you."

"Nuts to that," Luther said. "She's worth over a million dollars. I told you she'd been cheating you for years on that lease."

"Stop it right now, Luther. Momma can't help the way she is."

"Debra's right," Hank said. "People her age don't change. There's no point fussing about it."

"As long as she's happy and Daddy's happy, I don't care," Debra said.

Luther got up and stretched. "I got to get home. Got to be at work at seven tomorrow." He melted into the dark yard, and soon Simon could hear the sound of his four-wheel-drive truck climbing the dirt road back to his cabin.

Simon drained the last of his second beer, and kissed Debra good night.

When he went back into Rae's house she was sitting at the kitchen table drinking a cup of coffee and reading her Bible.

"You don't fool me," she said. "You all were across the way drinking a beer."

"You're a sharp one, Aunt Rae," Simon said. He pecked her on the cheek. "I'm off to bed. Coming?"

"I got two more verses here," she said. "I'm behind schedule as it is."

Aunt Rae reread the New Testament every year. She also read the local newspaper, *North Carolina Farmer,* and *The Biblical Recorder*. Anything else was a waste of her time.

Simon had left his cell phone in the bedroom when he went down to dinner. He checked his messages. Judy Smith, the history department secretary, wanted him to call her in the morning. Chuck Lysacht had called— Simon's house wasn't going to fall down, but the utility porch might separate from the kitchen wall. Chuck said he'd get a jack from the home store and shore it up.

Simon had asked Julia to call him, and she hadn't. He tried not to call her, but lost that battle.

Julia lifted her receiver just as the fourth ring died away, as if she decided at the last minute not to let her answering machine pick up. She knew her caller was Simon; she would have recognized his cell-phone number on her caller ID. Simon felt a brief surge of hope.

"Hi," he said. "I'm in Boone. Did you get my message?"

"Yes," she said. "And the roses are beautiful."

"I'm glad you like them. I am so sorry, babe. You know I…"

"I don't really want to talk about this right now."

"You're still angry," he said.

"You know," she said, "it could take some time to get over being abandoned on your doorstep. It was very embarrassing. The kid mowing the lawn next door kept staring at me. The postman going down the other side of the street looked at me oddly, and by golly, when he came back from the other direction, I was still sitting on your stoop with my little suitcase. Not to mention the woman who dropped off the kids on the corner, the…"

"Haven't I apologized enough? I'm sorry. How many times do I have to say it?"

"It's not just that, it's everything."

"What everything? I wasn't aware there was an everything."

"At our age, well, at my age, I guess I'm trying to say that I need to think about where our relationship is going."

Damnation. Simon was afraid of this.

"Julia, honey, you know how I feel about you," Simon said.

"I do, I just think, well, it hasn't been too long since

your divorce, and maybe a separation like this is a good idea," she said. "Like a cooling-off period."

Simon didn't want to cool off.

"Okay. I get the picture," he said. "Let me know when I've groveled enough, and if you can lower your standards enough to be seen with me. Good-bye."

Then he hung up, and instantly regretted it. He redialed Julia's number, but she didn't answer. Simon flung his cell phone across the room, but luckily, it bounced off his bathrobe hanging on a chair and fell onto the rug. He retrieved it, and it was working. He called her again. Still no answer.

Simon knew that he wasn't exactly Julia's dream man. He was a tenured history professor at a small Southern college who would rather teach than rack up prestigious awards and honors. The Pulitzer Prize that he had already won was most likely the high point of his career. He was perfectly happy with that. Julia, on the other hand, expected to marry someone wealthy and ambitious. She had been engaged twice, once to a banker who was the oldest son of an Old Raleigh Family, and once to a lawyer well on his way to an eighty-hour workweek. She never mentioned them to him.

And then, there was the truth that Simon hadn't admitted to himself since last Friday night. He had forgotten that he and Julia had a date that night. Maybe he wasn't as devoted to her as he thought he was.

Simon hated overanalyzing his feelings. It wasn't manly, and made him feel like those pitiful people on afternoon talk shows. He'd get some sleep and concentrate on his plan for the next day.

After Simon turned off his light and pulled up the worn, soft sheets and the quilt he remembered that he'd forgotten to talk to Aunt Rae about Roy Freedman's trial.

SIX

SIMON AWOKE TO the odor of warm brown sugar and cinnamon. It was only seven thirty, but Aunt Rae had been up long enough to bake a coffee cake from scratch. The cake rested, as yet untouched, on a cut-glass cake plate on the kitchen table. Aunt Rae sat at the table reading the *Watauga Democrat,* pink reading glasses resting well down on her nose so that she had to tip her head up to focus on a page. She wore a faded blue-print housecoat, white Keds tennis shoes, and blue lace ankle socks. The minute she noticed Simon standing in the kitchen doorway she got to her feet.

"Do you still drink your coffee with all that milk and sugar in it?" she asked.

"Don't wait on me," Simon said. "I'll get it."

She was already across the kitchen at the stove pouring coffee into a blue-flowered china cup on a matching saucer. There were no mugs in Aunt Rae's kitchen. Ugly old things, she called them. She would just as soon drink out of a tin can. She still fixed her coffee in an old-fashioned percolator that boiled the coffee until it was dark as molasses. The pot sat on the stove all day, over time reducing the contents to a sludge that should carry a warning label for caffeine. Aunt Rae drank most of it herself, the last cup just before she went to bed.

"Cut you a slice of coffee cake," she said to Simon.

"I used the recipe that called for apples and raisins. That's your favorite, isn't it?"

Simon was way ahead of her. He already had a knife in his hand, deciding how big a piece he wanted.

"You don't need to do all this," Simon said. He lifted a wedge of coffee cake onto a plate and cut into it with the edge of his fork.

"You could use some spoiling. You got no one to look after you properly."

"Don't remind me," Simon said.

Aunt Rae brought him his coffee, and a refill for herself.

Simon helped himself to another piece of coffee cake. Aunt Rae finally served herself, eating while finishing her newspaper.

She had stopped reading by the time Simon finished his second cup of coffee. She folded the newspaper neatly into rectangles, squaring the sides perfectly, so it would fit tidily into her recycling box.

"Do you have to go to the store today?" Simon asked her.

"No, Debra opens this morning. But I've got a lot of paperwork to do."

"Have you got a few minutes now?"

"For you, honey, of course."

"I meant to ask you last night about what you remember about Eva Potter's murder and Roy Freedman's trial."

Aunt Rae seemed disappointed in Simon's choice of subjects, but she assumed her remembering posture, leaning back in her chair and stroking her chin.

"I was real scared when I first heard what happened," she said. "I was home all day alone with a baby. Eva was murdered on our property. You know how Fat Boy

Road dead-ends at the New River? There's a flat place there, a river beach, where Eva and Roy went for their picnic. It was a lover's lane in those days.''

Simon was shocked. This was the first he'd heard that Eva had been killed so close to his home.

"I know that spot," Simon said. "Luther and I used to play there. I had no idea she died on our property."

"Gives you the willies, don't it?" Aunt Rae said.

"How come I never knew about this?"

"Who would tell a young'n such a thing?"

"Come to think of it, the actual location of the murder wasn't mentioned in the newspaper, or in Sheriff Guy's notes."

"Daddy worked hard to keep it quiet. It was easier to do that back then."

"Do you remember if anyone thought Freedman might be innocent when he was arrested?"

Rae shook her head. "I don't think so," she said. "Besides, he confessed. Why should anyone think he was innocent?"

"He says the sheriff and Potter's father threatened to lynch him."

Rae got up to pour herself another cup of coffee.

"Times was different then. If the sheriff was sure Mr. Freedman had done it, he'd do what he could to make him talk. Now, he wouldn't actually hang him, but I wouldn't put it past him to rough him up, scare him good to get him to talk. No way he would permit a lynching. He had deputies on duty at the jail twenty-four hours a day to make sure nobody messed with Freedman."

"Roy was threatened while he was in jail?"

"Honey, this was 1958. The man was a Melungeon, he wasn't from around here, he courted this girl even though her daddy forbid it, and now she was murdered.

What do you think? There was a crowd camped outside the jail for a couple of days. Not a mob, the sheriff wouldn't put up with that, but they sure weren't protesting against the death penalty.''

"What about the trial? Did you go?''

"No, but Daddy and Melvin went. It only took a few minutes. There was a plea bargain, and he got off with life in prison. Melvin was real disappointed there wasn't more of a show.''

"Did you know his lawyer? Was he competent, do you think?''

"He came up from Asheville. I guess he was able. I never heard different. What could he do, anyway? Everyone in town knew Freedman had confessed.''

"Doesn't it seem possible that he confessed out of fear? You said yourself he was a Melungeon, and that there was a mob outside the jail.''

"I said it wasn't a mob.''

"I bet it looked like a mob to Roy.''

"Well, he could have taken the confession back later, couldn't he? They moved him to Asheville and then to Raleigh. Far away from here.''

Exactly what Simon thought.

"Now that you mention it, though…''

"What?''

"What you said, earlier, about did anybody think he could be innocent. I do recollect Daddy and Melvin talking about that at supper after the trial. They always got along so well, but they sure had an argument that evening. I had forgotten about it.''

"What did they argue about?''

"Daddy said he didn't see how you could convict a man of murder without a corpse. But then Melvin said there was so much blood at the scene, and the bloody

knife, too, and the picnic things, and Eva's sister June
had seen Roy and Eva drive off together, and why was
Freedman's truck missing? Melvin didn't doubt that
Freedman had killed the girl.''

"Certainly the circumstantial evidence was damning,
that must be why the sheriff was so sure Roy was guilty.
I just wish he'd taken the trouble to collect a few actual
facts."

"What kind of facts?"

"The basics—fingerprints, blood typing, tire marks,
witnesses."

"Why don't you ask him about it yourself?"

"What do you mean?"

"He's up at the same rest home as your uncle Mel."

"He's still alive?"

"All of eighty-nine years old. Pretty spry, too, I
hear."

BACK IN LUTHER'S BEDROOM Simon got organized. He
knew Watauga County well, but he reacquainted himself
with its geography, marking the locations pertinent to
the Potter murder on a county map. The Potter homeplace, now a garden nursery, according to his aunt, was
further up Jefferson Road, a few miles north of the Shaw
homeplace, across from Meat Camp Baptist Church.

Simon could get to the river beach where Eva died by
walking to the end of Fat Boy Road and crossing a small
field. The murder was now a part of his family history,
his own life, even if he'd never heard of it until now.
The favor he was doing Roy Freedman had become personal to him.

He had so many questions to ask he hardly knew
where to start. He christened a new reporter's notebook,
the size that fit into a jacket pocket. He had a photo-

graphic memory, but the act of physically writing down his notes stimulated his thinking. This was something he had a hard time convincing his students. They thought that creating a file on their computers automatically stored information in their brains.

All the action in Eva's murder took place in a small geographical area, negotiable on foot, with one glaring exception. If Roy murdered Eva, and subsequently drove the corpse in his truck miles away and dumped her and the truck off the Blue Ridge Parkway, how did he get back to the Potter place by suppertime? It was too far to walk. If he hitchhiked, who picked him up? Did anyone see Freedman's truck on the main road or on the parkway?

If Freedman didn't murder Eva, and really did wander the woods for hours in a fog of unrequited love, did anyone see him?

Why wasn't the murder scene searched for more evidence? Was anyone other than Roy questioned? Nineteen-fifty-eight wasn't the Dark Ages, after all.

Did anyone else have a motive for killing Eva?

If Sheriff Guy had investigated these issues, it sure wasn't clear from the file Simon had read in Raleigh. Perhaps the sheriff just didn't see the need to write it down. If Simon's grandfather had convinced the sheriff to leave the actual location of the murder out of the file, what else might be omitted?

Then again, maybe nothing sinister went on during the original investigation. In 1958, the law commonly used persuasive methods of interrogation that weren't permitted today, and circumstantial evidence supported Freedman's confession. Simon reminded himself that Freedman probably was guilty. He hoped so. He hated to think an innocent man had been in prison for forty years.

Simon planned to approach all the actors in this drama carefully. He didn't want to put anyone on the defensive, or make anyone angry. That might affect the kind of information he got. He decided to present himself as a harmless professor researching something banal like legal procedures in the fifties. He would contact the district attorney's office first, and then the sheriff's office, before he did anything else. Talking to ex-Sheriff Micah Guy would be crucial. He hoped the old man would be willing to tell him the truth.

Simon looked up the phone numbers for the Balm of Gilead Rest Home, the Watauga County Sheriff's Office, and the district attorney's office. First Simon talked to a brusque assistant district attorney who told him he could investigate any damn thing that happened in 1958 he wanted to. The ADA was completely uninterested in a decades-old case, especially one that had been resolved in the prosecution's favor.

"I wouldn't waste too much of your time on this, Dr. Shaw," the ADA said. "Guys in prison will try anything they think might get them out."

Simon called the sheriff's office next. He wanted to get his blessing, and, with luck, an introduction to Sheriff Guy's nephew-in-law, a current deputy sheriff. Maybe he could maneuver the deputy into suggesting that Simon talk to the old sheriff, so that the deputy would think it was his idea.

"I don't know what I can do to help you," Sheriff Corey Hughes said. "But if you can be here after eleven thirty and before I have to go to my Rotary lunch, I'll be happy to talk to you."

Next Simon called his uncle Mel. Simon could hear

the pleasure in the old man's voice when Simon asked if he could visit him. Uncle Mel, it turned out, had a heavy social schedule. In the morning he had a checkers game and lunch at the senior center, and then he was scheduled to work in the church garden, but if Simon could come over late in the afternoon, they could visit and Simon could stay for dinner. They were allowed to have guests as long as they gave Mrs. Rinehart notice. They were having one of her specialties tonight, pot roast. Simon said he'd be there.

Simon found Aunt Rae in her office, poring over a Christmas-tree industry publication, taking notes on the contents. She had changed into a lemon yellow polyester pantsuit. Simon tucked down the tags hanging out over her collar, but he couldn't do much about the snag in the material between her shoulder blades. Simon wished she'd spend some money on herself. But if he said anything to her, she'd just snort and allow that her clothes had plenty of wear left in them, thank you very much, and it was no wonder young people today owed so much on their credit cards.

"I'm off, hon," Simon said to her.

Aunt Rae frowned. "I thought I could take you on a tour of the farm. Then we could have lunch, catch up on things."

"I promise I'll do that while I'm here," Simon said, determined not to let her make him feel guilty. "But I need to work on Roy Freedman's case. Let me get that out of the way."

Aunt Rae snorted. "If I know you, when you're done, you'll go right on back to Raleigh."

Simon put his arms around her. She rested her head briefly on his shoulder.

"I won't. I promise."

"You'd think your own people would be more important to you."

"Don't give me that. You never have visited me. I've invited you to Raleigh a dozen times, and you've always got an excuse, like doing the taxes or organizing some church thing."

"Will you be home for dinner?"

"I'm eating with Uncle Mel," he said.

"That old codger. He isn't even blood kin to you."

"Have a nice day, Aunt Rae."

BEFORE HE LEFT the house Simon returned Judy's phone call.

"See?" he said. "You did need me, after all."

"Don't gloat, I'm just doing you a favor," she said. "I could just leave it on your desk and wait for you to find it."

"What are you talking about?"

"A package came for you."

"And?"

"It smells. Awful. And it gets worse every day."

"What does it smell like?"

"In a word, poop. What should I do?"

"What's the return address?"

"Interesting you should ask. It reads, 'Unemployment Line, in Hell.' Postmarked Berkeley. And did I mention it smells terrible?"

"Okay. Now I know who it's from. I reviewed a manuscript for a university press written by an assistant professor at Berkeley."

Simon had felt sorry for the author even as he'd mailed his evaluation, but what could he do? The manuscript was fashionable, cynical, unsubstantiated drivel, the thesis planned to attract attention from journals and critics, not to explain the subject in any enlightening way. The guy wouldn't get tenure if he wasn't published, and Simon felt for him, but he wasn't going to recommend a manuscript for publication that didn't meet his standards.

"I take it you weren't kind."

"Afraid not. I advised against publication. I guess the author took it badly."

"What do you want me to do?"

"Pitch the box into the Dumpster."

"I've got these long tongs I use to reach the top shelves in the supply closet. I'll use them to put the box in a plastic trash bag first."

"Good idea. Anything else happening?"

"It's quiet as the grave here."

AS SIMON DROVE DOWN Jefferson Road toward the turn-off to Fat Boy Road, he was surprised to see a small subdivision had sprouted up on the Howards' property, like a patch of puffball mushrooms after a heavy rain. A sign at the entrance to the subdivision read HOWARD'S COVE. The houses were what a Realtor would call starter homes. Designed like mountain chalets, they varied just a little from each other in style and color. The lawns were green and planted with the usual azaleas and such. Children's toys in the yards, satellite dishes on the roofs, and minivans in the driveways completed the suburban scene. Simon wouldn't have dreamed that the Howards would sell any of their farmland for a subdivision. Shaking his head, he pulled away from the shoulder of the road and crossed over to his family's property.

Simon drove down Fat Boy Road until it dead-ended at an old metal gate, chained closed, with a no trespassing sign wired to it. He climbed over the gate and discovered that modern-day hikers, or lovers, still found their way to the romantic spot. A narrow trail of flattened vegetation led down to the beach, through a field waist-high in wildflowers. Swatting at the little no-seeums flitting around his eyes, Simon walked twenty yards or so to get down to the beach. He and Luther had come here as kids to play, but once Mel had caught them swimming in the dangerously swift water. Both sets of parents went ballistic, as Simon's teenage neighbor Danny would say, and forbade them to visit the beach again.

The little beach was a lovely, private, quiet spot, naturally paved with stones worn smooth by the river. Along the riverbank on each side trees trailed branches in the water, creating hidden spots for trout and frogs. A ring of black stones circled the remains of a recent fire. A soft-drink can bobbed in a little pool, trapped close to shore by rocks and weeds. Simon fished it out with a stick and crushed it, putting it in his pocket to throw away later.

Simon climbed onto a log that lay across the beach and shaded his eyes to look across the New River, the oldest river in the Americas. The river was about fifty feet wide, flowing quietly, quickly, and smoothly north. Simon had canoed the New several times, gliding past forests and pastures, summer homes and cabins, livestock and crops, as it moved through Watauga County.

The New's ancient drainage hadn't altered for 500 million years. Archeological evidence showed that humans had lived on the New for thousands of those years. Eva Potter certainly wasn't the first human being to die on its banks.

Simon tried to picture murder happening on the little beach. It wasn't easy, violence didn't fit into such a bucolic scene. Roy and Eva would have parked Roy's truck where Simon had left his own car, and toted the picnic basket between them to the beach. They spread out a blanket, maybe smooched a little, and ate lunch. Then what? Roy proposed, and Eva rejected him, because he was Melungeon, Roy claimed. Would he have stabbed her to death right that minute? Roy would have had to have a violent, volatile temper to do such a thing. Simon hadn't seen evidence of it in his own living room. Maybe Eva said more hurtful things to Roy than he reported to Simon. Or, if you believed Roy's story, he stalked off after Eva rejected him, angry and hurt, and spent hours brooding, wandering around the woods, arriving back at the Potter place hours later to hear of her murder.

Before Simon left the beach, he took a good look at the Harliss property, the abandoned place on the other side of Fat Boy Road. It was rocky, high, and heavily shaded. A steep cliff dropped down to the river. No wonder it had never been developed.

THE WATAUGA COUNTY Sheriff's Office was located in downtown Boone, a block away from King Street, Boone's historic main street. The street climbed steeply, so the flat-roofed beige building was built deep into the steep hill beside it. Several letters were missing from the sign on the outside wall. The office's special vehicles, a Jeep Cherokee, and, of all things, a Humvee, were parked out front. Squat and low, modified with a rack of lights on its roof, the sheriff's star painted on the doors, and wooden rails enclosing the truck bed, the Humvee looked like it could go anywhere in Watauga County.

Simon walked up a steep flight of steps from the street and followed a sign marked visitors through a door. He was the wrong kind of visitor. He found himself in the

visiting quarters of the jail, where relatives talked to in-
mates through wire windows. There weren't any chairs,
just cement stools anchored to the floor, and the area
was exposed to the outdoors. Paint peeled off the walls,
revealing several other colors, all ugly, underneath.
Simon backtracked outside and went in the only other
door he could see, and found himself in the front office
of the sheriff's department.

He told the receptionist his name, but she cut him off
before he could continue.

"I'm glad you're early," she said. "The sheriff's got
to break your appointment, but he wanted to speak to
you for a minute."

She pressed a button on her desk, and almost immediately the sheriff came into the reception area. Sheriff
Corey Hughes didn't fit the common image of the Southern sheriff. He wore civilian clothes, as an elected offi-
cial should. Hughes was a tall, rangy, fit man, with a
full head of well-cut brown hair, wearing a well-tailored
business suit with a bright star gleaming on his lapel.
He wore black cowboy boots and carried a Stetson hat,
the kind you see country singers wearing on compact-
disc covers.

"You're a history professor?" he said, shaking
Simon's hand. "Interested in the Potter murder? That
was way before my time. Things have changed around
here."

"I know," Simon said. "I just wanted to ask…"

"I'm sorry, I've got to leave. When the county com-
missioners call a budget meeting, I need to be there, or
I'll find myself short a car and two deputies next year."

"I—"

"One of my senior deputies, George Lyall, knows

Sheriff Guy very well. Lyall said he'd be glad to talk with you. Would that be okay?''

Simon said that would be just fine, and thought to himself that nothing could be better.

"He'll be out here in just a few minutes," the sheriff said. He hadn't yet let go of Simon's hand, and gave it a final squeeze before going out the door.

The receptionist gestured at a chair, and Simon sat down. She went back to her typing.

Looking around, Simon could see why the sheriff couldn't miss any budget meetings. The reception area held one cheap desk and a couple of uncomfortable wire chairs, one of which Simon was occupying. The rest of the small room was crammed with file cabinets and lockers, with cardboard boxes stacked on top. Past the receptionist's desk he could see down a narrow hall to an open area where two deputies questioned a suspect in an orange jumpsuit.

Simon studied a composite picture of the sheriff's office staff hanging on the wall opposite him. The oval photos were arranged by rank, and included Rex, a black German shepherd with a star on his collar.

Chief Hughes's photo was the largest, of course, displayed at the top of the picture. Arranged under his photo were photos of the chief deputy, who was a woman, and four other men, one of whom was Senior Deputy George Lyall. His title was Chief of Administration and Communication.

A few minutes later, Deputy Lyall himself came into the reception area. Lyall was a slender man in his fifties, with gray hair cut close to his head and bright blue eyes. He carried himself erectly and confidently, as if he had once been in the military, or wanted you to think so. Lieutenant's bars decorated the shoulders of his deputy's uniform. He shook hands with Simon, hard, as if he wanted to prove his strength rather than greet him.

"I understand you're interested in a murder that happened in Watauga County while Micah Guy was sheriff?" he said. "He was my first boss, he hired me, and we got to be good friends. I was married to his niece, for about two minutes. She lives in Nashville. I look after him now. He hasn't got anybody else."

"I'm writing an article on law enforcement in North Carolina in the fifties," Simon said. "I saw the newspaper articles on Eva Potter when her body was found, and I thought while I was visiting my family I'd study her case."

Surprising how easy it was to lie to Lyall about what he wanted to do. Simon wasn't a good liar, so there must be something about Lyall that made it easy.

Lyall shrugged. "I don't mind telling you what I know," he said. "Come on back to my office."

Deputy Lyall led Simon through the building. Equipment, lockers, and furniture lined all the available hallways.

"Want a quick tour of the office?" Lyall asked.

"Please."

Lyall opened a nearby door. "This is the booking area," he said. The room held a couple of folding chairs, a card table, and a what looked vaguely like a portable photocopier on a stand.

Lyall patted it. "New fingerprinting unit," he said. "The suspect places his hand in this slot here, and the computer maps his fingerprints. Then the prints are checked with the FBI, the State Bureau of Investigation, and the military, even Interpol."

"No more inky fingers," Simon said.

"That's right. And we usually know within a few minutes if the prisoner has a record."

Deputy Lyall opened another door.

"This is my area, dispatch and communications." The small room was packed with computer equipment, monitors, and four officers wearing headphones. "All this was installed just a year ago, under my supervision. We take all the nine-one-one calls for Boone and Watauga County here—city, county, fire, university, if you dial nine-one-one in Watauga, this office answers the call, and dispatches the appropriate people. Every two hours I get a computer-generated log of our calls, including what comes through the receptionist."

They passed another room, the civil division, where a mountain of paperwork surrounded two harried plainclothes deputies glued to their telephones.

"These guys are too busy to even say hello," Lyall said. "They deliver all the summonses and subpoenas for the court system. Of course, they have to locate the subject first, which is often an interesting process."

They passed the entrance to the jail, too. Simon looked through a barred iron door and down a dark, bleak hallway into the cell block.

"This ain't no country club," Deputy Lyall said. "That's the way we like it."

Lyall ushered him into an office not much bigger than a closet, and shut the door. He sat behind his desk, and Simon took the only other chair in the room. Lyall leaned back, making a temple with his hands and covering his lower face. He waited for Simon to speak.

"I'm interested in the Eva Potter murder, as I told Sheriff Hughes," Simon said.

"Yeah," Lyall said. "So I hear. I don't know why,

though. That murder was solved. The murderer is in prison. What's interesting about that?''

"I'd like to use it as a case study of Southern law enforcement in the fifties. Both Freedman and your uncle are alive, so I can interview them personally. Then there is the Melungeon aspect..."

Lyall leaned across his desk. "I know what you want to do. You want to show that Sheriff Guy was a greasy redneck who railroaded a man because of his race?"

Simon had made the wrong impression. He compensated as quickly as he could, the way all Southerners did, by asserting his family affiliations. Mentioning local family was like a secret handshake that let Lyall know Simon belonged to the tribe.

"Not at all. Just the opposite. I grew up here, did you know that? My aunt and uncle are Rae and Melvin Coffey. My dad taught at ASU."

Lyall's expression changed.

"You're Luther's cousin?"

"That's right. I don't have any left-wing preconceptions about the Potter murder. I just find it interesting, that's all."

"But you might write about it?"

"Maybe. But I'd disguise names and such."

"Oh, well. In that case."

Simon took out his notebook and pen.

"Could I ask you some questions?"

"I don't know much about the Potter murder. I read the file when I put a bunch of departmental papers in storage, but that was years ago."

"I thought you might have talked to Sheriff Guy about it."

"Why should I?"

"Even when the body was discovered recently?"

"Micah is eighty-nine. He watches wrestling and those religious shows on television all day. He doesn't care about anything else."

"I'd like to talk to Sheriff Guy. Would that be okay, do you think?"

"You'd be wasting your time. Micah's mind is going. His doctor thinks he might be developing Alzheimer's disease. You couldn't trust anything he said."

"What about the physical evidence?"

"County incinerator, years ago."

Lyall didn't move when Simon stood up and thanked him. He was left to find his own way out of the office.

Simon was disappointed that Lyall didn't think he could interview Sheriff Guy profitably. Didn't Aunt Rae say Guy was still sharp? But Lyall would know his condition best, he supposed.

SIMON DROVE a couple of blocks further down King Street and turned in at his cousin's car-detailing business, Coffey's Detail Den. Every bay of the eight-bay building was busy, with a line out the back. Luther's business was a high-class operation. There was no drive-through, automated car wash here. Every automobile got detailed by hand, from washing through waxing and vacuuming. The deluxe option involved chamois cloths and special waxes and cost $150. At the height of the summer season, the vehicles were Jags, Mercedes, BMWs, and Caddys. Their owners handed their keys over and sauntered down King Street to pass time at the Mast General Store, the antique stores, or to have lunch at the Red Onion. Today there were a few pickup trucks in line—owned by locals getting the mud scraped off their wheels while they drank orangeade and ate tuna sandwiches at the Boone Drug Store.

Simon found Luther inspecting a scratch on the hood of a Carolina-blue Mercedes SUV with Charlotte tags.

"I don't know," Luther said to the owner, a deeply tanned man in khaki shorts, polo shirt, and leather deck shoes. "We can try. But I believe you're going to need to take it to the dealer and get the paint touched-up."

"It'll never match," the owner said.

"If you paint the whole hood, it should look okay."

"Just do your best, that's all I can ask." He handed over his keys and went off down the street.

Luther waited until he was out of earshot. "People who want to drive off-road ought not to do it in a Mercedes Benz," he said. "Some of these people have more money than sense."

"Business looks good," Simon said.

"It's been excellent so far this summer," Luther said. He stretched, getting the kinks out. "But I wish, if I was going to have a seasonal business, that I'd picked one that was busy during the winter, instead of the summer. God, what a beautiful day."

"Yeah," Simon said. "I spent an hour down by the New this morning."

"Wish I was drifting down it in a rubber tube, drinking beer right now."

"Let me take you to lunch."

"I got to go home for a couple of hours. Expecting a load of gravel for the driveway. Come on with me. I've got some leftover barbecue and cole slaw from the Rotary pig pickin' last week." He looked over at Simon's car, critically. "Leave your T-bird here and we'll clean it up."

Simon gave his keys to Luther, who tossed them to an employee in the next bay over.

"Do my cousin's Thunderbird next," he shouted,

over the din caused by industrial-sized vacuum cleaners and pressurized water sprayers.

"Before this Caddy?" the man shouted back.

"Yeah, its owner won't be back for hours."

Simon heaved himself up into the passenger side of Luther's black four-wheel-drive truck. When Luther started the engine, Simon was almost blasted out of his seat by Alabama singing "Tennessee River." Luther turned the volume on the CD player down.

"I'm surprised to see you driving a three-year-old car," Luther said. "I thought you were the last of a dying breed, trading in every two years."

"Usually that's so," Simon said. "But I'm trying to find a 2002 Thunderbird. Don't want to buy anything else until I know if I can get one."

"Oh, man! I've read all about that car. It's got a chrome grille and chrome wheels, soft and hard tops, that porthole back window, not to mention a 252 horse-power, DOHC 3.9 liter, V-8 engine. I'm hyperventilating just thinking about it. Can you get one?"

"I'm on a waiting list. I'm sure I'll have to pay more than sticker."

"Get a black one, with a tan interior. With the full cabin accents package. Please! I'll come to Raleigh just to touch it."

"I'll do my best."

"Don't ever sell it, unless it's to me."

"I won't. If I get one, my trade-in days are over." Suddenly Simon remembered the money he'd sent to Tess. That could make buying a new car rather difficult for a while. But then, he remembered, the way things were going with Julia, he probably wouldn't be dating anyone, and he could save his entertainment budget.

They drove east out of town toward the turnoff to Shaw's Knob, very slowly, because of the traffic.

"This road carries more cars than I-40 between Raleigh and Greensboro, I swear," Luther said.

"Maybe the bypass will help."

"That thing won't get built in my lifetime. No one wants it going through their land."

When they turned onto Jefferson Road, Simon felt that time warp sensation again. Suddenly they were in the country, where the two-laned road wound around tight curves, farmhouses nestled in coves, and sun shone brightly on the crops growing in the cleared fields. Between the tourists, summer people, skiers, and students, it was hard to find that down-home feeling in Watauga County anymore.

Then, a half-mile past Aunt Rae's, just as suddenly, the pastoral scene vanished when the new subdivision that had sprung up on Howard land across from Fat Boy Road came into view.

"That took me by surprise when I came by this morning," Simon said, pointing toward the cluster of starter homes ranged around a small cul-de-sac.

"Yeah," Luther said. "It's a shame, isn't it? But then, folks have to live somewhere. And you can hardly blame Mrs. Howard. She needed the money, and the developer paid plenty. She says she's not going to sell off any more land, but who knows? The people who live there seem nice. Mostly young couples. They walk their dogs up and down Fat Boy Road."

Luther turned his truck onto Fat Boy Road, bumping along the graveled road until they got to Luther's cabin. Shaw's Creek and Fat Boy Road ran along the bottom of the holler—the narrow gulch between the two mountains that were Shaw's Knob and the Harliss place. The road stopped at the gate Simon had climbed over earlier in the day, while the creek flowed on into the New River. The holler ran east to west, so it was sunnier than some.

"Hold on," Luther said, as they turned into his drive-way. Simon braced himself as the truck jounced over a deep ditch.

"I see why you need gravel," he said.

"Washed out in the last rain," Luther said. "Every time we scrape the road, or fill in the ruts, the water breaks through somewhere else."

They parked next to Luther's cabin. Built by their great-grandfather as the headquarters for his moonshining operation, the one-story cabin still had the original bars on the windows. The hand-split wood siding was painted dark brown. A motley assortment of rocking chairs, stick furniture, and a squeaky porch swing furnished the front porch, which extended the length of the cabin. A three-foot-tall plastic Santa Claus, lit from inside by three hundred-watt bulbs, topped the metal roof. Luther left it there after Christmas a few years ago when he realized what a great navigational aid it was to anyone looking for his place at night.

The cabin backed right up against the slope of Shaw's Knob, which rose steeply a few feet away from the back door. Luther's driveway continued on up the knob, intersecting with the dirt roads that crisscrossed the Christmas-tree farm. Only a four-wheel-drive vehicle could use the farm roads.

Except for a small area that Luther mowed, the land surrounding the cabin was kept natural. Tall pine trees, hickories, oaks, and sugar maples towered over rhododendron and laurel, which in turn shaded the mosses, lichens, and ferns that thrived in damp leaf litter. The

great laurel was blooming soft pink now, but the rhododendron season was long over.

"The gravel won't be here for a half hour," Luther
said. "Come inside and let's get something to eat."

Luther's cabin was less than a thousand square feet,
even with a new bathroom. There were two small bedrooms, a compact living space, and a kitchenette. The
stone fireplace in the living area looked great, but didn't
draw worth spit. A big propane stove sat between the
fireplace and the kitchen door. It heated the house well,
roaring in the winter when the temperature registered
below freezing and clicking on for a couple of hours
most mornings in the summer, when the temperature
could be in the fifties. When Luther built the new bathroom addition, he ripped out the original small bath, re-
making it into a storage closet. He'd once grown marijuana for his personal use in there under a grow light,
but had given it up when his boys were old enough to
ask questions. He'd insulated the place and covered the
insulation with cheap paneling and put up pine shelves
to hold his model-car collection. A sofa, recliner, television, and gun safe took up all the space in the living
area.

Luther still displayed his wedding picture on the man-
telpiece of the fireplace. He and his ex had exchanged
vows on the infield of the North Wilkesboro Motor
Speedway, dressed in white formal Western wear. Simon
had been the best man. Mercifully, he'd been allowed to
wear jeans and a black blazer.

Luther took a couple of cheap light beers and a Styrofoam box out of his refrigerator. Simon popped the
top of his can and drank half of it while Luther piled
two plates with pork ribs, boiled potatoes, and greens.
He heated the plates, one at a time, in the microwave.

Then they took their plates and beers out onto the porch. The pork, seasoned with Lexington-style barbecue sauce, which contained catsup and brown sugar, fell off the ribs and melted in Simon's mouth. He preferred it to the Eastern variety, which was just vinegar and hot pepper. When they were done eating, Luther lit a Marlboro, holding it so the breeze blew the smoke away from Simon.

"How are you'n Momma getting along?" Luther asked.

"Pretty well. She's only made me feel guilty a couple times."

"You going to sleep over here tonight?"

"I better not. I should stay at Aunt Rae's longer, I think."

Simon realized something was wrong. Their plates sat on the floor of the porch, untouched.

"Where are the dogs?"

A look of deep pain crossed Luther's face. He crushed his cigarette out in his plate.

"They're both dead."

"Oh, man. I am so sorry!" Simon couldn't remember a time when Luther hadn't had a couple of dogs at his feet. "What happened?"

"Carter had cancer. He had chemotherapy, but it didn't work. Then Stumpy, he got slashed up by a raccoon one night. I took him straight to the vet, but that raccoon must have been rooting around in something real nasty, because Stumpy got such a bad infection that three kinds of antibiotics couldn't stop it. I had to put both dogs down within three days of each other."

"I am so sorry."

"Worst time of my life, except for when I got divorced."

"I'm surprised you haven't replaced them."

"I've reserved two puppies, half-sister and half-brother to Carter. They'll get weaned just about the time I get the boys in August, and I'll bring them home then. We'll have lots of fun with them."

"How are Jim and Bo?"

"About the same. Jim's smart, makes great grades—his mind must have come from the same place yours and your daddy's did. He's quiet, though. I wonder a lot what he's thinking. Bo's just the opposite. The only thing, and I mean the only thing, he thinks about is sports. He's convinced all he has to do in school is pass—that he'll play pro ball someday and be rich and famous. I can't convince him he needs a fall-back plan."

"You got by without one."

"It's a different world today. Did you know you need a college degree to be a policeman some places? Before long you'll have to go to community college to get a job flipping burgers."

They were interrupted by the gravel truck coming down the road. It stopped at Luther's driveway and tipped up its load.

"I'm going to help them fill in that rut," Luther said.

"Need some help?"

"Nah."

"I'm going to take a walk, then."

SIMON WANDERED DOWN the familiar road, following the curve of the creek. There had been plenty of rain recently, so the creek ran high and fast, draining water off the mountain into the New River. The sound was rhythmic and soothing. Tall weeds, rocks, and boulders lined the creek banks, but every now and then a narrow track led down to the water's edge. Luther had built a small dam across the creek near the cabin so his boys could cool off on hot days. The pool got about three feet deep before water plunged over the homemade rock spillway.

Simon came up to the old wooden bridge that crossed the creek and led up to the abandoned Harliss place. An old pickup was parked in the lay-by, so he assumed someone was fishing nearby. He ignored the tattered no trespassing sign nailed to a tree, just as he and Luther had throughout their childhoods, carefully picked his way across the rickety bridge, and walked uphill. It wasn't long before he was straining. His lungs weren't accommodated to the low oxygen level in the mountain air, and his legs weren't used to the grade. When he was a child, he and Luther had run up this hill, but now he stopped, bent over, and puffed for a few seconds. He wondered if the old shack they'd played in had fallen down. He thought he remembered that it wasn't that far up the track. He forged on, brushing aside tree branches as he went.

Suddenly a shotgun blast rang out, echoing around the holler. Lead shot sprinkled at his feet. The noise was so loud Simon clapped his hands over his ears first, before he thought of doing anything else. His eardrums throbbed with pain. Then he crouched, putting his hands up in the air. His heart pounded so hard it felt like it might break out of his chest. A flock of birds, screaming, tore out of a tree ahead of him. Keep your head, Simon thought to himself, don't move. He looked up at the shooter.

A mountain man stood in front of him, brandishing a double-barrel shotgun. Simon could smell the gunpowder. The man wore denim overalls, a dingy white undershirt, and work boots. Long brown hair hung down his back. A brown beard reached to his chest.

"Don't shoot," Simon said. "I'm harmless, I swear."

The man lifted the gun to his shoulder and sighted down the gunsight.

"Okay," Simon said. "Okay. You just tell me what you want me to do, and I'll do it."

The man didn't move. He didn't speak, and he cocked the second barrel of his shotgun.

Simon stayed crouched low with his hands over his head. Don't run, don't shout, he told himself, don't stimulate him.

"Whatever I've done, I'm sorry," Simon said. "Just let me leave, okay?"

The mountain main turned his gun slightly aside, and fired. The sound echoed around Simon again. A spray of shot shredded the vegetation a few feet away. It was buckshot, not birdshot. If he ran, the man could reload and kill him, for sure. He could survive a load of birdshot in the back, but not buckshot.

SEVEN

"HEY, THERE, ROCKY," Luther said.

Luther stood next to Simon, breathing heavily from the exertion of running flat-out up the path. He held his own shotgun with the stock pressed tight into his right armpit and his right hand grasping the barrel close to the trigger.

"This is my cousin, Simon Shaw," Luther said, extending his free hand to Simon to pull him to his feet without taking his eyes off Rocky. "He doesn't look like much, I know, but he is blood kin to me. Don't shoot him, okay? My momma and them would be real upset."

Rocky relaxed his grip on his shotgun a little, and cocked his head slightly, like a puppy that's not sure of his name. Not a bright boy, our Rocky. You could almost see the wheels turning in his brain.

"I forgot to tell him you all were home," Luther said. "Or he wouldn't have come up on your property without leave."

You all? Simon wondered how many more demented people with firearms lurked in the woods.

Then Simon heard another person come crashing down the trail from above. With each footfall the ground trembled and brush rustled from the passage of a large body. Neither Rocky nor Luther seemed to notice. From the sounds of it, Simon wouldn't have been surprised to see a Sasquatch appear out of the brush. Instead a very large woman hove into view. She wasn't just fat, she was big, at least six feet tall, and what you might call sturdy. The woman had long gray curly hair worn loose to her shoulders, wore a faded denim skirt with a wide flounce, a T-shirt from a 1987 Alabama concert, and work boots with thick white socks. She stopped next to Rocky, bent over with her hands on her knees, red-faced and winded from running down the mountain.

"Put that thing down, honey," she said to Rocky, between gasps. Rocky placed his shotgun carefully on the ground next to her, turned, and walked back up the path. He hadn't spoken a single word. The big woman picked up the shotgun, stood up, still breathing hard, and broke it open expertly, draping it over her arm.

"Is everyone all right?" she asked.

"Just swell," Simon said. "I get shot at every time I take a walk."

"I'm sorry about that," the woman said. "My boy's been in the hospital so much of his life he doesn't know how to act."

"Simon," Luther said. "Let me introduce you to Big Momma Harliss. That was her son, Rocky, who greeted you so warmly. Big Momma, this is my cousin, Simon Shaw."

Big Momma looked doubtfully at Simon. "He doesn't look like he's kin to you," she said.

"His momma wasn't from around here," Luther said. Big Momma processed that damning information while she continued to inspect Simon.

"From the looks of him, she must have been a foreigner," Big Momma said. "Where was she from?"

"New York City," Luther said.

Simon was furious. He was annoyed by being referred

to in the third person, his ears throbbed with pain, and he didn't like being called a foreigner. The adrenaline still lurking in his system, no longer needed for flight, fueled his anger. Luther, who still had hold of Simon's arm, felt his muscle tension building.

"Big Momma and Rocky just moved back here," Luther said to Simon, "since your last visit home, I think. They don't like company much."

"Oh, if he's your cousin, he's all right," Big Momma said to Luther. She extended her hand to Simon. "Come visit us anytime. I'll explain to Rocky. He won't bother you again."

Urged by a nudge from Luther, Simon took her hand. It was rough and callused.

"Big Momma," Luther said, "I've got to get back to work. Let's go," he said to Simon.

Luther bodily turned Simon around and led him down the mountain. They crossed the rickety bridge at the creek and Simon felt as relieved as an outlaw crossing the Rio Grande a minute before a posse of Texas Rangers reached him. Now that he was safe, he let his anger overcome him.

"Jesus H. Christ," Simon said. "That gorilla could have killed me. What century are those people living in?"

"Calm down," Luther said. "You were on his property, you know."

"Since when has trespassing been a capital offense? And what's wrong with Rocky? Did his mother marry her brother, or what?"

"Nothing that simple," Luther said. "Vietnam. He came back like that."

"Oh," Simon said. "Well. Poor bastard. Still, he's dangerous. He shouldn't be permitted to own a gun."

"I don't think he would have shot you."

"So that's why you came after me, toting your shot-gun?"

"Okay. It was a touchy situation. It's my fault. I should have warned you."

Inside Luther's cabin Simon dropped onto the sofa. His heartbeat wasn't quite back to normal, and his shirt was damp with sweat.

The door of the gun safe that took up a big part of Luther's living room hung ajar.

"Look at this," Luther said, grinning. He broke open his shotgun, and showed Simon the empty chambers. "I keep my ammo in a lockbox in the back of the closet, just in case the boys figure out the safe combination, and I didn't have time to get it." Luther placed his shotgun inside the safe, closed the door, and spun the dial.

"Want a Coke?" he asked.

"Please."

Luther got Cokes for both of them, then plopped down on the sofa next to Simon. He placed a hand on his chest.

"Whew," Luther said. "I'm not in good enough shape to run up mountains."

"Thanks for rescuing me," Simon said.

"You're welcome. After the gravel truck left, I looked around for you, and then I heard the shot. I realized you must have headed up the path to the Harliss place."

"Is Rocky always that friendly?"

"He's confronted a couple of other people who started to hike up the track toward their shack. Fired over their heads."

"Someone ought to tell the sheriff."

"He's been up here to talk to them," Luther said, "but no one wants Rocky to have to go back to the Veterans Administration Hospital. He's been there for years, and now that his momma's out of prison, they're trying to live on their land."

"She was in prison? What did she do?"

"Murdered her old man."

"Second murderer I've met this week."

Luther crumpled his Coke can and tossed it toward the trash. He missed. Simon made his shot.

"Come on," Luther said, "I've got to get back to work. I'll tell you Big Momma's life story in the truck."

Full afternoon sunlight streamed into the holler, filtering through leaves and branches, making moving patterns on the ground. Simon hated to leave Luther's porch. He'd forgotten how peaceful it could be here. Maybe someday he'd build a summer place of his own on this road.

"Want to go up over the knob?" Luther asked.

"Sure," Simon said.

They got into Luther's truck, he shifted into four-wheel-drive, and they started to climb the farm road up the hill behind Luther's cabin. Aunt Rae wasn't the sort to waste herbicide on a road, so the big truck plowed through tall weeds and grasses that blocked the way. When they got to the top of the knob, Luther stopped so Simon could look out over the hundreds of Frasier firs growing in neat, symmetrical rows. It was a pretty sight. Frasier firs were beautiful trees, with their even, conical shapes, thick branches, and fat green needles.

Between the trees the common wildflowers bloomed— black-eyed Susans, purple coneflowers, daisies, and Queen Anne's lace. He also recognized orange, spotted Carolina lilies and a stand of red-hot pokers—tall green plants topped with foot-long red spiked blossoms. Simon noticed, amidst the green, a dead fir tree. It had turned a burnt orange color, but retained its shape and needles, looking for all the world like a Halloween tree.

At the summit of the knob, Luther stopped again, next to the family burial plot. No one had been buried there since Simon's grandparents, but it was meticulously maintained. A split-rail fence surrounded it. Roses, the old varieties that spread everywhere, rambled around the gravestones and tangled around the fence. Luther and Simon parked in the sunlight for a few minutes. Luther lit a cigarette, rolling down the truck window and sticking his hand out the window.

"I thought you were going to quit smoking," Simon said.

"Someday I will. There aren't enough places in the world where a man can smoke anymore, and I don't in front of my boys anyway. Not to mention the expense."

"So," Simon said, "tell me about the Harlisses."

"Big Momma's people were what some would call white trash, but really they were just poor people trying to get by. Big Momma's first husband, Rocky's daddy, died in a stock-car crash. Big Momma cleaned houses for summer people, foraged for herbs and galax, made wreaths for the greenery businesses at Christmastime. She wrote some bad checks and went to prison. When she got out she found a regular job at the commercial laundry. She worked there for years."

"What about Rocky?"

"Rocky was your average redneck kid. Made his spending money working in the fields, drove way too fast, barely stayed in school. After high school, he joined the service. Went to Vietnam just in time to help invade Cambodia. Maybe the shrinks at the VA know what happened to him there, but I never heard. Anyway, Big Momma looked after him as best she could. Then she married a long-distance truck driver. He turned out to be a mean bastard. Beat her up, threatened to turn Rocky out. So she killed him. Antifreeze in his iced tea. She pleaded to manslaughter, went to jail, and Rocky had to go to the VA mental hospital in Asheville. He just couldn't manage on his own."

Luther crushed out his cigarette in the truck ashtray and started up the truck.

"That crappy piece of land is all they've got. Years ago there was a good crop of ginseng and herbs, but it's all gone now. Some distant relative paid the taxes while Big Momma was in jail. I remember my momma kept going down to the courthouse to see if she could buy it cheap."

"Why did Aunt Rae want it?"

"Because it's there, and butts up against ours. You know how people are about land around here. Anyway, Big Momma got out of prison a couple of years ago, sprung Rocky, and came home. They're living on Rocky's disability pay and that's it. If they can't manage, he'll have to go back to Asheville and I guess she'll end up on welfare."

"They're not living in that old shack where we used to go try to trap snakes?"

"Yeah, but they've fixed it up some. Besides, they don't have anywhere else to go."

SIMON'S THUNDERBIRD, gleaming like it had just come from the showroom, was parked at the far edge of the Detail Den's lot. Luther dropped him off there.

"Say hey to Daddy for me," Luther said. "Tell him I've cleaned his shotgun so it'll be ready for the Exchange Club turkey shoot Thursday night. He's been worrying me to death about it."

SIMON'S UNCLE MEL had the finest head of hair Simon had ever seen on a male human being. He was vain about it, too. It was pure white, thick as a teenager's, worn long enough to curl over his collar. He complemented it with an equally thick white moustache.

"I am so glad to see your face, boy," Mel said, holding him at arm's length. "You look good. How long's it been?"

"Too long," Simon said.

Mel seemed fit and healthy. His fair skin, wrinkled and blotched with years of sun exposure, creased deeply as he smiled at Simon. He wore a perfectly-ironed blue short-sleeved shirt, khakis, and new athletic shoes. Divorce appeared to agree with him.

"I'm sorry about you and Aunt Rae," Simon said, "although this looks like a real nice place."

The lobby of the rest home had a cathedral ceiling and big windows that let in plenty of sunlight. A cluster of potted plants basked under one of the windows. Chintz sofas and chairs, centered on a large hooked rug, faced a wall of books, knickknacks, and framed photographs. A felt banner appliqued with flowers, birds, a cheerful family group, and the phrase, HONOUR THY FATHER AND THY MOTHER hung on the wall opposite the entrance. Mel took Simon's arm and led him through a connecting door and down the single hall of the rest home.

"Your aunt Rae is a fine woman, a fine woman," he said, "and we had many good years, but it just got so we couldn't live together."

There were six doors on each side of the hall. Every door had a handmade angel on it holding a scroll with the name of the room's occupant printed on it. The angels were all different, supposedly reflecting the personality of the resident. Mel's angel wore overalls and a John Deere baseball cap. Its wings were made of tin foil edged in blue lace.

"Come on in," Mel said, opening his door. Uncle Mel's room was spacious and sunny. Simon recognized all Mel's own things, including a photo of Rae in her wedding dress. Mel's worn recliner faced a big-screen television. Mel saw Simon regarding the television with disbelief, and guessed his thoughts.

"Thirty-six inches," he said. "And we've got satellite," he added. "The NASCAR package, all the baseball games, too. And movies. You know Rae never would go to the movies. She always said it was a waste of time and money. There was a John Wayne festival on one of the channels last weekend. I watched every one."

Uncle Mel sat down on his recliner, tipped the footrest up, and pointed out another chair to Simon.

"Are you okay, really?" Simon asked him, sitting down.

Uncle Mel grinned at him. "For ten years I've dreamed about retiring. It's even better than I thought it would be. I'm having such a good time I should hire someone to help me enjoy it."

"I'm glad," Simon said.

"Luther tells me you're looking into Eva Potter's murder. I remember that day well. Did you know Sheriff Guy lives here, too?"

"I was hoping to talk with him, but Deputy Lyall tells me his mind is gone."

Uncle Mel frowned. "That's just not so," he said. "He might be a little forgetful, at eighty-nine who wouldn't be? But you'll meet him at dinner. He sits at my table. You are staying for dinner, aren't you?"

"Wouldn't miss it," Simon said.

"We've got some time to kill," Mel said, pulling the table with the checkerboard on it between them.

"No," Simon said. "Please, no."

"Come on. Play a game with me."

"Why? So you can embarrass me?"

"I enjoy being smarter than a Ph.D. at something," Uncle Mel said.

"Oh, all right," Simon said, looking down at the board. "What's this position?"

"The Fugitive King," Mel said.

Experienced checkers players didn't often play complete games. They worked puzzles instead. That way they bypassed the boring beginning and middle parts of a game and skipped to the challenging endgame. Checkers puzzle books filled with famous endgames tested the player to see if he or she could finish a game the way the experts did. Some of the puzzles were as challenging as any chess game ever was.

Mel picked up his checkers book, opened to the layout of *The Fugitive King,* and carefully covered the solution with a piece of paper.

"Can't we just play a regular game?" Simon asked.

"Come on," said Uncle Mel. "Let's see if you remember anything I taught you."

"How many moves?"

"You're red to play and win in forty-seven moves."

"I know, you take offense, and I'll defend."

"Coward. Just try it. I've been working on it for a week. I want to see how you approach it."

Simon studied the board. His Uncle Mel had a special tournament board, checkered in white and green. The green squares, where the pieces rested, were numbered from one to thirty-two, going from right to left, so that play could be annotated.

Red had three kings ranged to the left middle of the board, and one pawn. White had one king in a very strong defensive position on the lower right perimeter. Four white pawns guarded him.

"You've got to corner that king without losing your kings to his pawns."

"I've figured that out, thanks," Simon said.

His first three moves must have been correct, but his uncle howled at the fourth. Simon retrieved the piece and started the move over. After an hour, with his uncle's prodding, Simon had only made it correctly to move ten.

A distant bell sounded.

"Dinner," Uncle Mel said.

"Thank God," Simon said. "Does that mean we can stop playing now? My brain hurts."

"Sure," Mel said. "Don't feel bad. *The Fugitive King* requires very skillful play. I haven't gotten past move thirty-nine yet, and I've studied it for a week."

INSIDE THE dining room hung another colorful felt banner, this one featuring a cornucopia spilling over with fruits and vegetables, accompanied by the message FEED MY SHEEP. Mouthwatering odors wafted from a steam table near the kitchen door. Mel and Simon went to admire the spread. Pot roast, fried onion rings, mashed potatoes, squash casserole, and rolls filled the serving units. A nearby table held individual salads and peach cobblers.

Uncle Mel exchanged greetings with some of the other residents, introducing Simon to them. Most of the men were like Uncle Mel, elderly, but not frail or ill.

Simon and Mel heaped their trays, then unloaded them at one of the small dining tables. An elderly gentleman with a cane already sat there. He was very thin, and carried a Bible in a zippered case with him.

"Meet Micah Guy, sheriff of Watauga County," Mel said, introducing Simon to him.

"Not for years," the old man said. He had a firm handshake and a steady, clear voice.

"Can I bring you some dinner, Sheriff Guy?" Simon asked.

"No, thanks. Mrs. Rinehart always brings me mine." Mrs. Rinehart, a plump middle-aged woman, wore a pink uniform, but she was distinguished from the aides by the stethoscope that protruded from her pocket and her nursing-school pin. She had a mass of dark hair streaked with gray piled on top of her head in a neat bun, blue eyes, and large, capable hands. She wore a plain, heavy silver cross around her neck.

Mrs. Rinehart placed a plate in front of Sheriff Guy. It was long on meat, vegetables, and salad, but short on starch.

"I've got diabetes," Guy said, by way of an explanation.

"Do you mind if I join you?" Mrs. Rinehart asked. "You have some extra room at this table today. Mr. Pettigrew went to see his new great-grandbaby."

Finally everyone was served and seated. Mrs. Rinehart sat at their table; two aides and a man who looked like he was the maintenance man sat at the others. Simon picked up his fork, but Uncle Mel restrained his hand.

"Wait for the blessing," he whispered.

Mrs. Rinehart tapped on her glass, and the room fell silent.

"Sheriff Guy," she said, "would you do the honors?"

Guy got to his feet, steadying himself with one hand on the back of his chair, the other clenching his Bible to his chest. He closed his eyes.

"Lord," he said, "bless this food that you give us for the nourishment of our bodies, and bless the Balm of Gilead Rest Home."

Simon moved to take up his fork, but his uncle rested his hand on Simon's. Sheriff Guy wasn't finished.

"Give us, Lord," Guy said, "the strength to battle the devil and his evil works, to combat perversion and socialism, to cleanse ourselves of our sins, so that we may be worthy of salvation."

Simon's food was getting cold.

"Let your spirit enter the sinners amongst us, so that they may give up ungodliness, and be saved, Amen!"

"That was some prayer, Micah," Mel said. "I didn't know all that heaven stuff belonged in the blessing."

"I'm an old man," Guy said. "It's time for me to think about salvation."

"This is wonderful food, Mrs. Rinehart," Simon said. It was, too. The meat was so tender it could be cut with a fork, the squash casserole was thick with onions, and the mashed potatoes were so creamy Simon didn't bother to add butter to them. Halfway through the meal, a quiet Hispanic woman, also dressed in pink, but wearing an apron, came out from the kitchen with pitchers of sweet iced tea to refill their tall glasses. She poured Micah's from a separate pitcher, and he added two envelopes of artificial sweetener to it.

"The worst part about being a diabetic," Guy said, "is not having really sweet iced tea. This fake stuff just doesn't taste the same."

"Mel tells me you do all this good cooking," Simon said to Mrs. Rinehart.

"I do plan all the menus and do most of the cooking for the midday meal, although Mrs. Hernandez's help in the kitchen is invaluable, of course. And she does breakfast and supper. Please have seconds. It's against state regulations for us to keep leftovers. It'll just go to waste otherwise."

"They feed us all this so we'll sleep all afternoon and won't pester them to death," Mel said, leaning back in his chair and rubbing his stomach.

"If this is lunch, what's dinner?" Simon asked.

"Soup and sandwiches," Mrs. Rinehart said. "A light meal at night is best for the digestive tract."

Simon joined several other residents, including his uncle, at the steam table again. Sheriff Guy didn't quite finish his first plate. He opened his Bible, reading while he sipped his iced tea.

"Simon is researching the Eva Potter murder," Mel said to Micah.

"Really," Guy said. His hand holding the glass of tea trembled a little. "That was a long time ago," he said.

"I wonder if I could ask you some questions about it," Simon said.

"Roy Freedman's guilty," Guy said.

"I don't doubt that," Simon lied. "It's just that I'm studying law enforcement in the fifties, and..."

"He confessed," Guy said.

"I know," Simon said. "I read the file. I was wondering if you collected any corroborative evidence..."

"Didn't need any," Guy said, wiping his face with his napkin. "He confessed. And thank God this happened before Miranda and such ruined law enforcement.

In the old days we cared about getting justice for victims, not coddling criminals."

"Now Micah," Mrs. Rinehart said. "We talked about Eva Potter's murder at Bible study the other evening. You remember, you said then..."

"Excuse me," Guy said, interrupting her. "You know I watch *The Old Time Gospel Hour* this time every day. And Deputy Lyall is coming by to see me."

Sure enough, Deputy Lyall entered the dining room. When he saw Simon sitting at the same table with Guy, his expression could have frozen blood.

"What are you doing here?" he asked Simon.

"Visiting my uncle, Mel Coffey," Simon said, nodding at his uncle. Lyall looked over at Mel.

"I didn't know you had kin here," Lyall said.

Obviously not, Simon thought. You wouldn't have told me Sheriff Guy was senile if you thought I might meet him and find out differently.

Lyall turned away from Mel and Simon, and helped Guy to his feet, where the old sheriff got a firm grasp of his cane with one hand.

"You go on to your room, Micah," Lyall said. "I forgot my cell phone in the truck. I'll get it and be right with you."

After Lyall and Guy had left the dining room, Mel turned to Mrs. Rinehart.

"I'm worried about Micah," Mel said. "He doesn't look well."

"I checked his blood sugar this morning. He's fine," Mrs. Rinehart said.

"He's gotten so preoccupied with death and his so-called sins. He's not enjoying his life anymore."

"He's eighty-nine," Mrs. Rinehart said. "He's preparing to meet his maker. It's good for his soul to reflect upon eternity.''

She turned to Simon.

''If you'd like to talk to me about Eva's death, I'd be happy to cooperate.''

Simon looked at her in surprise.

''You don't know who I am, do you?''

''No, ma'am.''

''Rinehart is my married name. I'm June Potter Rinehart. I'm Eva's sister.''

THE REST-HOME WING was a long addition that intersected the modest ranch that was June Rinehart's home. She led him into a room decorated in pink and mint green, offering him a seat on the rose-patterned sofa.

''You run a good place, Mrs. Rinehart,'' Simon said. ''Your residents seem happy and healthy.''

''Thank you,'' she said, taking a chair opposite him. ''I took care of my father and my husband during their final illnesses. I believe the Lord called me to do this work. I prayed on it, then I built this rest home, and I've been blessed with a good reputation. It doesn't pay very well, I'll never be able to retire. Sometimes I wonder why good works aren't better rewarded, but then we shouldn't question God's plan for the world, should we?''

''Why are your residents all men?''

''Men this age are helpless if their wives predecease them. They've never cooked a meal, done laundry, or shopped in their lives. Some of them don't even know what their medications are for. So they come here. I'm a registered nurse, so I can give them their medicine.''

''I'm...''

''I know who you are. You're Simon Shaw, the professor from Raleigh. Your mother was Rachel Shaw, I knew her when she was head of the public health department. She was doing good work here—the Lord must have had a good reason for taking her to his bosom so early.''

Simon let that one go by.

"I'm looking into your sister's murder," Simon said. "Roy Freedman contacted me in Raleigh and asked me to. He says he's innocent."

"Yes, I know," she said. "He told me the last time I saw him."

"What?" Simon said. "When did you see Roy?"

"After they found Eva's corpse I got to thinking about Roy, about his immortal soul. I don't wish eternal damnation on anybody, even him, so I went to Raleigh to tell him I forgave him and to beg him to accept Jesus as his Savior."

"What did he say?"

"He said he didn't kill Eva." She shook her head sorrowfully. "If he doesn't confess, he'll never get right with God."

"You were there, Mrs. Rinehart, weren't you, when your sister died, that night, when Roy came back to your house?"

"Yes," she said. "The sheriff and Daddy were in the living room talking about getting together a posse to look for Roy. Momma and I were in the kitchen. She was crying so hard I thought she would strangle. Then what should happen, but Roy comes right in the house. He looked like he had been crying himself, and his clothes were a mess."

"He says your father and the sheriff beat him and threatened to lynch him. Did you see anything like that?"

"Daddy sent me and Momma upstairs. I gave Momma some pills the doctor had left to make her sleep and stayed with her. I don't know what happened, but Daddy came upstairs later and said Roy had confessed and that the sheriff was taking him to jail."

"Was anyone else there who might have witnessed something?"

"No," she said. "Just Daddy, and he died years ago. We had another boarder, but he left town before all this happened. But I'll tell you," she said, leaning toward him. "Sheriff Guy has been rattled ever since they found Eva's remains, and since I told him that Roy claims he didn't kill her, he's had to take sleeping pills. Something is troubling him. I've been praying on it."

WHEN SIMON GOT BACK to the Shaw homeplace his aunt Rae was sitting on the front porch, rocking and reading her Bible. He sat down next to her and patted her hand. The night was very cool—Aunt Rae wore a shawl over her shoulders. It was probably too hot and humid in Raleigh to sit outside. That made him think of Julia.

"Did anyone call me here?" he asked.

"No," she said. "Were you expecting a call?"

"Not really," Simon said. He had kept his cell phone on all day in hopes that Julia would call and accept his invitation to come for the weekend. It was just Tuesday—plenty of time for her to call him. Of course, they wouldn't want to stay with either Aunt Rae or Luther. The Mountain Inn was the nicest hotel around, with spectacular mountain views, a three-star restaurant, and heated swimming pool. Maybe he should make a reservation for the weekend, just in case.

Aunt Rae closed her Bible firmly and started rocking faster. She compressed her lips, and leaned toward

Simon. This was bad. He knew she was getting ready to speak to him seriously about something, and he thought he knew what it was.

"I saw Pastor Jones outside the post office today," she said.

"Oh, no," Simon said. "Not again. How many times have we talked about this?"

"Don't interrupt me. This is important. He would like to see you in church Wednesday night."

"And I'd like to go on *Oprah* to talk about my next book, but that's not going to happen, either."

"Don't sass me."

"The last time I agreed to go to church with you, when Pastor Jones called for all the sinners to come up to the front of the church to be saved, every damn person in the church turned to look at me. It was humiliating."

"They care about you. They cared about your momma and daddy."

"Don't bring them into this."

Aunt Rae started to cry, silently, big tears rolling down her cheeks.

"Don't do that," Simon said. He pulled out his handkerchief and gave it to her to sop up her tears.

"Your poor momma and daddy."

"Listen to me," Simon said. "Mom and Dad are not in hell. You read the Bible every day—do you just skip over Matthew nine, verses sixteen and seventeen? That's where Jesus says what we must do to go to heaven. He said we must obey the Commandments and care for the poor. That's all. He didn't say we have to be dunked by Pastor Jones, or that we shouldn't believe in dinosaurs, or that we can't drink a beer."

Aunt Rae clutched her Bible to her chest with one hand and covered her eyes with Simon's handkerchief with the other. Simon kept one arm around her and patted her back until she stopped crying. He leaned over and kissed her on the cheek.

"Don't worry about me," he said. "I'm fine."

"Here," she said, handing him back his handkerchief. "You put this in the laundry room, in the basket with the whites, and I'll wash and starch and iron it for you before you go." She shook out the handkerchief. There was a small rip in one corner. "On second thought, throw this one away. There's a sale at Penney's. I'll get you some new ones. The kind you don't have to iron, since you got nobody to take care of you."

"Good night, Aunt Rae," he said. "Sleep tight."

"I'll try," she said. "It's hard, when I've got so many troubling thoughts in my mind."

Aunt Rae lumped everyone who didn't attend her little country independent Baptist church or one like it into the same category, the unsaved/damned, whether they were Jewish, Muslim, or Catholic, it made no difference to her. He wondered what it would be like to believe, really believe, that most of the people you knew, including members of your own family, were destined to burn in hell while you sat up in heaven on a cloud, strumming a harp for eternity.

When Simon got up to his room, one of Billy Graham's books, dog-eared and well-thumbed already, lay neatly on his pillow. The woman would never stop trying to convert him.

Aunt Rae's determination to save him wasn't all about Simon's Jewish mother. Aunt Rae had adored Rachel Shaw, who married Rae's bachelor brother and gave him a son just when Rae had given up hope. Besides, Aunt Rae's form of primitive Christianity accorded Jews a vital role in the Second Coming of Christ. Somewhere in Revelation, she believed, God instructed the Jewish people to perform two very important tasks. First, they had to rebuild the temple. Difficult, to say the least, since the Dome of the Rock now stood on the temple mount. After that little task was completed, the Jews had to convert to Christianity. Why they would do that after going through all the time and trouble it would take to rebuild the temple, Simon didn't know. So Simon's aunt was conflicted, theologically-speaking—should she send Simon to Israel with a shovel, or ply him with fundamentalist Christian literature and save his soul? It was an amusing situation only if you didn't live in the middle of it.

There was little anti-Semitism in the Appalachians, because the mountain people believed Jews deserved respect for practicing the "old religion" of the Bible, the religion of Jesus. The first Jewish residents in the mountains were educated Orthodox merchants, and the simple country people respected them for their knowledge of the Old Testament, their mastery of the Hebrew language, and their piety. Even into modern times, newborn babies were often taken to the nearest Jewish person, sometimes miles away from home, who would whisper Hebrew into its tiny ears. This was supposed to give the child a great advantage in its spiritual life. Many times as a boy Simon would hear his doorbell ring, and go into the living room to find his mother holding a baby wrapped in a worn quilt in her arms, whispering bits from the Haggadah to it, much to its parents' delight. Simon's mother explained to him that this was pure superstition, but she never refused, no matter what time of the day or night, and seemed to enjoy it immensely.

Tomorrow was Wednesday. Aunt Rae wouldn't stop

pestering him to go to Wednesday night services. He'd
better plan to move in with Luther.

He sat down on the bed in Luther's old room, and
checked his watch. It wasn't too late to call Julia. Her
phone rang four times, then switched into the message
mode. He again left her his numbers, and reissued his
invitation to come up to Boone for the weekend. After
he hung up the phone he wondered if she was screening
her calls. He hoped not, because he wanted to think she
wouldn't play courtship games with him. He'd tried to
make up as best he knew how. If that wasn't enough, it
just wasn't. His stomach roiled. He didn't want to lose
her. To distract himself, he went over his notes of the
day and the county map.

He hadn't learned much of importance about the Potter murder, but he had many new questions. He wrote
them in his notebook, adding to an already extensive list
of queries. Why hadn't Roy Freedman told him about
June Rinehart's visits? Why had his aunt Rae tried to
buy the Harliss property, and why hadn't she told him
about it? Why had Deputy Lyall told him that Micah
Guy had Alzheimer's disease? The former sheriff was
excessively preoccupied with his mortality, but other
than that seemed mentally competent. Lyall didn't know
Simon's uncle lived at the same rest home, and that he'd
have the opportunity to talk to Guy. And why didn't Big
Momma take Rocky's shotgun away, and avoid the possibility that they'd both be arrested?

Simon was also intrigued by the geography of the
murder. Was it significant, or just coincidental, that all
the events of the murder took place in a small area, and
that the area was near Simon's family home? He decided

tomorrow that he'd talk to Big Momma again, and visit the old Potter place. He wished he could ask Roy Freedman a few more questions. Perhaps he could. He'd call Chaplain Mitchell tomorrow and find out.

EIGHT

SIMON DROPPED his bag and briefcase to the floor outside the kitchen with a significant thud. Aunt Rae, sitting at the kitchen table with the newspaper, pricked up her ears, as he had intended.

"You're leaving?" she asked. "You must be really mad at me."

"No," Simon said. "I'm not. But I know you won't stop trying to get me to go to church tonight, and I'm not going to go. I don't want us to have the kind of scene we had the last time I was here. I'm going on over to Luther's."

"You could just come to the fellowship hall for supper before the service. Everyone wants to see you."

Simon leaned over to kiss her.

"I love you, Aunt Rae. But you're not going to win this one."

Aunt Rae sniffed.

"I ain't giving up. You're young yet. Wait until your bones start to creak and your blood vessels get stopped up. You'll get interested in heaven fast then. But don't wait too long. Remember, Noah built the ark before the flood."

"I am interested in heaven. I just don't think I have to check my brains at the door to get in."

Aunt Rae insisted on fixing him bacon, eggs, and pancakes for breakfast. Four strips of bacon, two eggs fried in the grease, and four pancakes with syrup, to be exact.

ON HIS WAY TO Luther's, Simon stopped at the grocery store to buy Luther a case of good imported beer. Luther couldn't afford it himself, and it was the one gift Simon could bring his cousin that he would truly enjoy.

Simon dropped the beer and his luggage at Luther's cabin. He noticed Big Momma fishing off her bridge. After he stowed the beer in Luther's refrigerator, he walked down the driveway and across the road to speak to her.

Big Momma wore the same clothes he'd met her in, except she wore a clean man's white V-neck T-shirt, the kind that comes three to a pack at Wal-Mart. She sat on the edge of her bridge with her legs dangling off it and a line in the creek. The current towed her line downstream, where the red cork bobbed near a quiet pool of water under an overhanging tree. If there were any trout in the creek, that's where they'd be. Simon hoped that she wasn't trying to catch lunch, and remembered his ample breakfast with some guilt.

Big Momma patted a spot on the rickety bridge next to her, and Simon sat down, gingerly. Big Momma laughed at him.

"I know this bridge is on its last legs, but if it can hold me, you'll be okay. Just don't drive over it."

Big Momma reeled in her line and inspected her worm, jamming it more securely onto the hook before flinging the line back into the water.

"Thanks for not calling the sheriff on Rocky yesterday," she said. "He's already given us one warning."

"Luther explained your situation to me," Simon said.

"But maybe you shouldn't let Rocky have that shot-gun."

"I know," she said. "But he's never actually shot directly at someone, and he is a man. A man don't feel right without his gun."

"You could replace the buckshot with birdshot," Simon said.

"That's a good idea," she said. "Why didn't I think of that? I tell you, my brain don't work as good as it used to."

Simon introduced the subject he was really interested in.

"Big Momma," Simon said, "I'm looking into a murder that happened around here in 1958."

"That dirty Melungeon killed Eva Potter."

Simon counted to ten, reminding himself that people like Big Momma weren't likely to outgrow their preju-dices.

"You remember when it happened?" he asked.

"Not directly. I heard about it somehow."

"You weren't living here then?"

"I was in prison. Got sent up for passing bad checks."

"Oh," Simon said. He didn't know what else to say, so he watched a waterbug fight the stream's current.

"It wasn't all bad," Big Momma said.

"What?"

"Prison. I got my GED, so I got a good job when I got out. My mistake was killing my second husband."

"I can see that."

"Oh, he deserved killing. But I should have hired someone to do it instead. I was asking around, but then I lost my temper when he ate half of Rocky's birthday cake before Rocky even had a chance to blow out the candles. I got the idea how to do it when one of our dogs died just from licking his paws where he stepped in a little pool of antifreeze. I put a cupful in my husband's coffee water. He liked his coffee sweet, see. That was the last coffee he ever drank. He was dead by the next morning.''

Big Momma reeled in her line, inspected the intact worm again, and threw it back in the water.

''You know what he did to me?''

''Who?'' Simon asked. ''Your husband?''

''No,'' she said. ''That Melungeon. Him and his buddy, I don't remember his name. They stripped my land here of ginseng. The only thing on this land worth a nickel and they stole it all while I was in prison the first time. 'Seng don't always come back as good, you know.''

''I'm sorry,'' Simon said. ''It was a rotten thing to do.''

''If I'd had the money from that 'seng, I might not have married that worthless second husband of mine, then I wouldn't have killed him and gone back to prison.''

Simon left Big Momma fishing off her bridge. For a time he rocked on Luther's front porch and drank a mug of coffee he'd found left in Luther's coffeepot and warmed up. Big Momma's attitude toward Rocky and his shotgun puzzled him. Simon had the distinct impression that Big Momma had no intention of confiscating Rocky's shotgun, or of substituting lethal ammunition with birdshot. Everyone in the area must know by now to stay away from their property. She was risking a lot by letting him keep that gun. What if Rocky took a pot shot at a bicyclist, or someone walking a dog?

SIMON CALLED Chaplain Mitchell on his cell phone.

''Find out anything?'' Mitchell asked him.

"Just more questions," Simon said. "Does Roy have telephone privileges?"

"Not yet," Mitchell said. "But he's out of solitary confinement, so it shouldn't be too long."

"Can you ask him something for me? A woman named June Potter Rinehart visited Roy after Eva Potter's corpse was found. She's Eva's sister. Can you ask Roy about that visit? I'd like to find out what they talked about. She says she was just out to save his soul, but I'd be interested in knowing if they talked about anything else."

SIMON DROVE OUT Fat Boy Road to Jefferson Road, turning right instead of left, and went toward Meat Camp Baptist Church and the old Potter place. He followed the narrow road for a couple of miles, driving slowly as it twisted and dipped around hills and down into the coves, little valleys cleared of trees generations ago. Farmland was fertile in the coves, deep in loam that washed down the mountains and collected there. Most sheltered a home, often a picturesque farmhouse, but just as often a modern brick ranch.

Simon pulled off on the shoulder of the road opposite Meat Camp Baptist Church just to absorb the sights, sounds, and smells of the country. He got out of his car, climbed onto the warm hood, leaned back on the windshield, and folded his arms behind his neck, letting his head fall back so he could feel the heat of the sun on his face. Beside him was a field thick with immense bright yellow sunflowers, every one of them nodding its head in his direction, like an audience agreeing with a speech. Honeysuckle draped the fence that separated the field from the road, its odor sweet as caramelizing sugar bubbling on the stove. Dozens of butterflies fluttered around, gorging on nectar. Simon recognized the giant yellow Monarchs, but didn't know the names of the tiny yellow ones, or the big black ones with red spots on their soft wings. Occasionally a car passed by. Whoever was inside waved at Simon, and Simon would raise a hand in return. The driver didn't know Simon, and Simon didn't know him, but it didn't matter. They were pleased to see each other anyway.

Across the road Meat Camp Baptist Church sat high on a hill. It was a small, plain, white clapboard country church, just the steeple rising in front to proclaim its lofty purpose. It wasn't the original church, of course. Its predecessor was built in 1851 near Meat Camp and the old Buffalo Trail, which crossed Jefferson Road a few miles further on.

The Buffalo Trail was a wide, prehistoric road blazed by millions of buffalo migrating east from the prairies to winter on the Atlantic coast, thousands of years before humans settled the Americas. The buffalo crossed the Appalachians to spend the season where it was warm, then returned to the deep grasses of the Midwest in spring.

Simon liked to fantasize about this prehistoric road trip, envisioning the vast herd of buffalo making their way east, stopping to graze in the lush valleys, drinking their fill from clear, cold mountain streams. He couldn't help but finish his daydream by imagining the big animals frolicking happily in the Carolina surf off Pearlie Beach.

Simon reluctantly abandoned his reverie, got back in his car, and drove just a mile further down the road to the Greenwood Nursery, the old Potter homestead. He parked on a graveled drive in front of a restored farmhouse. The bright white clapboard walls, green trim on windows, doors, and gables, and the scrubbed, varnished wood floors of the porch, gleamed with attention. Bentwood rockers, the expensive kind cushioned in green-checked canvas, lined the front porch. A profusion of red-blossoming columbine twisted around the porch columns and wound around the railings.

Simon went up to the front door and rang the bell. There was no answer. He wandered around back, where he noticed an old barn with a half dozen cars and pickups parked inside. He ventured down a graveled path that curved around the back of the barn. There he was met by two black Labrador retrievers, tails wagging furiously, vying to lick his hand. They led him behind a row of conifers to a commercial greenhouse. Acres of cutting flowers bloomed in a field behind it. Two Hispanic men worked, bent over, in the field, carefully cutting mature blossoms, tying their stems together gently, and placing the bunches in boxes. Insects filled the air around them.

Simon knocked at the greenhouse door, and this time he got a response. A small, plump, middle-aged woman in jeans and an embroidered denim shirt opened the door. She had on heavy gardening gloves and carried a pruner in one hand.

Simon introduced himself. This was the part of his new avocation he disliked, telling strangers that he was poking around some old tragedy and asking them personal questions about matters that were really none of his business. He never warned them that he might uncover secrets that they would wish he hadn't, secrets that might change their lives. This time he was spared the conversation.

"Oh," she said, "I know who you are. You're Professor Simon Shaw, Rae Coffey's nephew. I heard all about you at church last Sunday.''

The woman took off her gloves and extended her hand. ''I'm Elizabeth Sheets,'' she said. ''My husband and I own this place.''

Simon shook her hand.

''I'm glad to meet you,'' he said. ''So you must know I'm looking into the murder of Eva Potter in 1958. I understand she lived here with her family.''

She took his arm and led him toward the house.

''I didn't know a thing about the murder, about this house being her home, until I read it in the newspaper when the girl's skeleton was discovered. Imagine, she was still in the truck where it went off the parkway all those years ago!''

''Yes, I...''

''Our hired men, bless them, they're good people, but they drive too fast—there are no speed limits in Mexico, you know—one of them will wind up off the road and down a mountain like that one day if they don't slow down.''

''The roads can be dangerous up here, that's for sure.''

''Rae told me about your parents, but goodness, you don't want to talk about that, do you?''

Simon didn't.

They reached the porch and she showed him to a rocker.

''Have a seat. I'll get us some lemonade and cookies.''

Simon suspected that Mrs. Sheets had been waiting for his visit ever since Aunt Rae had told her about him. He'd be lucky if he got away from here before dark.

Mrs. Sheets brought out a tray and set it down on a

wrought-iron table between Simon's rocker and the one she took. Simon sipped his lemonade. It was the real thing, cloudy with lemon pith, and not too sweet. He bit into an oatmeal cookie, chunky with nuts and raisins. Suddenly he didn't care if Mrs. Sheets talked all afternoon. It was a sunny day, flowers bloomed everywhere, chickadees and cardinals gorged at the bird feeders, and hummingbirds hovered like tiny helicopters over the red flowers of the trumpet vines. One zoomed by him an inch from his ear, sounding like a miniature jet fighter.

"Mrs. Sheets…"

"Call me Elizabeth, honey," she said. She leaned toward him, her voice lowering into a whisper. "Don't you want to know everything?"

"Yes, ma'am," Simon said, taking another cookie. "Everything."

"Well," she said, rocking vigorously. "My husband and I bought this place in 1967, from old Mrs. Potter and her daughter, the one that remained, June. They couldn't keep it up after Mr. Potter died. That was before land prices got so outrageous, so high no one can buy a decent size farm anymore, only developers can afford it, and they build houses. Then the people who buy the houses so they can enjoy the country complain about the cows, the smells, and their allergies. I don't understand it."

Mrs. Sheets paused for a sip of lemonade.

"Eldon, my husband, and I had no idea that our place was the setting for a murder! After it came out in the paper, I was so curious I just had to find out everything I could. I pumped all the old-timers at church for information. I found out that the Potters boarded these two men, Earl Barefoot, who was a farmhand and forager, and Roy Freedman, who was an ASU student, except it wasn't ASU then.''

"I don't understand why Roy didn't live closer to campus,'' Simon said.

"Honey,'' she said, "he was Melungeon. This was 1958. No one in town would rent to him. And the college couldn't find him a roommate. But he had a pickup truck, so he could drive to campus.''

"It's hard for me to picture that kind of attitude today, as cosmopolitan as Boone has become.''

"Wasn't it stupid? My husband, Eldon, is part Cherokee, you know, and our daughters have the most beautiful dark brown eyes, almost black. But anyway, Roy was a nice young man, I understand. Not bitter at all, which you would think he would be, being the victim of prejudice and all. Made up his own bed everyday, cleared the table after meals, helped tote the laundry for Mrs. Potter.''

"You found all this out from people at church?''

"Some of it when June Rinehart came by here a few weeks ago.''

"Mrs. Rinehart came here?''

"Yes, she said that finding Eva's body made her think about her old home. She wanted to see it again. Of course I let her. She wandered all over the house. Said that the wallpaper with violets on it in Roy's old room really brought her childhood back to her. That had been her grandmother's room. After she died, that's when the family started to take in boarders.''

Before Simon could form the question, Mrs. Sheets leaned forward in her chair, poised for action.

"Would you like to look around, too?''

THERE MUST BE good money in flowers. The interior of the Sheets home was as beautifully restored as the exterior. Wide, pegged floors were sanded and refinished, the stone chimney and mantel cleaned and repointed. Antiques filled the living and dining rooms.

Elizabeth Sheets led him upstairs. She gestured toward the front of the house.

"The two big bedrooms are in front," she said. "The Potters had one, and June and Eva shared the other. They used the main bathroom."

Mrs. Sheets led him down the hall.

"See up there?" she said, pointing to the ceiling. "See that soffit? The Potters built a wall here, with a door that led to the back, to divide the boarders' rooms from the family's. My husband and I removed it."

Two steps down the hall she stopped in front of a door and opened it. The small room had one gabled window and a small closet.

"The other one across the way is identical," she said. "Eldon and I redid them for our girls. They're both in college now. The Potters added a tiny bathroom over the back porch for the boarders. My husband and I redid that, too."

Mrs. Sheets's cell phone rang. She answered it.

"What?" she said, and listened for a minute. "All right," she said. She clicked off the phone and turned to Simon. "I've got to run out back. You stay here if you like. I won't be long."

Alone at the back of the Potter home Simon tried to picture Roy Freedman's life in that room. It wasn't easy. The Sheetses had decorated it for a teenage girl, painting it sage green, and filling it with white, feminine bedroom furniture and green chintz fabrics. Simon went across the hall and opened the other room, where he supposed Barefoot had lived. It was identical in size and shape, but painted pink with wicker furniture and rose-printed fabrics.

Simon was halfway down the stairs to the first floor when he remembered that June had mentioned the wallpaper in Roy's old room. What wallpaper? He went back upstairs and back into the green room. On a hunch, he opened the closet door. Like most renovators of old homes, the Sheetses hadn't bothered with areas that couldn't be seen. The interior of the closet was still covered with faded wallpaper. He switched on the light, and noted the bunches of purple violets, each tied with a tiny pink ribbon, strewn over the closet walls. He turned off the light, and went back down the stairs, thinking. When June had visited her old home, she had looked into the closet in Roy's room. What an odd thing to do.

Simon met Mrs. Sheets on the porch.

"I don't suppose you could remember exactly what day June Rinehart visited you, could you?"

"Certainly," she answered. "It was July thirteenth. I know because we were on our way to the Doc Watson Music Fest in Sugar Grove. We were late because we waited while she looked around the house."

WHEN SIMON ARRIVED back at Luther's cabin, Big Momma had left her fishing spot on the bridge. Simon was alone, and he luxuriated in it, stretching out on the hammock tied between two pine trees in the front yard. He listened to the sound of the water in the creek rush over the rocky bed, and watched a couple of male hummingbirds duke it out over a perch at a hummingbird feeder. They were aggressive little guys, dive bombing each other, wings buzzing like angry giant bees, until one finally flew off, vanquished.

SIMON'S CELL PHONE rang. It was Chaplain Mitchell at Central Prison.

"I talked to Roy," he said. "And he confirmed what June Rinehart told you, that she visited him shortly after Eva's body was found. According to him, she wanted him to 'buy into all this Jesus stuff,' as he put it. He told her he didn't kill Eva, but she didn't believe him."

"Did he say why he didn't mention it to me?"

"Didn't think it was important."

"Maybe it isn't. June is certainly religious enough to do something like that. Her home and business are full of angels and crosses and such."

"There's something else," Chaplain Mitchell said. "Roy only told me about one meeting. But when I checked the guest register, it showed that June Rinehart had visited him twice."

"Twice? Really?"

"That's right, July tenth and July fifteenth. I'll ask him about it the next time I see him."

"Don't do that," Simon said. "At least, not yet. Let me poke around some more up here."

Simon clicked his cell phone off. June Rinehart had visited her old home between two visits to Roy Freedman. He was beginning to feel uncomfortable with his place in this story, like a moviegoer who's missed the first half-hour of the show, trying to piece together what he's missed while keeping track of the present.

DUSK FELL OVER Shaw's Creek. The sun set quickly, falling behind the steep mountains that lined the holler. Simon turned off the porch light so he could enjoy the night coming. The air grew cold, and out in the woods an owl hooted. In the moonlight, the creek water looked like flowing milk.

Luther had gone straight to church after work, so Simon was on his own for a few hours. He made two toasted peanut butter and jelly sandwiches, opened a beer, and went back out to the porch. While he was inside Simon selected some of Luther's collection of traditional Appalachian music, and ironically, the first cut was a rendering of "Down to the River to Pray." A woman's voice, singing alone, joined by others as the song went on, cried "Oh, sinners, let's go down to the river to pray," so they could pray about "that good old way, and who should wear the robe and crown, oh lord, show me the way." The music and lyrics laid bare human longing for spiritual consolation. Listening to it, Simon didn't know whether to feel inspired or depressed.

The next song was "Oh, Death," that poignant a cappella plea for another year of life. "Won't you spare me over to another year," it began, in the rusty voice of Ralph Stanley. In the song Death visits an old man, announcing, "I am death, none can excel, I'll open the door to heaven, to hell. I come to take the soul, leave the body and leave it cold." He assures his victim that "no wealth, no land, no silver, no gold, nothing satisfies me but your soul." You'd have to have no heart at all not to feel apprehension listening to those words. Except those, maybe, who had been born again, and were convinced that they'd get immortal life in the good place by "accepting Jesus" and clutching their inerrant Bibles to their bosoms.

Simon avoided choosing between Christianity and Judaism mostly because of the pain it would cause the other half of his family, but he was more attuned spiritually to his Jewish half. He didn't think any religion could offer better advice than the Ten Commandments.

They were in everybody's good book now, but the Jewish people received them first. The historian in him respected that.

Simon didn't think it mattered whether God actually dictated the Ten Commandments to Moses, Moses thought of them himself, or a remarkable tribe of humans had developed spiritually in advance of the rest of the primitive peoples around them, to the point where they could understand what God's law should be. What mattered was the law itself.

Simon had problems with the conservative Baptist concept that good works weren't essential to salvation. He thought people ought to try to be good, and that atonement was an excellent idea. Yom Kippur was the only Jewish holiday he observed. His Jewish grandfather, who had died when he was a child, told him often that no one should pass up the opportunity to do *mitzvoth*. Helping out Roy Freedman might qualify as a *mitzvah,* he thought, if he stretched the concept a bit.

Simon heard Luther's truck turn onto Fat Boy Road. He got up and turned on the light in the plastic Santa Claus to welcome him home. He was relieved to see Luther. His introspection had been descending into brooding, but his cousin would shortly turn his attention to more important things, like beer.

Luther bounded, there was no other way to describe it, up the porch steps. He was dressed in khakis, a short-sleeved dress shirt, and tie that he must have changed into at work.

"Don't listen to that mountain gospel stuff by yourself," Luther said. "It might make you think, and you already do too much of that."

"You're right," Simon said.

"Here," Luther said, handing Simon a paper plate

covered in plastic wrap. "Coconut cake. From the church supper."

Simon didn't bother to get a fork. He picked up the hunk of cake with his hand and bit right into it.

"Now," he said, "this is heaven."

"Best in town. Mary Anne Hunter brings it almost every week. There was lots left over tonight. Momma took some to Daddy and some to Sheriff Guy."

Simon was surprised.

"Aunt Rae went to see Uncle Mel at the rest home tonight?"

"Right after services. It don't mean nothing. They're still fond of each other. They just can't live together anymore. I don't think that's going to change."

Luther went inside and changed the CDs. Simon already knew what he'd select—Creedence Clearwater, Alabama, or the Allman Brothers. Luther brought three imported beers back out on the porch, handing one to Simon.

"Man, I love this beer," he said, tipping one back and draining it. "Thanks for getting it."

"You're welcome. How was church?"

"Fine. Great sermon. We prayed for you."

"That was good of you."

The two men listened to music and rocked.

Halfway through his second beer, Luther checked his watch.

"I've got to be at work at eight tomorrow. I'm going to bed."

"I'll be along in a minute."

Halfway into the cabin Luther turned on his heels and came back outside.

"I almost forgot," he said. "I checked the messages

here at the cabin earlier today, and your girlfriend called you.''

Simon pretended nonchalance.

"Oh?" he said.

"She said to call her if you got in before eleven."

"Thanks," Simon said. Luther went back inside, and Simon heard his bedroom door close.

Simon thought about waiting until tomorrow morning to call Julia, hoping she would wonder where he was. But, he remembered, he disliked relationship games, and he had rung off rather abruptly the last time they talked.

Simon dialed Julia's home number. She answered on the second ring.

"Hey babe," he said, "are you still mad at me?"

"Not so much," she said.

Thank God.

"You were entitled," Simon said.

"Maybe. But I could have been more understanding. It's not like I don't get wrapped up in my own work sometimes."

This was good.

"So," Simon said. "Can you come up this weekend?"

"I might be able to," she said. "Wait, let my check my calendar."

"We don't have to stay with my aunt or my cousin. I'll get us a room at the Mountain Inn. It's got a great view of Grandfather Mountain. Then you could meet my family at dinner one night."

"Oh," she said, and Simon heard pages flipping. "Your family. Sure. I'd like to do that. But you know, I just checked my schedule. I can't make it this weekend. Maybe some other time."

"Sure, whatever."

"Besides, I'll see you when you get back to Raleigh. Okay?"

"Of course."

SIMON WOKE UP when Luther got up at dawn.

He'd spent the night tossing and turning, dreaming repeatedly about getting baptized in the Watauga River by Jesus himself. He was relieved to be fully conscious. The crowd of white-robed spectators at the baptism hadn't seemed very friendly.

Luther heated up two packages of sausage biscuits in the microwave for breakfast. Simon told him about his telephone conversation with Julia.

"Bummer," Luther said. "But are you sure she blew you off? Maybe she really did remember a conflict."

"I don't think so," Simon said, spreading strawberry jam on his sausage biscuit. "You know what I think? I think she didn't realize until we talked last night that if she visited me here, I'd expect her to meet my family. That's when she decided not to come. I don't think she's committed enough to our relationship to bother."

"Ouch," Luther said. "But do you care, really? I mean, what could be better? She's good-looking, she makes her own money, and she doesn't want to marry you."

Simon jellied another biscuit.

"But I want to remarry someday," he said. "I want the whole thing, the kids, the minivan. I want to have what my parents had, what Debra and Hank have. I thought I wanted to marry Julia. I'm not sure, now. I feel like the guy in the Paul Simon song, you know, okay for an off-night."

Luther threw a piece of his biscuit off the porch onto the ground and watched two squirrels fuss over it.

"You know what I think?" he said. "You're on the rebound, that's what. Didn't you meet this woman right after your divorce? Wasn't she the first woman you dated?"

"Yeah." Simon threw a chunk of his biscuit at the squirrel who lost the dispute over Luther's piece. The animal snagged it with his left paw and shoved it in his mouth.

"You're young. Don't you read the papers? Guys get married and start families late these days. You got plenty of time. Hell, have fun. You should have no trouble finding dates."

"You're right about that. The women just line up outside my front door and wait for their turn."

"You don't have the right attitude. You're not ugly, you're not mean, you love kids, and you have a job for life. Of course, if you want them to actually like you, that's harder."

"I know."

Luther slapped his shoulder.

"Lighten up," he said. "I'm just messin' with you."

It wasn't like Simon hadn't heard these sentiments before from all his friends and relatives. Maybe he should pay attention to them.

"Do you think about remarrying, Luther?"

"Sure, a lot. But no more kids. My two boys are enough. Any woman who marries me has got to bring her own children with her."

"Your future wife might have her own ideas."

"It won't do any good. I'm a sports model."

"You're kidding."

"No, I'm not. Did it right after Bo was born."

The two squirrels perched on the porch rail now, chattering for more handouts. A couple of bicyclists, outfitted in matching spandex, bent low over their expensive mountain bikes, cycled silently and swiftly by. Luther went inside the cabin and came back outside with a couple of pretzels, which he broke in pieces and lobbed out into the yard. The squirrels broke and ran for them. A couple of crows swooped down from the trees, cackling, to share in the bounty.

"I know," Luther said. "Come with me to the Apple Barn on Saturday night."

"The dance hall? I don't know if I'd fit in there."

"The only thing you have to do to fit in is be available. And I've seen you two-step, you're pretty good. Saturday nights the place is packed wall to wall with women. Most of them come alone, too. Lots of them are your type. Teachers, librarians, nurses, not just us rednecks."

"I wasn't thinking that, and you know it."

"Oh, hell!" Luther said, smacking his forehead. "I forgot! You're on your own for the weekend. I'm going to jail."

NINE

"EXCUSE ME," Simon said. "I must have heard you wrong. Where are you going?"

"To jail," Luther said.

"What for?"

Luther went back to the coffeepot to refill his mug, sat back down, and crossed his legs.

"I got ten days for paying my child support late," Luther said. "I'm working it off on weekends. I found out today that I can go in Thursday night, and be done with it by the end of this weekend."

"I didn't know you needed money. I can lend you whatever."

Luther shook his head.

"It's not that. It's just that nothing gets my ex's attention except money. She was trying to tell me that I couldn't take my boys to the Southern Five Hundred. Since she got married to that pharmacist, she suddenly thinks our boys are too good for stock-car racing."

"I didn't think you could withhold child support for any reason."

"You can't. But she tells me this so close to their visit I don't have time to take her to court. So I just held back her check. She gave in quick. She's building a swimming pool, I hear. But the judge wasn't impressed with my tactics. He still gave me the ten days. It was worth it.''

''I hope so.''

''Look, could you do something for me while I'm inside?''

''Sure, name it.''

''Eat with Daddy tonight and take him to the Exchange Club turkey shoot. I had planned to, but when the deputy sheriff said I could finish serving my time this weekend if I went to jail tonight it seemed like a real good idea.''

''Sure, I'd like to spend the time with him.''

''Let's have another cup of coffee on the porch, then I've got to go to work. I'll come back here around five to pick up some things for the weekend—I'm due at the jail at six. Daddy will be expecting you about then. I'll call him as soon as I get to work and tell him.''

They took their second mugs of coffee outside, sat, rocked, and watched a young mother pushing a stroller down the road, with a toddler on one leash and a Dalmatian on the other.

''Luther,'' Simon said. ''I want a serious answer from you.''

''Uh, oh.''

''For what reason would you spend forty years in jail for a crime you didn't commit?''

''Is this about your Melungeon friend?''

''Yeah.''

''Forty years,'' Luther said. ''Man, I wouldn't do it for any damn reason.''

''Sure you would. Think about it.''

''Well,'' he said. ''For my boys, I guess. Momma and Daddy, maybe.''

"So to protect someone you loved, you'd go to jail for life."

"I suppose so."

"How about to protect something, rather than someone? Would you go to jail to keep a secret?"

"I don't know. Why do you ask?"

"Roy Freedman, if he's innocent, must be hiding something. Something so big he's been willing to stay in jail to protect it, until now."

"I thought you said he was forced to confess."

"He was. But he's had forty years to take it back. And I feel like some of the people I've been talking to up here are being less than honest with me. Like they're hiding something, too."

"What people?"

"Like Big Momma, for example. Why on earth would she let Rocky threaten people with that gun? No one wants to trespass on her property. What if the sheriff gets tired of it, and arrests them?"

"What could she be hiding?"

"I don't know. And what about June Rinehart?"

"The woman who runs Daddy's rest home?"

"She's Eva's sister. Why did she visit Roy twice in prison? And why is she needling the old sheriff about his sins?"

Luther sighed. "I'm getting lost. Tell me this Freedman guy's story from the beginning."

Simon told him. When he got to the part about visiting Eva Potter's old home and finding violet-sprigged wallpaper in the closet, Luther smiled widely.

"Man," he said, "you're clutching at straws. The guy is guilty."

"I'm not so sure, and it's driving me crazy."

"What are you going to do now?"

"I'm giving up on trying to get people to tell me the truth. I'm going to go to the library."

SIMON SAT CROSS-LEGGED on the floor in the stacks of the Appalachian Reading Room in the library at Appalachian State University, a mound of pamphlets and documents in cardboard folders scattered around him. He was interested in two issues that seemed critical to him in resolving his questions about Eva Potter's murder. First, was the geography of the murder and related events just coincidental or was it an important clue? Second, what could Roy Freedman, or June Rinehart, or Big Momma, or Sheriff Guy, or Deputy Lyall, or all of them, possibly be hiding? And, if they were hiding something, was it the same something?

After a couple of fruitless hours spent reviewing Watauga County history he already knew, Simon moved to the map room. He was getting hungry, but damn, by the time he was done, he was going to know everything that had ever happened on Shaw's Creek.

Simon made a complete reference map marked with all the items he thought might be useful to his investigation. He had brought with him a current county road map, tracing paper, and a box of colored pencils. First he lay a piece of letter-sized tracing paper over that section of the county map that enclosed the murder site, the Potter home, the old Harliss place, and the Shaw homeplace. He traced all the highlights of the county map onto the tracing paper. Then he photocopied the traced page, enlarged to the biggest size available, producing a hard copy he could edit and refer to.

Carefully Simon added the other modern features he wanted on his chart. With a green pencil he highlighted the overgrown, forested parts of the area, switching to a lighter green pencil to shade in pastures and cleared acreage. With a brown pencil he marked Shaw's Knob, Howard's Knob, and the higher, unnamed summit of Big Momma's property. In blue he traced the south fork of the New River, Howard's Creek, and Shaw's Creek. He labeled Fat Boy Road, Jefferson Road, and Howard's Road. Squares in black pencil depicted the complex surrounding his aunt's house, Luther's cabin, Big Momma's shack, the Potter Home, Meat Camp Baptist Church, and Howard's Cove. He marked the river beach where Eva Potter was murdered.

Then Simon carefully examined every map of Watauga County in the map collection, one at a time. The collection contained maps of all kinds, photocopies of antique charts, tourist maps, federal survey plans, geological diagrams, and amateur historical maps. If there was a clue to Eva Potter's murder buried in the geography of Watauga County, he would find it. If he recognized it. From amateur historian Gailard Stout's detailed historical map of Watauga County, Simon transferred the locations of the original Meat Camp, the Buffalo Trail, the old narrow-gauge railroad line, and an abandoned Fire Service watchtower, to his own map.

A geological map of Watauga County interested him, even though Watauga possessed fewer minerals and ore deposits than counties to the east. Watauga's only two gold mines, long exhausted, were located near Grandfather Mountain and just north of Boone. The flakes of gold Simon and Luther found in Shaw's Creek when they were kids washed down from the latter's old workings.

Simon leafed quickly through the photocopies of antique maps in the collection. The earliest was dated 1770. Nothing was labeled in the vicinity of Boone, which didn't exist then, except the New River. The next map he found, dated 1808, showed Meat Camp, the New River, Howard's Knob, and the Buffalo Trail.

On Bradford's famous map of 1838, just a few years before the first Shaw bought his farm, Jefferson Road was a dirt path which connected Boone to the Buffalo Trail. Another path, marked by tiny dashes, probably an old animal track, ran parallel to the stream later named for the Howards and the Shaws, crossed Jefferson Road, and continued toward the New River, where Fat Boy Road was today. Interesting. The creek was named Wennyma Branch then. The tiny script on the map was barely decipherable. There seemed to be a W scrawled below the dashes designating the path, with a mark connecting it to the path. The word *wennyma* was Cherokee, he was sure, he could tell from the phonics of it. He shouldn't be surprised; the Cherokee named everything in their environment, and white settlers often continued to use the Cherokee place names. *Watauga,* for instance, meant whispering waters, and *Appalachia* was Cherokee for endless mountain. This was the first time he had heard that Shaw's Creek had an earlier name, or that Fat Boy Road followed an older trail along the creek. He made a note to go looking for a Cherokee dictionary later.

At the end of the morning, Simon had a colorful historical and geological map of a small section of Watauga County, but nothing on it struck him as a clue to solving the Potter murder. That Cherokee word for the creek did interest him, though.

For the fun of it he searched the stacks for a Cherokee dictionary. He found several, but they translated directly from the English to written Cherokee, without indicating pronunciation. He needed someone who could speak Cherokee to help him decipher what *wennyma* meant.

Of course, the word could be so far removed from the original Cherokee that it was meaningless, but he wanted to find out. It was the only fact he'd turned up in a morning of hard work that had surprised him.

SIMON MADE an appointment by cell phone before he left the library to the one man whom Simon knew could help him with the Cherokee name of Shaw's Creek. He paused for a while before he called, a lump forming in his throat. Gordon McLeod was Professor Emeritus of Appalachian Studies at Appalachian State University. He was part Cherokee, fluent in the language, and an expert on the history, culture, and folklore of the Appalachian Mountains. He was also a close friend of Simon's parents. Simon had seen little of his parents' friends since they died, avoiding the pain it would cause him. On the phone McLeod had been gracious, not alluding to the time that had passed without any contact with Simon, and suggested he come by his home right away.

Simon postponed the meeting for a half-hour so he could grab a bite to eat. He drove the length of the university on his way to find a fast-food restaurant. He hadn't seen the results of the new construction at the university. The campus was stunning. He turned around and drove back through the campus to get a better look.

A new brick and stone Convocation Center anchored the entrance to the campus. New classrooms, science buildings, and residence halls lined both sides of the main street that went through it. Confined between a tall mountain and the town of Boone, the university couldn't grow much bigger than its 12,500 students, and that was just fine with its board of advisors. "App," as it was affectionately known to all, was the only campus of the UNC system that would likely stay small, and, in

Simon's biased opinion, student-friendly. He once thought about applying to teach there himself, but decided that he wanted to live and work away from his hometown and his father's shadow.

Simon drove to a hamburger joint and sat in the parking lot, wolfing down a double-cheeseburger, fries, and a chocolate milkshake.

Fortified by carbohydrates, he went on to the McLeod's home, a modest stone ranch in a part of Boone favored by university faculty. It looked much as Simon remembered it from the McLeod's yearly brunches, except the garage had been converted into another room. Simon parked on the street outside, setting the parking brake carefully on the steep hill.

The front door opened before Simon got to the end of the slate walk. McLeod came out onto the front porch. The two men hugged unashamedly for a minute.

"Son," McLeod said, "it is so damn good to see you. Where have you been? Don't say anything, I know it's painful. Come inside."

McLeod had aged, of course. He never could see well, and the lenses of his glasses were as thick as the bottoms of Coke bottles. He was bald, thin, and slightly stooped. Simon calculated his age. He had been some years older than Simon's father, which made him close to eighty now.

"Professor McLeod," Simon began.

McLeod chuckled. "Please," he said, "call me Gordon. We're colleagues now. Come into my study."

McLeod's energy belied his looks. He might shuffle, but he shuffled eagerly and quickly into the room that had been the garage.

"I did this when I retired," Gordon said. "My wife

says it's my career crammed into a fifty-by-twenty space."

"It's great," Simon said. "If I had a place like this, I'd never leave it."

Floor-to-ceiling bookshelves stuffed with books, periodicals, and thick, worn file folders lined three walls. The fourth wall, which faced the front yard, contained a large bay window. McLeod's desk stood in front of it. A computer with a huge monitor took up most of the space on it.

"I see worse than ever," Gordon said. "With this contraption I can still read and write."

McLeod sat down on a battered leather sofa and patted the space next to him.

"You've done a little writing yourself," McLeod said. "The Pulitzer Prize! Your dad would have been beside himself with pride, or jealous as hell, I don't know which."

"Both, probably," Simon said, sitting down.

"Then," McLeod said, "there's the detective thing. One day I open *People* magazine, and there you are, solving murders, a forensic historian! What a hoot."

Simon groaned. "Don't remind me," he said. "My friends have never let me live it down. And it doesn't help that Kenan College keeps a link to the spread on its Web site."

"Don't be absurd," McLeod said. "Historians used to be out in the world doing interesting things. Think of Churchill, Roosevelt, McCauley, Herodotus. They didn't sit around universities being stuffy. They were active in society. Your notoriety is good for the profession."

"You're very kind," Simon said. "But how are you?"

"Other than old? Just fine, nothing to complain about.

Mary and I are healthy, we've got two married children, five grandchildren, and enough money to travel some. What's to complain about?''

"I'm glad," Simon said. "I've missed you. I'm sorry I haven't visited more."

"It's all right," McLeod said, patting Simon's knee. "We'll keep in touch better now. Of course, I'm not sure I would have heard from you today if it weren't for this little question you have."

Gordon was smiling broadly at him, so Simon didn't try to apologize.

"Yeah, I guess so."

"Let's have it then."

Simon told him the story of Eva Potter's death and Roy Freedman's request, at the point of a shotgun, for Simon's help clearing himself of her murder.

McLeod listened intently, never taking his eyes, huge behind his thick glasses, off Simon as he talked.

"Interesting, very interesting," McLeod said, once Simon had finished. "Extremely interesting. There's the Melungeon issue, of course. You've read about the new DNA studies? Fascinating. Of course, your Mr. Freedman would have experienced considerable prejudice. And the legal issues are critical, also. I agree with you that the central issue is, was the confession forced, and why has Mr. Freedman been content to stay in prison if he's not guilty? Now, that Cherokee word you mentioned? What has that got to do with all this?"

Simon unfolded the map he had made in the library.

McLeod took it over to his desk and held it under a magnifier that transferred the image onto McLeod's computer monitor.

"Picasso, you're not," McLeod said.

"No," Simon said. "But you do see, Shaw's Creek

was named Wennyma Creek before my illustrious ancestors bought the property. And there's a W written there that seems to refer to the trail.''

"Yes,'' McLeod said. "The word doesn't strike a bell. It's probably a combination of words, or a Scots-Irish version of what the Cherokee word or words sounded like. I've got a phonetic Cherokee dictionary on my computer. Let me play with it a little.''

The old professor booted up his computer and called up a dictionary. The typeface on the screen was huge. Simon read over McLeod's shoulder for a time, until he got tired of scrolling through words in a language he didn't know, so he went to wandering around the study, looking at the books, pictures, and memorabilia of McLeod's academic life. It was all there, the sheepskin diplomas phrased in Latin, the book jackets, photographs, Native American pottery, and, incongruously, a brass rubbing of a knight. Simon's own book, *The South Between the World Wars,* stood facing out on a shelf, he noticed with a pang. When he picked it up and opened it, a newspaper clipping about Simon's Pulitzer Prize fell from among the book's pages.

Simon replaced the clipping and the book, then turned to find McLeod had stopped scrolling and was staring at him. He had an intent, eager, almost suspicious look on his face.

"What have you found?'' McLeod asked him.

"What do you mean? Nothing, at least, nothing yet,'' Simon said.

"You swear? You wouldn't keep something from an old professor, would you?''

"Gordon,'' Simon said, crossing over to him, "What does *wennyma* mean?''

"My best educated guess is that it means place of wealth, or place of rich things, or maybe way to riches."

"Oh, my," Simon said.

"You're surprised?"

"Yes, I'm surprised. I mean I think I'm surprised."

"Tell me what you believe it means."

"I don't know. At least, not enough to say anything yet."

McLeod got up from behind the desk and walked over to Simon, who still stood next to the bookshelves.

"Promise me something," Gordon said.

"Of course," Simon said.

"Please let me know how all this turns out. I'm curious as hell."

"I am, too, and I swear you'll be the first to know."

McLeod said good-bye to Simon at his front door. Simon shook hands with the bent old man, and knew he'd be back to see him soon. He'd waited too long to renew old relationships, and he was glad he had some time left to enjoy this one.

TEN

IT COULDN'T BE.

Simon waited until he got back to the cabin before letting his imagination shift into high gear. He tried to restrain his churning mind, taking a cold Coke out onto the front porch of Luther's cabin. He avoided looking across the creek at the Harliss property until he felt more relaxed, watching instead a junco urging her fluffy, ungainly child to fly.

When Simon finished collecting his thoughts he allowed himself to stare at the peak of Big Momma's land. It was rocky, rugged, and ringed with clouds, at least five hundred feet higher than Shaw's Knob. Hadn't Big Momma said no one ever climbed up there? His imagination leapt forward again. "Preposterous," he said, out loud. But he wondered how he could explore the place without anyone knowing what he was doing, especially Rocky, whom he expected was just as eager to shoot trespassers as ever. He certainly did not want to tell Big Momma anything. Disappointing her would be a terrible thing to do.

Suddenly, Simon's temples throbbed, warning him that the barometer was falling quickly. He rose from his chair and walked out into the road and inspected the creek. The water rushed by deeper and faster than it had this morning, splattering against rocks and spraying into the air. He looked west, where dark clouds gathered and filled the sky. A leaf skittered across the road. The breeze brought him the scent of damp honeysuckle. It was raining to the west of Boone, and the storm was coming this way.

The Appalachians were a temperate rain forest, a fact the western North Carolina tourist bureau didn't publicize. Four rivers had their headwaters in Watauga County, supplied with water by eighty inches of rainfall a year, the highest average rainfall on the East Coast. A storm could whip up so quickly the local TV weatherman would hardly get on the air before torrents of rain began to fall. Flooding was a major problem, too. Rain poured off the slopes into creeks and streams so quickly that waterway banks overflowed, filling the narrow hollers with water, which then raced down into valleys with amazing force. The raging water pushed cabins off their foundations, broke bridges into sticks, and washed entire roads away, rock beds, asphalt, guardrails and all.

Simon idly wandered down Luther's driveway. Poke branches hung over the shoulder of the road. Clumps of poke berries, purple on red stems, dragged the branches down with their weight. He and Luther made ink from the berries when they were kids, ruining a set of clothes every summer. Simon stopped at the Harliss's creaky bridge across the creek. A downpour that raised the creek level a few feet would surely wash it away. He wondered how it had survived this long.

"Pitiful, ain't it," Big Momma said, from her side of the creek. "We don't dare drive the truck over it, but it's safe enough to walk along the side beams." She stomped on one of the heavy wooden beams that stretched across the creek. With its partner, it held up the boards that made up the bridge. With her stomp the boards quivered and rattled, but the beam itself seemed solid. A new rope stretched over a beam between two trees on each side of the creek.

"Insurance," Big Momma said. "Think there's a storm coming. Come on over," she said, waving him across. "Come sit with me and Rocky and have a cup of coffee." Simon's hesitation must have shown in his face, because she quickly added, "it's okay. Rocky won't do nothing. I still feel bad about that the other day."

Simon crossed the bridge, one hand sliding along the rope, and followed her up the hill. The dirt road leading up to the cabin needed a good scraping and a couple of loads of gravel.

As if reading his thoughts, Big Momma said, "there ain't no use fixing up this road as long as can't nobody drive across the bridge."

Simon hiked alongside Big Momma until they came out of the woods into a small clearing. Big Momma's home was no longer the derelict shack that Simon remembered exploring with Luther when they were kids.

New concrete blocks were inserted into the foundation to fill the gaps, shoring the house up into a more or less level condition. More concrete blocks stepped up to the front door. Irregular sheets of black, orange, green, and brown asphalt siding covered the old rotten clapboard walls; fresh tar paper coated the roof. A new propane tank leaned against an outside wall.

Someone had recently mown an area around the house. A spot about ten feet square that got enough sun grew tomatoes, peppers, squash, and corn. Behind it, on the edge of the woods, Simon saw a bright blue porta-potty, tastefully surrounded by a bed of marigolds.

A small campfire burned a few feet away from the

door of the shack. A coffeepot rested on a grate over it, steam rising from its spout. Rocky sat in a lawn chair next to the fire, whittling a heavy stick. When he saw Simon and his mother, he abruptly got up and walked away, dropping the stick and the knife.

"Rocky says he would love to sit and jaw with you," Big Momma said, "but he's got work to do. We got propane for the stove, but we still heat with wood. We need about three cords to get through the winter. Rocky hopes you will excuse him."

"Of course," Simon said. Soon after Rocky went into the woods, Simon heard the rhythmic sound of Rocky chopping wood.

Big Momma indicated that Simon was to sit in the chair Rocky had just vacated, and she took another. Simon looked down at his feet. Rocky's whittling tool was a six-inch-long hunting knife with a tapered point. Bright streaks along the blade showed that it had been recently honed. The long stick he had been whittling was three feet long and carefully sharpened to a point. Thinking of that man with an axe in his hands made Simon shudder.

"Want some coffee?" Big Momma asked.

"Sure," Simon said.

Big Momma reached into a plastic tub of mismatched dishes and pulled out two mugs. With a heavy towel she grasped the handle of the metal coffeepot and poured thick black coffee into the mugs, and handed Simon his. There was no sugar or milk in sight, and Simon hated to ask for fear she didn't have such luxuries. He sipped from the mug; the coffee was scalding hot, bitter, and gritty with grounds. Big Momma drank half her mug in one gulp.

"The place looks good," Simon said. "You've done a lot of work on it."

"Thanks," she said. "It's slow going. We have to save up from Rocky's check every month. I never put nothing into Social Security."

Big Momma turned to point to the utility pole next to the house and the wires strung from it. Simon took that opportunity to pour out the rest of his coffee on the ground.

"We've got lights and a telephone now," she said, "and the Vietnam Veterans found us a good refrigerator. Luther give us an old television set. Rocky got an antennae way up there," she said, pointing to the top of a tall pine on the edge of the clearing, "and we get three channels. NASCAR's on TV now, did you know? And we got the well pumping without having to replace it."

"I'm impressed," Simon said.

"Now we're saving for a bathroom," she said. "I got used to indoor plumbing in prison. More coffee?"

"No, thank you," Simon said.

Big Momma tilted her head back and sniffed the air, like an animal.

"Rain's comin' for sure."

"I think so, too."

"Not until after midnight, though." She sighed. "Hope the road don't wash out again."

"Fat Boy Road? Since when does it wash out?"

"Ever since we come back, it washes out two or three times a year. Luther says it started when the last hurricane came through. Down where the road curves around that big boulder, you know, and the road climbs a little. When the creek rises, the water surges right across the road and overflows into a new channel. That water takes a chunk of the road right out, a couple feet deep and wide. Nothing can pass. It's usually two or three days before Luther or Hank can bring a load of gravel to fill it up.''

Simon didn't understand why his family would permit Fat Boy Road to be impassable for any length of time.

"It needs a dry-weather bridge," Big Momma said. "You know, a concrete ditch with sloping sides that a car can drive across, but that would channel the water when the creek overflows, and wouldn't wash out. 'Course I know that would cost big money.''

Simon hoped that Big Momma didn't see the heat rising in his face. Fat Boy Road was part of the Shaw homeplace. Economy was one thing, but would it be too much for his aunt to build a dry-weather bridge so two neighbors could use the road? It was Big Momma's only way out of the holler. Luther could drive his four-wheel drive up over Shaw's Knob by the system of dirt roads that crisscrossed it to service the Christmas-tree farm, but that option wasn't open to the Harlisses.

"I kidded your aunt, the last time she tried to buy my land, that she didn't fix the road so we would want to move out." Big Momma laughed, as though that was the silliest idea in the world.

It wasn't silly to Simon. Would his aunt make the Harlisses' life even harder than it was to get something she wanted? In a New York minute. Now he was really angry.

"I'll take care of it," Simon said.

Instantly Big Momma looked worried.

"I shouldn't have brought it up," she said. "I wouldn't want Miz Coffey to be angry with me."

"I'm half-owner of this property," Simon said. "That road needs to be fixed. I'll make sure it gets done, and I won't mention your name.''

"That would be wonderful," Big Momma said.

Repairing the road would hardly dent Aunt Rae's bank balance, and it would be real Christian of her. He'd look up some real good Jesus quotes from the Bible to reinforce his request. Again, he wondered why his aunt wanted to buy the Harliss property, which then reminded him of another question.

"Big Momma," he said, "have you ever noticed any Indian sign on your place?"

"There ain't been Indians here in a hundred and fifty years. They all live on the Qualla Reservation now, near Cherokee."

"I know that. I mean old sign."

"Like what?"

"Oh, unusual marks on trees, painted rocks, caches of arrowheads, piles of stones, things like that."

Big Momma frowned.

"Can't say that I have," she said, "but then I ain't exactly completely explored the place. I didn't live here when I was a young'n. We lived up over the feed store where my daddy worked. Plus it's hard going up toward the summit, and I don't need to break a leg on top of everything."

ONCE BACK ON Luther's front porch Simon could not quiet his mind. He felt that he was no closer to figuring out if Roy Freedman was guilty of killing Eva Potter than he was when he first got up to Boone. But he'd uncovered enough questions related to the murder that he felt there had to be something to Roy's declaration of innocence.

Simon went inside to get his notebook, and stayed inside because of the chill of the evening. The propane stove clicked on, and Simon sat on Luther's sagging sofa, flipping over the pages of his notebook. He read over the same old questions he didn't have answers to.

Why hadn't Sheriff Guy gathered any corroborating evidence of Roy's guilt?

Why did Roy plead guilty, if he wasn't, and never challenge the plea until now?

Why did June Rinehart visit Roy in prison, twice?

Why did she visit her old home, and look in the closet of what had been Roy's room?

Why was Sheriff Guy anxious about Simon's questions, why did Deputy Lyall say the old sheriff was senile, and why did June Rinehart keep pressuring Guy to "repent?" Repent what?

Simon added more questions to his list.

Why did his aunt want to buy the Harliss place?

Why didn't Big Momma sell her land, instead of struggling to survive on it? Why did she let Rocky wave that shotgun around, when she could lose her parole and he could be committed for it?

Why did the Indians name the creek "Way to Riches"?

Simon unfolded his carefully researched, meticulously drawn research map of this little part of Watauga County. His instincts told him that the answers to his questions lay somewhere on Big Momma's rocky patch of mountain ground. Simon badly wanted to explore the Harliss place, but not badly enough to get shot by Rocky.

Luther's genuine cuckoo clock, brought back from his army tour in Germany, chimed. It was six o'clock. Time to go to the rest home and pick up Mel for dinner and the turkey shoot.

Simon decided to take Luther's four-wheel-drive truck because of the possibility of heavy rain. He parked his own freshly detailed car under Luther's metal carport. He stowed Uncle Mel's shotgun on the truck's gun rack and tossed a box of ammunition and a couple of waterproof ponchos into the backseat.

As SIMON DROVE into the rest home parking lot he saw an ambulance, light-bar flashing, pulled up to the front door. A lump formed in his throat. Quickly he parked the truck and ran into the lobby. Uncle Mel stood with a knot of other men inside near the door. Relieved, Simon put an arm around his shoulder. Mel turned to him, his eyes red-rimmed and his mouth set in a hard line to keep it from quivering.

"It's Micah," he said.

"I'm so sorry," Simon said. He gripped his uncle's shoulder and watched the sad drama unfold in the lobby.

Sheriff Guy lay flat on his back, eyes closed. Two paramedics tended him, one with a hand on his pulse and the other adjusting an IV line. He must be alive, Simon thought, or they wouldn't be bothering. June Rinehart knelt next to Guy, holding his hand tightly between hers. She raised her head to speak to an aide standing nearby, and saw Simon. To his surprise, she beckoned to him. When he didn't respond, she gestured more urgently.

Mel nudged him, so Simon reluctantly went over to Mrs. Rinehart and knelt down on the floor next to Guy. June leaned over the old man. His skin was beaded with sweat and his eyes were closed.

"Sheriff Guy," she said. "Professor Shaw is here. Isn't there something you want to tell him?"

The old man's eyes opened briefly, then closed again. The paramedics raised the stretcher and bore it outdoors, carefully loading it into the ambulance, which drove off. When it hit the main road, the sirens blared.

"That's too bad," Mrs. Rinehart said, as she got to her feet. "Sheriff Guy told me this morning he wanted to talk to you after all. Now he might not have the chance to unburden himself."

"What happened?" Simon asked.

"I think renal failure," Mrs. Rinehart said. "He has diabetes, you know."

"That ain't it," Uncle Mel said, coming up to the two of them. "You tell those doctors to look for something else," he said to Mrs. Rinehart.

"I'm so sorry, Mel," she said. "I know it's hard."

"It ain't his time," Mel said.

"He's eighty-nine years old," Simon said.

"That don't mean this spell is natural," Uncle Mel said.

Simon took his arm and urged him toward the door.

"Come on," he said, "let's go on. I've got my cell phone. We'll check on Sheriff Guy whenever you want. Let's get something to eat, at least."

In the truck Mel reached for Simon's phone.

"The power button's—" Simon began.

"I know how to work a cell phone," Mel said, "I'm old, not stupid."

Mel punched in a number. Simon assumed he was calling the hospital.

"Hey, there," Mel said into the phone. "Is the sheriff in? No? How about Deputy Lyall? Well, who the hell's in charge?"

Simon groaned as Mel proceeded to tell the senior deputy in charge at the sheriff's office that he needed to get on over to the hospital and check up on old Sheriff

Guy, that his illness wasn't natural, and that the deputy should investigate the possibility of foul play.

"I hope you know what you're doing," Simon said. "You've made a serious accusation."

"I know that. But Micah had just been to the doctor for his checkup. He was in pretty good shape. I'm telling you, someone wants to help him on to his reward."

"Why would someone want to kill him?"

"I don't know, but I aim to see that Sheriff Hughes finds out."

UNCLE MEL LOOKED more like his old self after a cold lemonade and a plate of chopped pork barbecue, cole slaw, and seasoned french fries at Woodalls', a popular barbecue restaurant on Blowing Rock Road. The pending storm must have kept the hordes of locals and tourists away for the evening. Mel and Simon had walked right under the pink neon pig into the restaurant and found a good table without having to wait.

"Maybe Micah'll make it," Uncle Mel said. "He ain't ever had dialysis. Maybe they'll put him on that and he'll get better."

"Maybe so," Simon said, but he doubted that dialysis would be in order for an eighty-nine-year-old man with diabetes. After their plates were cleared, and since there was no line of hungry folks at the door agitating to get in, Simon ordered them each banana pudding and coffee.

Uncle Mel scraped the bottom of his bowl, then leaned back, patting his stomach.

"I just saw one shotgun in the truck," he said. "You ain't shooting tonight?"

"You know I haven't used a gun in years," Simon said.

"I remember you were a good shot."

"When I was twelve, I could hit a Coke can off a fencepost at a hundred feet," Simon said. "But I just never took to it." In truth Simon got bored with target-shooting, and he didn't enjoy killing animals, even varmints.

"Where is that shotgun I gave you for your twelfth birthday? What kind was it? I can't remember."

"It was a Remington pump-action, four-ten gauge. Luther's got it. His boys use it sometimes."

"You ought to take it home with you, you should have some protection, as mixed up in murder as you've been getting yourself lately," Uncle Mel said.

SIMON PULLED Luther's truck onto the shoulder of the road near the target range. There were three other cars parked off the road. The weather must be keeping people away.

Simon and Mel followed a hand-painted sign down a track into a cleared field. A small hardy group of shooters gathered around a fire lit in an empty barrel. One was Hank, who greeted Mel and Simon with a quick handshake each.

"Hard to believe it's July," the only woman there said. "The temperature's really dropped." She wore gloves with the fingertips cut out, rubber boots, and a flannel jacket several times too big for her.

"This is some cold front that's coming through," a man in a wheelchair said. "It must be going to rain like hell later tonight."

The only other person at the shoot was a teenage boy, who appeared to be the son of the man in the wheelchair.

The Exchange Club had sponsored a shooting contest as long as Simon could remember. Everyone would throw money into a pot for whatever charity the club was sponsoring, and set out to prove he, or she, was the best shot in the field that night. It took as much luck as skill to win, since shotguns were the weapon of choice. Closest pellet to the center of a paper target took first place. The winner took home a turkey or ham, whichever the grocery store donated that week.

Mel introduced Simon around. The woman turned out to be Rose Purview, Simon's old elementary school librarian. Simon remembered that she seemed ancient twenty years ago. When she heard that Luther was spending the weekend in jail, she wasn't surprised, she joked, winking at Mel, only she figured it would be for something more serious. The man in the wheelchair was William Dart, a draftsman at the furniture factory, and the teenager was his son, Bill.

"We ain't going to raise much for the widows and orphans tonight," Dart said, "unless we increase our contributions some." He stuffed a twenty dollar bill into a coffee can labeled DONATIONS. Everyone followed suit, including Simon.

Three bare lightbulbs hung between two poles provided the only illumination. From the looks of the wire strung from the poles to a nearby power line, the Exchange Club still stole electricity from the electric company. The shooters lined up under the lights and squinted at a row of paper targets pinned to a fence about thirty yards away. After the first volley, Dart's pellets lodged the closest to the bull's-eye on his target.

"Y'all can't beat me tonight," he said. "I'm hot."

Dart's son prepared to shoot, and Simon noticed that his father bit back advice. The boy pulled the trigger, then rubbed his shoulder after the recoil.

"I don't think I even hit the target," he said. "What did I do wrong, Dad?"

"The kick from that gun is bigger than the one you used last time. You might try to aim a little lower to allow for the recoil," Dart said.

As the shooters exchanged small talk between volleys, it was obvious to Simon that every one of them knew exactly why he was in Boone. His mission was the subject of all the small talk.

"I knew Eva," Purview said. "It surprised me that she took up with a Melungeon, not that there's anything wrong with that," she added hastily. "She just wanted to irritate her parents. She wanted to go to nursing school, and they wanted her to stay on the farm."

Mrs. Purview took forever to steady her shotgun in shaky hands, but when she did finally fire, her pellets lodged within an inch of the target.

"So," Simon said, "you think she went out with Roy so her parents would let her go to nursing school?"

"It's possible. I'm sure they'd rather that than have a passel of brown grandbabies. Back then they thought that way," she added hastily.

"She rejected him when he proposed," Simon said. "That's supposed to be why he killed her. Do you think he did?"

"Didn't know the man," she said. "I just understood from talk at the time that Eva wasn't serious about him."

This looked bad for Roy. It would be hard to learn your girlfriend wouldn't marry you because of your race, but even worse to find out she didn't much like you to begin with.

Dart rolled up to the line in his wheelchair. He had to hold his shotgun at an odd angle to shoot from a sitting position, but he didn't hesitate to fire, scoring a bull's-eye.

"Way to go, Dad," Bill said.

"That turkey is my destiny," Dart said. "I can smell it deep-frying in my outdoor cooker now."

Bill took his stance. This time his shot was more accurate.

"Good job, son," Dart said.

Mel and Hank took their shots in turn, aiming carefully, while Dart wheeled himself over to Simon.

"I hear from Luther you met the Harlisses the other day."

"Sure did. Luther forgot to warn me."

Dart shook his head. "I worry about those two. I was with Rocky in 'Nam," Dart said. "He was a good boy, but not too bright. I worry about anyone who takes him by surprise. He's several bricks short of a load."

"I agree. And he ought not to be armed."

"You know," Dart said, "after an experience like Vietnam, you come out of it either anxious as hell, or so glad to be alive, nothing bothers you. I guess I'm lucky to be in the last category."

Simon instinctively glanced at Dart's chair.

"Yeah," he said. "'Cong mine field. But it could have been a lot worse. I'd rather be in this chair than dead, or in and out of a mental hospital. My girl still loved me, too. We got married as soon as I could wheel myself down the church aisle."

"Your son seems like a nice kid."

"Thanks," Dart said. "I like to take him shooting. It's about the only thing I can do these days that impresses him!" Dart wheeled his chair around. Mel and Hank were done shooting. They all searched for their shotgun shells, dumped their trash into a plastic bag Hank brought, and turned off the lights. In the dark they walked back to their cars. Dart was the acclaimed winner of the turkey, which he held in his lap as he rolled across the field toward the parked vehicles, with an occasional push from his son.

With powerful arms Dart hoisted himself into the passenger side of his car, while his son placed his wheelchair in the back, and went around to the driver's side.

Mrs. Purview carefully broke her shotgun, put it in the trunk of her Ford Escort, and drove off.

"Wait for me," Mel said to Simon. "I got to go piss in the woods. One of the disabilities of old age. I can't hold it."

Hank waited with Simon, smoking a cigarette, which Debra wouldn't allow in their house.

"Tell me," Simon said. "Why does Aunt Rae want to buy the Harliss place?"

"She covets the mistletoe and galax that grows up there," Hank said, "especially the mistletoe. I haven't actually heard her mention it for a while."

"She approached Big Momma Harliss about it recently."

"No kidding. I didn't know that."

"You don't suppose that's why Fat Boy Road washes out several times a year, do you?

Hank flashed him a big grin. "Could be. I just figured it's because she's cheap."

RAIN STARTED TO FALL before Simon got Mel all the way back to the rest home. It came in big, heavy drops, knocking aside branches and leaves as it fell. Treetops swayed, illuminated occasionally by flashes of lightning. Thunder sounded in the distance. The next time lightning flashed, the two of them counted the seconds until the next rumble. Ten seconds. The lightning strike was ten miles away.

Every light in June Rinehart's house and most of the

lights in the rest home extension blazed. Two Sheriff's
Office vehicles were parked outside the entrance.

"This can't be good news about Micah," Mel said.

Simon held the door open for Uncle Mel, but the two
of them barely had time to get inside before Deputy
Lyall appeared from inside the lobby, grasped Mel by
the collar, and shoved him up against the door jamb.

"What the hell are you doing?" Simon said. With the
palm of his right hand Simon shoved Lyall's chin back
until the deputy broke his hold on Mel and fell on his
backside.

His face burning with fury, Lyall pointed his finger at
Simon.

"That's assault on a deputy sheriff," he said.

"Put your hand on my uncle again, and I'll show you
assault," Simon said.

By now Lyall was on his feet, rubbing his neck.

"That hurt, damn you," he said to Simon. "And as
for you," Lyall said to Mel, "I want to know why you
were so sure Sheriff Guy was poisoned? What business
is it of yours?"

Mel and Simon were stunned.

"Poisoned? Is Micah dead?" Mel asked.

"Not yet, but he's critical," Lyall said, rubbing his
chin.

"Deputy Lyall," Sheriff Hughes's voice was calm.
He and Mrs. Rinehart came out of her private entrance
into the lobby. "Go home. You're relieved of duty for
two days."

"But…"

"You've been out of control all evening. Go home
and get a grip."

"Her," Lyall said, pointing at June Rinehart. "If Micah was poisoned, it must have been her. Ask her why

she waited so long to call an ambulance. I'll tell you why! Sheriff Guy left her half his life insurance in payment for living here. Fifty thousand dollars!''

"Don't you get the other half?'' Mel asked.

It seemed to them all that Deputy Lyall made an infinitesimal move toward his sidearm. Instantly Sheriff Hughes lifted Lyall's gun from its holster.

"Go home,'' he said to Lyall. "Stay there. Don't make me put a deputy outside your door. We'll find out if Sheriff Guy was poisoned, and who did it. You're not on this case.''

With the loss of his gun, Lyall's anger began to subside, and he realized he was in trouble.

"Sheriff, I apologize.''

"Just go on home.''

Without another word Lyall left the lobby.

"I'm sorry about that,'' Sheriff Hughes said, stuffing Lyall's gun into the waistband of his own holster. "He's real fond of Sheriff Guy.''

"What's happened to Micah?'' Mel asked.

"He's in intensive care with renal failure. The docs think it's poisoning because he just had a checkup, and his kidneys were okay.''

"What was the poison?'' Simon asked.

"They don't know yet. Lab results aren't in. At first the docs thought it looked like wood alcohol, you know, bad moonshine, but we told them that Sheriff Guy never drank anything stronger than iced tea.''

Sheriff Hughes put his Stetson back on his head.

"Don't you all worry,'' he said. "We'll get to the bottom of it.'' He looked significantly at Mrs. Rinehart. "You remember what I said, ma'am.''

The sheriff left, hunkering down into his jacket as he walked out into the rain.

"What did the sheriff say?" Mel asked her.

"He told me not to leave town," Mrs. Rinehart said.

"You're kidding," Simon said.

Mrs. Rinehart shrugged. "I expect it's just routine. Deputy Lyall is correct. I am one of the beneficiaries of Sheriff Guy's life insurance."

"No one who knows you would think for one minute…" Mel began.

"Thank you, honey. I wish Micah had called me when he became ill. He must have felt poorly for hours before he collapsed."

"He was fine Tuesday night at dinner. You were there, Simon, you remember?" Mel said.

Mrs. Rinehart took Mel's arm.

"I'll walk you to your room."

"Micah was the best checkers player in town, next to me," Mel said. "All the rest are just wood-pushers."

"Let me spend the night here with you, Uncle Mel," Simon said.

"No, you go on back to Luther's," Mel said. "It's going to rain hard, and you got to keep an eye on the creek."

IT WAS A TENSE drive back to the holler. When the lightning cracked, Simon saw the tops of the trees bending so far over it was a wonder they didn't break in two. The real danger, though, was that the roots of the biggest trees would just pull out of the wet earth and topple over, crushing cars and houses. Simon had seen that happen in Raleigh when Hurricane Fran struck there, and he was eager to get Luther's truck parked under the sturdy metal carport. He was forced to drive slowly. Sheets of water dimmed the streetlights and his headlights. Simon navigated by the yellow line in the middle of the road, and only knew the turnoff to Fat Boy Road by a reflective post sunk into the ground at the intersection.

A few feet down the road he saw a pair of headlights bearing down on him. Big Momma pulled up next to him in her pickup, and stopped. Both Big Momma and Simon rolled down their windows, and sheets of water blew into the cabs. Rocky sat next to his mother, staring ahead, his head nodding in four/four time, except that Simon didn't hear any music.

"This rain is worrying me," Big Momma said to him. "I don't need a tree to fall on this truck. Then I would be in sad shape. I'm going to park out in the middle of the Wal-Mart parking lot until the storm's passed."

"Where are you going to sleep?" Simon asked.

"We got sleeping bags in the back," she said. "We'll be fine under the topper."

Simon crept on down the road. Luckily he had lit the Santa Claus on top of the cabin before he left to pick up Mel, or he would have overshot Luther's driveway. Cautiously he drove up the muddy slope, and parked Luther's truck next to his Thunderbird under the carport.

He got soaked running to the cabin porch. Standing on the porch, all he could see was a blanket of rain covering the holler. His uncle had told Simon to keep an eye on the creek. He couldn't see the damn creek, but he could hear it. The rushing water and pouring rain together sounded like a train passing by.

Inside the cabin, flames crackled behind the grate of the propane furnace. The living room was much warmer than the boys' bedroom. Simon lifted an armful of blankets and a pillow off the bed and carried them into the living room and made up a bed on the sofa. He wasn't sleepy, but he didn't want to think about Roy Freedman or Micah Guy or June Rinehart, or for that matter, Julia, who hadn't called him to tell him that she missed him desperately and would drive up to Boone tomorrow, whatever the weather, after all.

Simon made a pot of hot decaffeinated coffee and spiked it with sugar, cream, and Southern Comfort. He found a stack of movies, and watched *To Kill a Mockingbird* and most of *Deliverance* before he fell asleep.

SIMON WAS AWAKENED the next morning by the telephone ringing.

"Good morning," Hank said. "You're not drowned."

"Should I be?" Simon said.

"Look outside."

Simon looked. A mighty river flowed through the holler. Its near bank was the slope up to Luther's cabin. The road was underwater.

"Wow," Simon said.

"You must sleep like the dead."

"I had a couple drinks."

"Are you all right there for a while?"

"How long is a while?"

"I don't know. Until the water recedes. Until I can get a dozen trees that fell across the farm roads moved, including the two across our driveway. Until I can get a load of gravel up Fat Boy Road. I'm sure it's washed away in the usual spot."

"I'm fine." Simon said. "Don't worry about me. Are you all okay?"

"Yeah. Like I said, lots of trees down that'll take a while to move. I've got to put the winch on the truck, and hope I don't have to hire a crane. You could walk out of that holler, you know."

"Have you been listening? I'm fine here. I see no need to go hiking anywhere."

"Suit yourself."

"Hank, Big Momma and Rocky Harliss went to spend the night at the Wal-Mart parking lot. How can I find out if they're okay?"

"Them and about twenty other families were parked there. St. Luke's and First Presbyterian sent their vans and rounded them all up and took them to the emergency shelter at the elementary school. They'll be fine."

After Hank rang off Simon walked down to the swollen creek. He marveled at its power. Charging white water rushed by him, choked with branches, clumps of plants with dirt still clinging to their roots, and even a tire. The holler sparkled, sunlight reflecting off the raindrops that clung to every twig and leaf. The rain had scrubbed the dust and dirt off every surface. There wasn't a cloud left in the bright blue sky.

It would be a couple of days, he expected, before anyone could get into the holler. In an emergency, he could walk out over Shaw's Knob, but the cabin was dry and warm, and Luther's kitchen was well-stocked with food.

It was perfect.

ELEVEN

SIMON FIXED HIMSELF a big breakfast of scrambled eggs, coffee, bacon, and toast. Then he combed Luther's cabin for the supplies he needed for his expedition. He wasn't in any hurry. It would be a few hours before the water receded enough for him to venture across the road to Big Momma's place.

He wished he knew exactly what he was looking for. He had twenty-four hours, forty-eight if he was lucky, to scour Big Momma's land for the reason an innocent man endured forty years in prison. He felt in his gut the answer was up there. It was also true that he had a vivid imagination, and that it had been seriously encouraged by learning the meaning of *wennyma*.

Luther's athletic son Bo was about Simon's size. Simon raided his closet for a fiberfill vest and a pair of hiking boots. He borrowed thick socks and a long-sleeved flannel shirt to protect himself from rattlesnakes, cottonmouths, and poison ivy. Luther's junk closet yielded a canteen and a sturdy walking stick. In the storage shed out back Simon found yards of thin nylon rope. He wound it into a thick loop he could carry over his shoulder. He cut the fingers off a pair of work gloves that were otherwise too large for him, and found Luther's utility knife in his toolbox.

Simon almost gave up looking for carabiners, but finally found two in the junk drawer in the kitchen. He didn't bother with his cell phone. He couldn't get service that far up the mountain without a satellite phone. Finally he emptied a tool belt of screws and pliers and such and packed it with all his gear.

Then he wrote a note to Luther or Hank, whoever came looking for him first, that he had been exploring the Harliss place and was probably lying somewhere with a concussion or a broken leg, and to bring water and painkillers.

Some water had receded off Fat Boy Road, but walking out in any level of rushing water could be dangerous. Simon eyeballed the distance between the water's edge at the foot of Luther's driveway to where he thought Big Momma's bridge was, if it was still there. If it wasn't, he'd just have to come on back and think of something else to do for two days.

He knotted one end of the nylon rope around a tree trunk, and estimated the distance between the tree and Big Momma's bridge. He tied that length of rope to his waist, looping the rest over his arm. Making sure that all his jury-rigged equipment was securely attached to his body, he ventured out, keeping the rope between him and Luther's tree taut. He reminded himself that he was in no hurry.

He slipped once, sliding onto his backside into the rushing water that coursed over the road. He easily pulled himself to his feet using the rope. He made his way to the tree where Big Momma had tied the guide line over her bridge. Water was halfway up his shins here on the edge of the creek, while the creek itself still rolled by fast and furiously. First Simon tested Big Momma's rope, pulling at it with all his strength. It seemed secure. He clipped a carabiner to it, looping the other end of his rope through it. Then he untied the other end of the rope from his waist, cut it with Luther's utility knife, and tied it to Big Momma's tree. It would serve as a guide rope between the bridge and Luther's driveway, if he needed it on the way back.

Secured safely to Big Momma's guide rope, Simon felt around with his feet for the bridge. He found it. Or rather, he found the support beam. The planks that formed the rickety floor of the bridge were gone. He jumped up and down on the beam. It appeared solid. He eased himself carefully across the creek, walking on the beam, tethered to the guide rope. A tree branch sailed by, painfully nicking an ankle. He tottered for a second, struggling for balance. He caught himself, and walked across the rest of the bridge and up the far bank to solid ground. His hands shook and his back muscles knotted from the strain of hauling himself across the bridge and keeping his footing. After unhooking the carabiner from Big Momma's rope, he sat on a fallen log for a few minutes and drank a few swallows of water from his canteen.

Adrenaline powered him up the slope to Big Momma's shack, which he was glad to see was still in one piece. He went around the back, where he noticed a narrow path winding up the hill behind the shack. Branches and vines met and intertwined over the path, forming a dark tunnel. This was as likely a route up the mountain as any, so he started to climb.

Sodden humus squelched under his feet. Once he slipped, but he caught himself with his walking stick. A broken ankle would not be a good thing. It wasn't long before Simon was sweating heavily under his fiberfill vest. He sat down and took it off, waiting for the breeze to dry him out. He drank most of the rest of his water, then refilled his canteen from a tiny waterfall that tinkled down the slope and cascaded over a rock near the trail.

Through a gap in the vegetation he could see the roof of Big Momma's house far below. He couldn't see most of Luther's cabin, just the tip of Santa's red hat.

After his rest Simon set off up the hill again. Head down, bent forward against the slope of the mountain, he didn't stop until his breathing was so labored his chest hurt, and the muscles of one of his legs began to cramp. He sat down to massage his leg and drink more water. The trees and vegetation were thinning now, and the summit of Shaw's Knob seemed to be directly opposite him. He must have about another five hundred feet to go.

Further along the trail his heart leapt when he saw the bushy stump sprouts of a chestnut tree, volunteered from old roots. Fifteen feet high, the bush had bloomed and set spiny burrs, each of which, if the bush survived to first frost, would produce up to two delectable chestnuts. Of course, soon the baby tree would die of chestnut blight, but repeated sproutings from dead stumps kept hope alive that someday a resistant tree could repopulate these mountains with the mighty giants. The chestnut tree once dominated Appalachian hardwood forests. Its delicious nut and lovely timber had proved irreplaceable.

Simon only spotted the camouflage netting because of that chestnut bush. He was examining the bush, trying to determine—ignorant of horticulture though he was—whether the chestnut had been attacked by blight yet. Out of the corner of his eye, he saw the netting, a huge expanse of it, stretching deep into the forest.

Simon felt sick. There was only one use for camouflage in these mountains. Big Momma and Rocky were growing marijuana. How stupid could two people be? If they got caught she'd be imprisoned again and Lord knows what would happen to Rocky. Fools. If they needed money, why didn't they sell out to Aunt Rae, and get an apartment with central heat, indoor plumbing, and cable television?

These old country people were so stubborn, they would suffer almost anything to keep their land. But who was he to question Big Momma's devotion? He wasn't about to sell the property that had his name on it, leasing it for peanuts to his family, and he'd even speculated about building himself a cabin up here. If he wasn't careful he'd soon he'd be trading in the Thunderbird for a pickup, get himself a couple of dogs, and take up fishing, porch-rocking, bird-watching, and country bluegrass.

Simon couldn't resist exploring. He bent over and lifted the edge of the netting over his head so he could get into the nursery. Once he saw what was growing, he sat flat on the damp ground and started to laugh, out loud, mostly with relief. The Harlisses weren't growing marijuana, they were protecting a stand of wild ginseng. The plants, scattered about the forest floor under the trees, ranged from under a foot to about two feet high, their stalked leaflets crowned with tiny red berries. Under the soil their roots grew long, thick, and wrinkled, just like the Chinese liked them.

The ginseng stretched far out under the netting, shaded by trees above, as far as he could see into the dark wood. That's what Big Momma and Rocky were guarding. Her land had been stripped before, and she wasn't going to let it happen again. Simon wondered if Aunt Rae knew about this big patch of roots and that's why she wanted to buy the property. Maybe Aunt Rae didn't think Big Momma knew about the ginseng, and maybe Big Momma was sure Aunt Rae had her eye on it. The spectacle of those two strong-minded women dancing around each other over thousands of dollars' worth of Chinese medicine was worth the climb.

The ginseng patch might explain why Big Momma so zealously guarded her land, and why Aunt Rae wanted to buy her property, but it didn't explain why Roy Freedman spent years in jail if he was innocent, so Simon found his way out from under the camouflage netting and continued his search.

Simon didn't dream of moving off the path. He wasn't an experienced orienteer, and knew he'd get lost quickly, even in his own backyard, so to speak, if he did. The old path was barely visible in the rocky terrain, and he had to pick his way carefully over it. He continued to climb and the already cool July mountain air grew crisp. He was glad for the fiberfill vest.

Then Simon saw the tree. He judged from its size and condition that it was over two hundred years old, twisted and gnarled from exposure to the mountain winds. When he got closer to it, he realized that the defect wasn't natural, but man-made. It was an Indian-trail tree. He had found his Indian sign.

No one knows how the practice of bending living trees into signposts began. It may have started when the Indians used unusually shaped trees as landmarks, then got the idea to create their own.

It was a simple operation. The sign-maker bent a sapling in the correct direction, placed a Y-shaped branch under the bend in the tree, and tied grape vines or sinew to a stake in the ground so a length of the tree stretched horizontally, while the tip grew vertically. Eventually the bend in the tree trunk became permanent, showing the way to fresh water, caves, game tracks, or river fords.

Simon stroked the rough wood of the tree reverently.

It was still healthy—its branches were heavy with leaves and new sprouts. He remembered the words of Cherokee Chief Medicine Wolf, who said, "Everywhere you see and walk, we have already seen and walked hundreds of years before you. To those who can read our signs, we have left a record of our presence that will stand many years longer."

The signpost tree further fueled Simon's imagination, as he recalled the stories and legends about Cherokee "treasure trees." In the early 1830s, when the Cherokees marched west on the infamous Trail of Tears, or were, in North Carolina, confined to the Qualla Reservation, they supposedly concealed all their valuables, marking them with trail trees, planning to return for the treasure. But four thousand Indians died, the rest grew old, and few made the return journey.

Simon ran his hand over the forked tree, its nose pointing straight down the trail Simon was following, though now that trail was barely inches wide.

Logic reminded Simon that he was probably on a wild goose chase. The Indian signpost tree could be directing him to a long-vanished hunting lodge, or a water source. But he wasn't going to stop looking for that "way to riches" now.

Simon looked at the sky. It was just a few hours until nightfall, and he was bone-tired. He figured he could search another hour, then he'd have to get home and start again tomorrow.

Twenty feet further along the narrow path a dell opened ahead of him. It was, maybe, sixty feet across, treeless, covered with rocks and moss. It was so perfectly round Simon speculated that it was the crater of a small meteorite that had hit the mountain ages ago. Simon cut a length of rope and tied it around a branch to mark the entrance to the path down the mountain. It might seem like a absurd precaution to an outsider, but with dusk coming on, it would be easy to get caught walking endlessly around the dell looking for the path back down the mountain.

Simon went out into the middle of the dell. Drifting cloud, trapped there after the storm, filled the cup of the dell. He walked though it up to his knees, giving the experience a dreamlike quality.

His footing obscured by the fog-cloud, Simon tripped over a root and fell headlong. Throwing out his arms to catch his fall, his left hand slammed against a rock, hard.

"Oh, crap!" he said, rolling over on his back and holding his injured hand in the other. "Oh, damn!" His wrist throbbed.

Once the first intense pain passed, Simon found that he could move the hand and his fingers, but a deep red mark at the base of his thumb threatened to develop into a serious injury.

It could have been worse, Simon thought. He could have broken a leg.

He turned over to curse the offending rock. It wasn't a rock. Simon completely forgot his injury. He used both hands to disperse the mist and scrabbled at the dirt that half-buried his find. With Luther's utility knife he pried out the packed earth that filled the hollow space below a concave cup of rock. The rock was definitely a primitive smelter, how old he didn't know. It might date from the Cherokee, or from those dedicated Spanish treasure hunters, Desoto or Pardo, or a lucky early Scots settler. The smelter was essentially a hollowed rock set over a rock-lined hole. Fire burning red-hot in the hole melted ore in the cup, and the liquid metal, whatever it was, separated from the ore's other components. The early

miners most likely dug out a hole in the dirt, shaped in
a rough square or rectangle, directly underneath the lip
of the smelter. The liquid metal would be poured into
the dirt mold and cooled, forming an ingot. Maybe an
object like an acorn or an animal's tooth or an initial
had been pressed into the mold, so that the cooled ingot
would bear a mark of ownership. Whatever else, a mine
had to be nearby. No one would carry ore far when one
could build a smelter a few feet from its source.

Simon stood up. Damn the cloud. He could see very
little of the dell, although it might not help if he could.
The mouth to the mine could be obscured by an ava-
lanche, or forest growth. If he was right and Roy Freedman found this mine in 1958, Roy might have disguised
the entrance himself. Simon went back to the path where
he had entered the dell, and slowly circled it, clockwise,
looking high and low. He found nothing.

The only interesting object in the dell other than the
smelter was an ancient stone that had fallen over the
edge of the dell and broken in two, obscuring a good
chunk of the bank that faced into the mountain. Curious,
Simon walked back across the dell to examine the stone.
He ran his hands over it, estimating that it was at least
250 million years old. Permian, probably, part of the
supercontinent of Pangea. He touched the boulder reverently. It was layered with streaks of white gypsum and
darker calcite, laid down by hypersaline waters as sea
levels rose and fell. There would be few fossils embedded in the boulder—the Permian was the age of the last
great extinction before the age of the dinosaur. Simon
looked around for a formation that could have expelled
the boulder. He could only think that it fell from further
up the mountain, moved by an ancient earthquake a very,
very long time ago. It had become a part of this place,

hosting five or six different kinds of mosses, a large rhododendron that had rooted in a crack, and a clump of wild orchids. With one finger Simon traced a sedimentary layer, walking from one end of the boulder to the other. As he reached the end that rested on the floor of the dell, a blast of cold air hit his legs. It came from a large gap between the boulder and the wall of the dell. Simon reached his hand into the gap. More cold air. He lay down on the wet grass, cloud floating around him, and reached his arm as far into the gap as he could, back toward the rim of the dell. He couldn't touch earth where the wall of the dell should be. His heart rate quickened. He flicked on his flashlight and crawled inside the opening. Shining the light ahead, he saw timbers roughly framing an entrance into the earth. He had found the mine.

After crawling back out from under the boulder, Simon spent some time sitting on the rock, knees up, with his arms enclosing them and his head resting on his arms, thinking. Dusk was beginning to fall. He had to get back home soon. Once night fell, he would get very cold and be in danger of losing his way. He was too tired to go into the mine now, anyway. Exploring underground required special preparation. He would get a good night's sleep tonight and come back tomorrow.

Before he left, Simon stuffed the coil of nylon rope into the hole leading to the mine. There was no point in hauling it down the mountain and all the way up again.

Working his way down the mountain was as exhausting as climbing up. With his flashlight in one hand and his walking stick in the other, he crept slowly downward, his leg and back muscles straining to keep his balance on the slope. He was relieved to get to Big Momma's shack, and even more relieved to see that the creek level had dropped below her "bridge," which now was just a beam and a guide rope. Poor woman. Simon hooked a carabiner to the guide rope and easily crossed over the slippery creek. Once on the road, he collected a last bit of energy to walk down Fat Boy Road toward the highway. Sure enough, the road had washed out near the bend in the creek. It was still impassable to vehicles. Good. He needed another day.

SIMON ENTERED the cabin through the outside entrance into the bathroom. He was cold, wet, and filthy. He dumped his equipment into a heap on the floor, stripped, and got into the shower, turning up the water as hot as he could stand it. He soaped himself twice before he felt clean. His left wrist throbbed where he had fallen on the smelter; he hoped it wasn't fractured.

After Simon finished showering he wrapped himself in two towels and a bathrobe, threw his clothes into the washing machine, started the cycle, and went into the living room, where he turned up the temperature on the propane heater. It might be July, but he was cold. The flames whooshed on with a warm glow. He took three aspirin and washed them down with two fingers of bourbon.

He went into the kitchen and checked on Luther's food supply. In the freezer he found a stack of old-fashioned TV dinners, the ones with fried chicken, corn, mashed potatoes, and a brownie. Simon didn't know you could find them anymore. He put two of the dinners in the oven.

In his bedroom Simon dressed in jeans and a Kenan College sweatshirt and athletic shoes. He picked up his cell phone off the bedside table and saw that he had a message. He knew without checking that it wasn't from

Julia. Women had more stamina than men. They could cling to an argument forever. That's why most men found themselves begging forgiveness almost instantly after an argument. They were going to lose anyway. Why wait to make up and get the good things that would follow?

In his case, though, Simon thought he'd apologized enough. If Julia couldn't meet him halfway in an argument over this incident, what did that mean about the durability of their relationship? He'd been divorced once. He'd rather spend Saturday night at home watching television with his cats for the rest of his life than go through that again.

The cell phone message was from Uncle Mel, who asked Simon to call him immediately. Simon didn't like the sound of Mel's voice. It was wheezy with stress, as if he was having trouble breathing.

Simon dialed Mel's room at the rest home.

"Thank God," Mel said. "Where have you been all day?"

"Cleaning up outdoors from the storm," Simon lied. "Are you okay?"

"Sure, I'm okay, but all hell has broken loose."

"Tell me."

"Micah Guy died from renal failure due to antifreeze poisoning."

"Oh, God," Simon said. "How horrible."

"Have you ever heard of anyone dying from antifreeze poisoning, other than dogs and cats? I haven't."

Simon had. Big Momma had murdered her husband with antifreeze.

"How does the sheriff think it happened?"

"Micah loved iced tea. He drank glasses and glasses of it every day. He had a little refrigerator in his room, and kept a gallon jar of the stuff on hand all the time. Mrs. Rinehart kept it filled up for him. Of course, he wasn't supposed to have sugar, so he used artificial sweetener. So, supposedly, Mrs. Rinehart laced his iced tea with antifreeze, which tastes real sweet, you know, and it killed him.''

"Has Mrs. Rinehart been arrested?''

"Yeah. Deputy Lyall says she had motive and opportunity. Micah left her half his life insurance, and she was in and out of his room every day.''

"Do you believe she did it?''

"Of course not. What do you think?''

Simon wasn't sure. For one thing, Mrs. Rinehart had been pestering Sheriff Guy to tell Simon something that she thought was important. How could Guy do that if he was dead? For another, he figured lots of people had access to Guy's jar of iced tea. All the residents, including Mel and the rest-home staff, could have doctored it, including, he remembered with a pang, Aunt Rae, who'd taken the old sheriff coconut cake the other night.

"I don't know. I assume the sheriff will investigate every possibility,'' Simon said.

"Mrs. Rinehart's very calm. When they came to arrest her, she said the Lord knew she was innocent, and that she'd be exonerated.''

"Who's taking care of you guys at the rest home?''

"Some manager from a home health agency. Our quality of life has plummeted, I can tell you. The corn bread was hard as a rock at dinnertime. Listen, can you get out of the holler yet?''

"No,'' Simon said. "I don't think so.''

"I thought maybe with your experience and all, you could help Mrs. Rinehart.''

"She needs a lawyer, not a historian,'' Simon said.

Simon felt he could best help Mrs. Rinehart by getting to the bottom of Eva Potter's murder. Sheriff Guy had been alive and well until Simon had stirred up that pot.

Simon ate both TV dinners. You'd have thought it was *coq au vin* the way he chowed down. He chased the food with Coke and bourbon, then fell asleep on the couch watching a *Law and Order* marathon on television.

At two o'clock in the morning Simon awoke in serious pain. His left wrist burned, black bruising had spread from the tip of his thumb down past his wrist, which had swollen to about twice the size of his other hand. Simon could still move his hand and fingers, but not without pain. To make matters worse, he felt a migraine coming on. And he intended to climb that mountain later today and find out what was in that mine, if he had to crawl the whole way.

Even if Simon could get to a doctor, he didn't want to answer questions about how he had injured himself. He just had one day more that he could work in isolation in the holler, and he didn't plan to spend it in the emergency room. And he didn't want Big Momma to know anything about the mine until he had explored it.

Simon went into the bathroom and went through Luther's medicine cabinet. He found nothing stronger than aspirin and cold remedies. He searched the bathroom vanity drawer, and there, under a package of expired condoms, he found a brown pharmacy vial half full of pills. It was oxymorphine, prescribed to Carter Coffey. Who the hell was Carter Coffey? Of course, Luther's dog that had died of cancer. Carter must have spent his last days in a very comfortable haze.

If Simon remembered correctly, Carter weighed about half what Simon did. So he promptly took two of the pills. In another drawer he found Luther's first-aid supplies. It was fortunate that Luther had an athletic son who suffered diverse sports injuries. Amongst the gauze, tape, and elastic wraps was a left wrist immobilizer. Simon strapped it on, and it fit. The gods were smiling on him. Maybe he could avoid doctors for another day. He went back to sleep, this time in bed, covered deep in quilts.

When he woke up Simon's headache was gone, and his wrist was less painful. He fixed a big pot of coffee, took another tablet of dog morphine, and planned his day.

Simon called Hank, catching him on his cell phone.

"What's happening?" Simon asked.

"I got a crane here lifting these trees off our driveway. Clearing it's taking a lot longer than I thought. I'm not sure I can get a load of gravel out to Fat Boy Road tonight."

"Don't bother," Simon said. "You've got plenty to do without worrying about me."

"Aren't you tired of being stuck there? You could walk out to the end of the road, and I could pick you up."

"I'm doing fine. Rather enjoying it, actually. Tomorrow will be okay."

"You sure?"

"Absolutely."

An hour later he was ready to go. He'd added a backpack to his gear, full of equipment he had scrounged from the cabin. Most important were a heavy-duty flashlight with extra batteries and a box of matches. He also broke the face guard off one of Bo's football helmets and duct-taped a small flashlight to it. He found a pair of catcher's shin guards and stuffed them in the pack.

He took a couple of Cokes and a few packages of Nabs crackers with him, too. He made a sling for his arm from elastic wrap, hoping he could protect it on the climb. Sadly, he left the dog morphine behind. He needed to be able to think. He'd just have to endure the pain until he was back at the cabin.

He left a note for Luther, or Hank, or whoever came to the cabin first looking for him, explaining the location of the mine and asking them to come rescue him quickly, although by then he'd most likely be dead from hypothermia.

Water had receded from the road, though it still ran high and swift between the banks of the creek. Simon moved quickly across Big Momma's bridge and up the track to the tiny dell with the ancient boulder in no time. There he sat cross-legged on the ancient rock, forcing himself to think carefully about what he planned to do next. Spelunking was dangerous, and he wanted to be as prepared as possible.

He strapped on the shin guards. He might have to crawl a long way underground and his knees would turn to jelly without protection. He put on his jerry-rigged caving helmet and headlamp, Bo's football helmet with the flashlight duct-taped to it, and strapped on the tool belt. He was beginning to regret his note to Luther. If he died in the mine, he thought he'd prefer to rot there than be found in this ridiculous getup.

Simon retrieved the nylon rope from its hiding place, tying one end tightly to a nearby tree. The other end he secured around his waist. Trailing the rope behind him while exploring the mine, dealing with slack and tangles, would be a nuisance, but going inside without it was unthinkable. Who knew how many forks and side chambers were in that mine? Exploring underground could be disorienting, and he didn't want to get lost. Thinking about the dark underground he was about to enter, he double-checked all his knots and equipment.

Simon squeezed under the ancient boulder and crawled to the mouth of the mine. He shone his flashlight on the timbering that framed it, looking for evidence of its builders. The timbers looked like they had been cut by a sharp, iron axe and fastened together with machine-made nails. That dated the timbering, but not necessarily the mine, of course, to no earlier than the middle of the nineteenth century. The timbers weren't chestnut, but poplar, a late addition to the Appalachian hardwood forest, so he thought maybe the mid-twentieth century would be more accurate. He crawled a couple of feet into the opening, flashing his light around and feeling the walls and ceiling of the mine. They were wet, slimy, solid rock. He detected no instabilities that would have made him feel unsafe.

He guessed the temperature inside the mine was about fifty degrees. Water dripped constantly, trickling down the walls of the mine, collecting in small puddles on the floor. Gray lichen spotted the walls, and a single cluster of thin, drooping, pale mushrooms clung to a rock shelf.

Ahead Simon saw more timbering spaced at regular intervals. He called out, and his voice echoed for a long time, the last echo fading far away. He crawled forward, glad he'd worn the shin guards, dragging the rope along with him. He protected his injured left arm by using his right elbow and forearm for support as much as he could as he crawled. It seemed to him that the floor of the mine sloped down, and soon he could stand, just slightly hunched, as he moved forward. Back and forth over the walls of the mine he moved his flashlight, but he saw no evidence of riches.

The ceiling of the mine dropped a bit, and he was thinking about getting to his knees again, when he noticed a chunk of rock dug out of the wall of the mine. He stopped and examined it closely. The large niche, about two feet square, had been chiseled out of the quartz wall. The blunt, irregular marks of a primitive mining tool slashed along the inside of the niche. Simon imagined a Cherokee with a fire-hardened stick and a rock mallet, chiseling something precious out of the wall. On either side of the niche two deep holes, about two inches square, might have held torches.

Simon moved further into the mine. Several other niches showed signs that ore had been removed from them. Then the modern timbering structures ended, the mine narrowed, and Simon seriously considered turning back. It was very cold and damp. And ahead of him was an obstacle course, evidence that the mine had been worked a third time, after the Cherokee and before the twentieth century.

Early nineteenth century miners used a primitive method of stabilizing mine walls and ceilings. They chopped down trees, cut them into long logs, and wedged the roughly-cut logs between the walls and ceiling at whatever angle they'd fit. The result was an obstacle course of tree trunks criss-crossing the tunnel that he'd have to climb over to get further into the mine.

Simon shook off his hesitation. He could do this. He wasn't that tired, his wrist didn't hurt too much, and he wasn't out of rope yet. More importantly, he hadn't found what he was looking for.

Simon shook his left wrist out of its sling. He needed both arms and both legs to negotiate the maze of timbers. He extinguished his big handheld flashlight, looping it into his toolbelt, and relied on the small flashlight taped to his makeshift helmet. Simon tugged on the nylon rope, pulling it until a pile of loops lay at his feet. It was remarkable that it hadn't snagged on anything. Carefully he climbed over the first log, wedged at waist-height between the walls of the mine. The next log was almost vertical, so he could edge around it. He went under the next one. And so he made his way deeper into the mine. He still had the feeling that the floor of the mine was sloping downward, and it made him a little claustrophobic, thinking of the tons of earth that pressed down on the ceiling above him.

Suddenly the way opened up, and Simon sensed a cavern ahead of him. He switched on the big flashlight. It illuminated a large space, roughly forty feet square. A taller man than he could stand upright, and he did, stretching his back in relief.

Evidence of several generations of mining activity was scattered everywhere. Chunks of rock and granite, some of them quite large, lay around the floor. A rusty pick and a crowbar leaned up against a wall. A hand pick, with a narrow head and short handle, lay at his feet. He picked it up; the wooden handle fell apart in his hand. Niches in the walls held lumps of wax, the remnants of dozens of candles. A glass lantern rested on a rotting board stretched over two nail kegs. A wooden chair, missing one leg, leaned up against the board. A deck of cards, barely recognizable squares of paper coated with mildew, lay scattered across the makeshift table. There was just the one chair pulled up to the table—was solitaire the last game played there?

Simon couldn't tell if the lantern was old or not—you could buy reproductions just like it all over Boone. He noticed that the glass bowl of the lantern was half-full of liquid. Suddenly, more than anything else, Simon wanted light, and lots of it. He struck half the box of matches in vain, the damp air extinguishing them one at a time. Finally, one match caught, he touched it to the wick, and settled the chimney over the flame. Light filled the space, and as he looked around, he saw it. A vein of white quartz two feet wide ran horizontally along one wall of the cavern. Running right through the middle of the quartz band, like a yellow line down the middle of a highway, was a ribbon of gold.

Simon was stunned. Even though he had hoped to find something valuable, he was unprepared for the sight of all that gold. He had believed that there was more to Eva Potter's murder than a lover's quarrel, and here was his evidence. When he examined the ribbon of gold, he could see that some had been gouged out of the vein already. With Luther's knife, he stabbed into the shiny ore. It was soft, and he had no trouble prying out a chunk. The inch-square yellow rock gleamed in his hand.

Big Momma and Rocky were going to be very rich indeed.

SIMON WAS chilled to the bone, hungry, and his wrist hurt badly. He wanted to get out of the mine and back to Luther's cabin where he could think.

He extinguished the flame in the glass lantern and flicked on his flashlight. Looping up his guide rope as he went, he started back. As he carefully worked his way back toward the mouth of the mine, he pieced together the history of the mine, as best he could from the clues he'd found. The Cherokee discovered the cave and mined the gold to fashion their famous jewelry. After they were ''relocated,'' a nineteenth-century settler found the mine and wedged the tree trunks between the walls as he tunneled far past the Cherokee workings. Whoever that settler was, he must have kept the location of the mine a secret, and died without telling anyone about it. In 1958, Simon was now sure, Roy Freedman found the mine while foraging for herbs on Big Momma's abandoned property, and added the modern timbering to further stabilize its walls.

The mine had to be a factor in Eva's murder. He didn't know how, or if Sheriff Guy's murder was related to her death. The obvious next step would be to confront Roy with the existence of the mine, and hope that he'd tell the truth. Otherwise Simon might never figure out the complete story, and June Rinehart's life could be at stake.

Crawling over a tree trunk, Simon in his exhaustion miscalculated and lost his footing. Stumbling to keep from falling, he careened into a dark cleft in the wall of the mine, where he finally fell flat. His chest crunched on something sharp on the floor of the mine. He lost his flashlight, and the light went out. His helmet light illuminated a very small area. Swearing, he groped for the big flashlight. He found it, and thankfully, was able to switch it back on, only to find himself staring into a slack-jawed human skull. In his fall he had crushed the rib cage of a skeleton.

Simon flung himself off the corpse, scuttling backward until he hit the wall of the mine, his flashlight trained on the corpse.

"Jesus H. Christ," he said. He found himself gripping the flashlight as if it were a weapon, with his injured hand pressed to his pounding heart. He raked the skeleton with the light. Whoever it was had been dead a long time. Dust hovered over its rib cage, where Simon had crushed it in his fall. So much for avoiding corpses.

"At least you're not gooey," Simon said.

In the light of Simon's flashlight the skeleton seemed to be laughing at him. The skull faced him, its lower jaw hanging loose, so that its open empty mouth gaped gleefully. The skull's staring eye sockets looked right at him.

Simon took a deep breath, and crawled over to the skeleton. The corpse's cause of death had to be the deep, round dent in one temple. Cracks radiated from the dent. The death blow couldn't have been a natural event—the shape of the dent was too symmetrical. Simon could think of a couple of handy items that could make that dent, like a walking stick with a round knob, a miner's tamp, or the upended handle of a shovel.

The skeleton had once been a man wearing blue overalls, a flannel shirt, heavy canvas coat, and work boots with natural leather soles. Gingerly Simon patted the corpse down. He found no identification, no wallet, nothing that could identify the victim.

He did feel the outline of a couple of coins in one pocket of the man's overalls. He had to work them out carefully, since the pocket was sealed shut by the damp decaying fabric. He finally removed three modern coins—a Jefferson nickel and two Jefferson pennies, all minted in the fifties. The earliest was dated 1956. Obviously the man died no earlier than 1956.

Now Simon really wanted to get out of the mine. Moving as fast as he dared, he reached its mouth, crawled out from under the boulder, and rolled over the damp ground into the dell. He lay gasping flat on his back, gripping grass with both hands, breathing as though he had been suffocating. He noticed that it was still quite light. He felt as though days should have passed while he was inside.

Later Simon barely remembered his trip down the mountain. In a daze he stripped off his clothes in Luther's bathroom, took two dog morphine tablets, and showered. Afterward he dressed and had two peanut-butter-and-peach-jam sandwiches on toasted bread and a beer. The alcohol and dog morphine created a pleasant buzz. He went outside and climbed into Luther's old hammock, turning his face away from the sun and pulling up an old quilt he had brought from the house. He swayed and thought, planning his next move.

He knew the identity of the corpse in the cave, who killed Eva Potter, and who murdered Sheriff Guy. But it was a complicated story, and proving it to the proper authorities required him to set a trap, a trap that he couldn't construct unless he kept the discovery of the skeleton and the mine to himself for a while longer. That was okay. They'd both been there a long time and would keep a few more days.

He heard the sound of a heavy truck on the road. Hank must have brought gravel to repair the washout. Simon reluctantly got out of his hammock cocoon and walked, stiffly, down the road. Sure enough, gravel flowed from the back of a dump truck into the washout. Hank's Ford truck and Big Momma's pickup were parked behind it. The dump truck driver stood on the load and guided the gravel into the deep hole in the road, while on the ground Hank and Rocky spread the gravel evenly with a shovel and a rake.

"Hey, there," Hank said. "Give us a hand."

Simon raised his injured left hand, still in the immobilizer.

"What happened to you?"

"Slipped in the mud and smacked it on a rock."

"Is it broken?"

"I don't think so."

Big Momma sat on a log nearby watching the work, so Simon went to sit down next to her. No one spoke to Rocky. They knew he'd walk off if they did.

"Big Momma," Simon said. "After these folks are gone, we need to talk."

TWELVE

"PROFESSOR SIMON," Big Momma said, "I don't know what to say. It's so nice here. Did you know there's two rooms, and a kitchenette? We don't need all this. Rocky and I could share a regular room. Did you know you give us a hundred dollars? Some twenties must have stuck together. We can't spend all this, or I'll never be able to pay you back."

"Don't worry about that," Simon said, cradling his cell phone to his ear. "Enjoy yourselves. I'm taking care of everything. You all just stay out of sight as best you can."

"There's a fried chicken place across the way. Rocky loves fried chicken. Can we go over there?"

"Sure. Just stay out of sight of the main road."

"Can we buy one of the movies off the television? There's one with aliens in it. Rocky loves alien movies. I could pay you back for that, for sure."

"Of course. You all lie low, and enjoy yourselves."

"How long before you tell us what's going on?"

"Not too long, I don't think."

Simon hung up. He didn't have much time. He needed to spread some gossip fast, just to the locals, though. Students, tourists, and retirees weren't suspects. They didn't live in Boone in 1958.

SIMON FOUND Aunt Rae in her kitchen, floury from rolling out biscuits. The radio played Elvis singing "How Great Thou Art" in the background.

"Hi, sweetie," he said.

"Don't you 'hi sweetie' me. I haven't seen or heard from you since you left this house on Wednesday morning."

Simon circled her waist with his arms and kissed her cheek.

"I've been busy, talking to people about the Potter murder. And I was stuck at Luther's cabin, you know."

"You could have got out if you'd wanted to."

She saw Simon's wrist.

"What happened?"

"Slipped and fell on it."

"Been to a doctor?"

"Nah. Been drinking heavily instead."

She slapped at him, and he ducked.

"Aren't you going to ask me to dinner?"

"I guess there's enough. Hank and Debra are coming. I invited your Uncle Mel, too."

Simon raised an eyebrow.

"Don't look at me like that," she said. "It don't mean anything. I feel sorry for Mel, with Micah Guy dying like that, and Mrs. Rinehart getting arrested. You did hear about that?"

"Yeah, I heard."

"Antifreeze, of all things."

"What time's dinner?"

"You're leaving?"

"Got a couple of errands to run."

"Six o'clock, just like always."

SIMON SLID ONTO the stool at the lunch counter of the Boone Drug Store between two old-timers. He ordered the drug store's famous orangeade, made from orange juice and Sprite.

"Hey," he said to the bearded man sitting next to him. He was eating a platter of baked pork chops, collards, mashed potatoes, cabbage, and biscuits.

"Hey, yourself," the bearded man said. "Do I know you?"

"I'm Simon Shaw, Rae Coffey's nephew," Simon said.

"Sure," the bearded man said. "I remember who you are. You're that professor from Raleigh. I'm Lucas Pride. I know your family well."

The bald man on the other side of Simon, reached out his hand to Simon, too. "I'm Avery Moss," he said. "I own the gas station out near Rae's store." Moss was about halfway through a plate of apple pie and vanilla ice cream.

"You need to get you some of these eats," Pride said, gesturing at his plate.

"I'm having dinner at Aunt Rae's."

"You ain't staying there?"

"No, I'm out at my cousin Luther's cabin. Watching out for things. He's in jail until Monday. And the Harlisses are gone, too."

"Where'd those two get to?"

"To Asheville. Rocky has got to check in at the hospital there, and get his prescriptions refilled where it's free."

"I don't like that man running loose," Pride said. "It's just a matter of time before he shoots someone."

"I knew him when he was a kid," Moss said. "He was okay then."

Simon paid his chit and strolled down the street to

Farmer's Hardware, where he found a group of local men sunning themselves in the rocking chairs lined up in front of the store. He sat down in the only vacant one, rocked a bit, then introduced himself casually as a member of the Shaw-Coffey extended clan, declared that he was staying at his cousin's cabin on Fat Boy Road, and thank goodness the Harlisses were gone to the VA Hospital in Asheville for a few days so he didn't have to worry about getting shot walking down his own road.

Then he ambled up the street toward the Sheriff's Office, stopping at the Candy Barrel next door to the Mast General Store for a bag of chocolate-dipped soft peppermints, Luther's favorite. He didn't expect either Sheriff Hughes or Deputy Lyall to be there late on Saturday afternoon, but a deputy was minding the reception area.

"Hey," he said to the deputy.

"Hey, yourself," he said.

"Is the sheriff in?"

"No," he said, peering at the computer screen. Simon had the distinct impression that the deputy didn't enjoy weekend reception duty.

"Deputy Lyall?"

"No. But they'll both check in later, I expect."

"Just out of morbid curiosity, is June Rinehart being held here?"

"Not anymore. She posted bail."

That was good news. Simon needed all his suspects available to fall into his trap.

"Then could I speak to my cousin, Luther Coffey?"

"Visiting hours is over."

"I just wanted to give him this," Simon said, holding out the bag of candy.

"I can take it back to him."

"Let me write him a note." Simon borrowed a piece

of paper and a pen. "I want him to know everything's all right at the cabin after the storm. There wasn't any damage to speak of."

Simon folded over the note and tucked it inside the bag. "Except part of Big Momma's bridge washed away. You can still get across the creek on one beam with the guide rope, though."

"I don't see how those people can keep living there. The woman's old, and her boy is half-crazy."

"I'll say," Simon said. "They're in Asheville right now, at the VA psych unit, getting Rocky his checkup and prescriptions."

"Wouldn't want him to run out of his medicine."

"No, we would not."

SIMON GOT BACK to Aunt Rae's at a quarter of six. Since her home was an alcohol-free zone, he popped another morphine tablet in the car before going into the house. He was beginning to feel a little guilty about abusing alcohol and canine prescription drugs to ease his pain in his wrist. If his wrist wasn't better by Monday, he'd go to the Emergency Room and get an X-ray.

He met Hank and Debra walking over from their trailer. Debra held a steaming casserole. Simon sniffed hungrily.

"What's that?" he asked.

"Hello to you, too," she said, pecking him on the cheek. "Creamed corn."

Mel's truck was parked right up in the yard outside the porch.

As they walked inside, they heard Rae talking.

"You always did park on the yard instead of on the driveway. This isn't a trailer park. Why do you do it?"

"To annoy you, why else?" Uncle Mel answered. The

three of them got inside the door just in time to see Aunt Rae ward off Uncle Mel's embrace.

"We're separated, don't forget," she said.

"Yes, ma'am, and I thank the Lord for it every day," he said, winking at them.

Aunt Rae ignored him, toting food into the dining room.

The five of them sat down at the table. They all knew better than to remark on the fact that Luther wasn't there because he was in jail, because they feared Aunt Rae might start to sermonize. No one wanted to mention Micah Guy's murder, or June Rinehart's arrest, either, because that could get Uncle Mel started.

Simon concentrated on heaping fried chicken, ham, creamed corn, steamed broccoli with cheese sauce, fresh sliced tomatoes, and hot biscuits onto his plate. He didn't know what was for dessert, but he intended to find out. Since he was destined to be single, and not have a wife to take care of him properly, as Aunt Rae predicted, he felt obligated to take advantage of home-cooked meals whenever he could.

Hank thought of an uncontroversial subject and broke the silence at the table.

"What did you do for two days up at Luther's?" he asked Simon.

"Read, listened to music, watched TV," Simon said. "I rather enjoyed it."

"Have you made any progress on the research you were doing on Eva Potter's murder?" Debra asked.

"Very little," Simon said, with his mouth full. "I expect Roy Freedman's guilty. What's for dessert?"

Aunt Rae brought a tray laden with plates of dark chocolate cake with fudge frosting from the kitchen. Debra refused a piece. Simon took the biggest one.

"When you reach middle age and finally start to put on weight, I plan to be there to enjoy it," Debra said to him.

Aunt Rae folded her napkin carefully, placing it in her napkin ring to use again.

"You all have coffee without me," she said. "I have lots to do to get ready for church tomorrow. I've got to iron my choir robe and read the lesson for Sunday School. And I've got to memorize a prayer," she said. She looked pointedly at Simon. "I'm leading the prayer for sinners."

Simon concentrated on his piece of cake, while Debra tried to distract her mother.

"Church should be full tomorrow, what with the Neely baptism and the reception for the pastor's birthday and all," Debra said.

Simon searched his plate for the last remaining crumbs, smooshed them together on his fork, and ate them.

"You could have another piece," Hank said.

"You're right, I could," Simon said, and carried his plate into the kitchen.

"You know," he said, his voice carrying from the other room, "I'm going to be alone on the creek until Luther comes home. Big Momma and Rocky have gone to Asheville so he can get his prescriptions filled free at the VA."

AFTER DARK Simon packed a backpack with two Cokes, half-frozen so they'd stay cold, two peanut-butter-and-jelly sandwiches, and a sweatshirt. He unlocked Luther's gun cabinet and removed the four-ten shotgun Uncle Mel had given him years ago. It was a small piece, often a boy's first gun, but it could do anything a bigger, more expensive shotgun could—knock a can off a fence post, kill varmints, or stop a man. He hadn't fired the gun in years, but he was confident he could if he had to. He hefted the shotgun in his hands, sighted down it, and tested the action. Luther had kept it in good working order. Simon found a box of four-ten ammunition and took five shells out, pleased to see they'd been loaded with buckshot. He stuffed them into the backpack, then slipped out the back door of the cabin. No one was around. He locked the shotgun and the backpack in the passenger seat of Luther's truck.

Simon tried not to sleep that night. He doubted anyone would try to climb Big Momma's mountain in the dark, but he couldn't take the chance. As far as he knew, there was no practical way to get onto her property except by way of the bridge, now just a log and a rope, over the creek. He would be bound to hear any car that came down Fat Boy Road at night. He settled in an armchair in the dark living room next to the window that faced the road, and concentrated on staying awake. He drank an entire pot of coffee, watched television, played countless hands of solitaire, and tried, without success, to read one of Luther's Western novels. He fell asleep around three o'clock in the morning.

He awoke at dawn, with a crick in his neck and a backache from sleeping in the chair. He peered out the window. Nothing. He slipped on a jacket and walked down to the road. He was no tracker, but he could tell no one had passed down the road in the night. The crusty, cold mud of the road was undisturbed except for the tracks he had made the night before. Back in the cabin he quickly ate a fried egg sandwich and drank another cup of coffee. He locked up the cabin, went outside, got into Luther's truck, and left. As he drove down Fat Boy Road he carefully left clear tire impressions. If anyone came down the road, they would know he was gone. Everyone around knew he was driving Luther's truck, and they would expect to see Simon's car parked at the cabin.

Simon turned left onto Jefferson Road and, shortly, left again, not into Aunt Rae's driveway, but a hundred yards before, into the driveway of the Christmas tree farm warehouse. The parking lot was deserted. All three loading docks and the office door of the blue corrugated metal building were shut. Simon skirted the mountain of wooden boxes piled up on the lot, used to ship Frasier firs and greenery, and turned up the dirt service road to the tree farm.

At the top of the ridge he turned onto another service road, one that took him the back way to Luther's cabin. A few hundred yards further along the road was blocked by a fallen tree. That was okay. He needed to stop about here, anyway. He didn't want anyone who might be on the Harliss property to hear the truck.

Simon took his backpack and shotgun out of the truck and walked down the road. When he got to the place where he might be visible from Fat Boy Road, he went off the road and made the rest of his way undercover. He passed Luther's cabin and stopped in the underbrush. He saw and heard nothing.

Quickly he crossed Big Momma's log bridge and went up the hill, passed behind her shack, and continued up the mountain. When he reached the dell he circled it, looking for a protected spot where he could see the mine and the path. He hid behind a fallen log, loaded his shotgun, and waited. He didn't really expect to see anyone until after church. When the sun was high overhead, he ate his sandwiches. He was struggling not to doze off when he heard someone coming up the path, and who-ever it was wasn't trying to be quiet.

Simon got to his knees, raised his shotgun, and laid his index finger alongside the trigger. For once, he was going to have the damn gun.

Deputy Sheriff Lyall walked into the dell. He was dressed for spelunking, wearing a miner's helmet, head-lamp, boots, and thick warm clothes. A hand pick hung from the belt of his gun holster. Simon stepped into the dell and raised his shotgun.

"Raise your hands, way high, Lyall."

Simon had never seen anyone look so surprised.

"What..." the deputy started to say.

"Shut up, and put your hands up."

Lyall did as he was told.

"Now take your left hand, unbuckle your holster, and drop it to the ground."

"I can explain," he said, but he did what Simon told him.

"So can I," Simon said. "Now kick the gun away."

Lyall did it.

"Have you got a satellite phone?" Simon asked.

Lyall nodded.

"Dial the Sheriff's Office, then toss the phone over here to me," Simon said.

THIRTEEN

THE LITTLE DELL teemed with more people than had been there in probably a hundred years. Big Momma and Rocky weren't among them, they were holed up in the motel with a banker and a lawyer Hank had recommended. By now Big Momma knew she could repay Simon for the motel room and fried chicken dinner.

Deputies from the Sheriff's Office laid a portable bridge, really just two wide metal tracks, across Shaw's Creek. The Humvee made two trips to get everyone up the mountain: the sheriff and two deputies, a crime scene photographer, Simon and Luther, and two archaeologists. When Simon had called Gordon McLeod to tell him about the mine, he'd given Simon the name of a professor at the ASU Archaeology Laboratory who would want to explore the workings. At Simon's urging, Big Momma had given the archaeologists her permission to go to the dell and protect the ancient mine and whatever artifacts they could find, much to the irritation of the sheriff, who was plenty displeased with Simon already.

The sheriff stood next to the boulder that led to the mine opening, arguing with the professor, who was dressed in spelunking gear and carrying a video camera. Two deputies and the photographer, also dressed for caving, waited nearby for the argument to be resolved. The archaeology graduate student sat on the ground, oblivious to the cold and damp, carefully removing dirt from around the smelter. Simon found her very attractive. She was petite, pretty, and, from the conversation they'd had in the Humvee, smart. She wasn't wearing any rings on her left hand, and he could have sworn she'd glanced at his wedding-ring finger, too.

Simon himself sat on the ground with his back to a tree, watching the activity. His left wrist was freshly cast, in a sling, and he was enjoying legal drugs. Luther, now out of jail, had taken the morning off to watch the fun.

"How much gold is in that mine, do you think?" Luther asked him.

"Lots."

"How much is lots?"

"I don't know. More than enough for Big Momma to build a house with many bathrooms and a bridge a tank could drive over."

"How on earth did you know it was there?"

"It seemed to me that the principals in this story, everyone from Roy Freedman to June Rinehart, were hiding something other than who killed Eva Potter. Before our illustrious ancestors settled here, this creek had a Cherokee name, 'Way to Wealth.' I looked for the wealth."

"So who did kill Eva Potter? And who's the dead guy in the mine?"

The group gathered around the mine solved their argument. The professor went in first, then the photographer, and then the deputies with a folding stretcher. It was going to be a tough job to get the corpse out of there.

Sheriff Hughes walked over to Simon and Luther. He

had been furious with Simon last night, when he'd taken the call from his office informing him that Professor Simon Shaw had found a lost gold mine, discovered a corpse, and that deputies had arrested Senior Deputy Sheriff George Lyall for trespass and larceny. He was still angry.

"I would like to know," he said to Simon, "what you thought you were doing. You should have called me with your suspicions, not set a trap. Anything could have happened."

"Deputy Lyall is in charge of communications. If I called you, he'd have heard about it, and it would have scared him off. I had to catch him in the act of visiting the mine."

"You trespassed on private property."

"Big Momma gave me permission to be here."

"You assaulted a sheriff's deputy with a firearm. That's a serious charge."

"What, am I on an alien planet? Isn't this North Carolina? I'm on a neighbor's land, with her permission, looking after her interests. I brought my shotgun to protect myself from snakes and such, like any good Southerner would. When Deputy Lyall appeared under such suspicious circumstances, surely I had the right to detain him until the proper authorities arrived."

"Okay, okay," the sheriff said. "Forget it."

"Did you call Chaplain Mitchell at Central Prison?"

"Yeah, we talked early this morning. He says Roy Freedman has corroborated your theory, and Freedman's ready to make a full statement. The chaplain says Freedman wants you to attend his allocution. He wants you to hear all the details."

"I can do that."

"June Rinehart's story agrees with your theory, too."

"Good."

"So give me a break," Hughes said. "Tell me everything, from the beginning. And please include who the dead guy is."

"The corpse is Earl Barefoot."

"The Potters' other boarder? According to the file on Eva's murder, he'd left town days before she was killed."

"He never left," Simon said.

"Start at the beginning, please."

"Roy Freedman and Earl Barefoot found the mine while foraging for herbs. Naturally they wanted to keep it secret, the property didn't belong to them. Their plan was to mine the gold on the sly. Earl pretended to leave town. Instead he came and camped up here, guarding the place."

"It might have worked," Hughes said.

"Yes, except Roy was madly in love with Eva Potter. He proposed to her down at the river beach. When she refused, he tried to change her mind by telling her about the gold. She didn't believe him. Roy will have to tell us the details, but at that point I think he went to the mine to get some gold to prove to her that he was going to be a rich man. Earl Barefoot ran into Eva, maybe while he was down at the river getting water. She told him that she knew about the mine. Earl was a rough man. Maybe he didn't like the idea that she knew about the gold mine, maybe she threatened to tell her father, I don't know. He killed her, drove her corpse up to the Parkway in Roy's truck, which Roy had left parked on Fat Boy Road, pushed the truck off the road with her body inside, and hitchhiked back. I don't know exactly what happened next, but when Roy found out Earl had killed Eva, he murdered Earl in a rage. I expect that the medical examiner will find that the dent in Earl's skull was made by one of the tools down in the mine.''

Luther had been leaning up against the tree, smoking, enjoying the spectacle. He dropped his cigarette onto the ground and crushed it with his boot.

''So Roy went to prison for Eva's murder, which he didn't commit, because that way he could still keep the mine secret,'' Luther said.

''That's right,'' Simon said. ''If he'd fingered Earl as Eva's murderer, he'd have to reveal the location of the mine so the authorities could find Earl's body. But then he'd go to jail for Earl's murder and conspiracy. But by confessing to Eva's murder, the mine remained a secret, and he thought there was a tiny chance he could get back to it someday.''

''A very small chance,'' Hughes said.

''Yes, but it was worth it to him. What difference did it make which murder he went to prison for? Then Eva's body was found, and June went to see him in prison to save his immortal soul,'' Simon said. ''Roy jumped at the chance to try to get out of prison, to get back to the mine. He insisted he didn't kill Eva, told June about the mine, the whole story. She didn't believe him. So he directed her to a hiding spot in her old house, in a closet, where he'd hidden a nugget of gold. She found it there.''

''And she hightailed it back to Raleigh,'' Luther said.

''Roy read about me in the newspaper, and he thought of a plan to recruit me to help them,'' Simon said. ''Sheriff Guy had mistreated Roy to get his confession, and their scheme was, since Guy was living in June's rest home, that June would needle him into telling me about it. I would arrive in Boone and start poking around in time to hear Guy's confession. Roy would get a new trial, or pardoned, and he and June would share the spoils of the mine.''

"But Big Momma and Rocky were living here," Luther said.

"Exactly. And this is where Roy and June's plan went awry. Deputy Lyall knew about the mine."

"How?" Sheriff Hughes said.

"The same way I did," Simon said. "Remember, he read a lot of old files when he reorganized your Records Department. He spotted the same inconsistencies in the Freedman case that I did. He confronted Sheriff Guy. He wondered what Roy Freedman was hiding, searched this mountain, and found the mine. He's been stealing gold a little bit at a time, not enough to attract attention to his lifestyle, until the Harlisses came home."

"It's still hard for me to believe that Deputy Lyall killed Sheriff Guy," Hughes said.

"He visited Guy Tuesday evening at the rest home and found me having dinner with my uncle. He didn't know Uncle Mel lived there, and he was sure that Guy would break down and tell me everything. He went out to his truck, got a can of antifreeze, and some time during the evening he laced Guy's iced tea with it.''

"Don't tell me, he got the idea to use antifreeze from Big Momma's case file," Hughes said.

"Why did he take the chance to come up here yesterday?" Luther asked.

"Think. The Harlisses have been here for a couple of years. He couldn't visit the mine. I spread it all over that Big Momma and Rocky had left town for a few days. Lyall couldn't resist the chance to fill his pockets. He didn't know when he'd get the chance again."

"I hope we can persuade Lyall to plead guilty," Hughes said. "I'd like to avoid the publicity of a trial."

Hughes walked off to the mouth of the mine, shaking his head grimly. Luther followed him, eager to see what the deputies brought out.

Simon tried not to stare at the grad student. She wore thigh-high hiking shorts, hiking boots, a sleeveless blue shirt, and a silver chain with a turquoise charm dangling from it. She'd pulled her long dark hair through a baseball cap. She had some meat on her bones, thank goodness. He was going to ask the woman to have dinner with him. If she turned out to be engaged or otherwise unavailable, he'd cruise the clubs with Luther over the weekend. Time to start his new role as carefree womanizer. Maybe he'd stay in Boone for a couple more weeks.

"By the way," Luther said, walking back to Simon. "I forgot to tell you. Julia called. She said she hoped you'd be back in Raleigh by the weekend."

EPILOGUE

SIMON AND ROY Freedman were alone in the conference room at Central Prison, except for the guard at the door. The court reporter had packed up her equipment and left. Chaplain Mitchell, who turned out to be a pudgy, peppermint-chewing Episcopal priest with a nicotine patch on one arm, had been called away to help cope with a violent patient in the prison infirmary.

"You see," Roy said. "It didn't matter to me which murder I went to prison for, I was going. I thought maybe something would happen to where I could get out, somehow."

"Then they found Eva's body."

"Yeah, I never knew where Earl had dumped her, so I couldn't tell her daddy and momma where her remains were. I would have if I had known."

"What happens to you now, Roy?"

Roy visibly brightened.

"Chaplain Mitchell, he called this professor at the UNC law school. He's going to make my case a class project. He thinks I can get pardoned for innocence, then get my sentences for conspiracy to defraud and for Earl's murder plea-bargained for time served. You know, it should qualify for second-degree murder. I killed him in a fit of rage, and all that."

"I'll say. That was some dent in his skull."

Roy rubbed his eyes. They were bloodshot and underlined with dark creases, as if he hadn't slept well in several days.

"It happened so fast. When Earl told me he'd killed Eva, he acted as if it was nothing, as if I'd agree that her telling her daddy about the mine was worth her life. I was so angry. I don't know, maybe if I wasn't holding a hand pick right then, I might not have hit him, I might have turned him over to Sheriff Guy, I wouldn't have spent most of my life in prison."

"You kept that gold mine a secret from its owners. They've been almost destitute for years."

"It was wrong, but there's no law against it. I never took any gold out of the mine but that little piece I had hid behind the light switchplate in my closet. Earl and I hadn't figured out how we'd sell it without getting found out yet."

"If you're released, what will you do?"

"June, I mean Mrs. Rinehart, said I could come work for her, her maintenance man is going to be retiring soon. She reminds me so much of Eva. She's an attractive woman, don't you think?"

AN ELDERHOSTEL MYSTERY

PAINTED LADY

PETER
ABRESCH

James P. Dandy and his ladylove, Dodee Swisher, embark on an Elderhostel adventure along the old Santa Fe Trail. But before the trip even gets under way, Jim sees a Native American woman plunge to her death from a Denver rooftop. He suspects that the woman was pushed.

Soon it's clear somebody thinks Jim knows the whereabouts of a priceless Mayan artifact—a misconception that is becoming dangerous to both Jim and Dodee.

Another grisly murder occurs on the historic trail through the Wild West, and mysteries old and new find Jim caught in a shoot-out with a killer determined to make this Dandy's Last Stand.

"...a suspect-rich plot with a revealing glimpse of small-town life... evocative descriptions of the desert and mountains of the Southwest."
—*Booklist*

Available April 2004 at your favorite retail outlet.

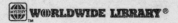

WPA488

DOROTHY KLIEWER

MURDER
IN THE SWAMP
A DEEDRA MASEFIELD MYSTERY

A woman's body is dragged from the fetid, swampy end of a
tiny lake. She is the latest victim in a string of murders, and
newspaper reporter Deedra Masefield is determined to break
the story. None of the longtime residents of this desolate
California town is above suspicion.

Barely surviving a plunge into the frigid, terrifying depths of
the swamp herself, Deedra discovers grisly secrets beneath
the surface and makes the stunning connection between the
murderer and his victims. She's finally got her killer story—
she's just got to live long enough to tell it.

Available April 2004 at your favorite retail outlet.

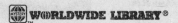 **W❂RLDWIDE LIBRARY** ®

WDK490

MURDER IN A HEAT WAVE

A MARTHA PATTERSON MYSTERY

A wilting summer heat wave is bringing out the worst in the tenants of septuagenarian Martha Patterson's Greenwich Village apartment building. She agrees to join the co-op board to help facilitate some badly needed change. It's a thankless job—and a deadly one when the president of the board, Arnold Stern, is murdered.

Martha soon discovers Stern was extremely unpopular. A trail of suspicion leads to several tenants, including her neighbor and good friend, an ailing archaeologist whose priceless Greek antiquity becomes a subtle but crucial clue. An innocent secret exposes the killer—and unravels a murder prompted by greed, jealousy...and undoubtedly, the heat.

"...the real prizes are the heroine's shrewd, unassuming intelligence and the authorial voice... consistently entertaining."
—*Kirkus Reviews*

Available April 2004 at your favorite retail outlet.

GRETCHEN SPRAGUE

 W⬤RLDWIDE LIBRARY ®

WGS489

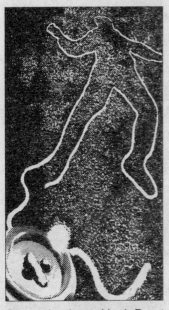

BUTTONS & FOES

A MANDY DYER MYSTERY

Dolores Johnson

Denver dry cleaner Mandy Dyer is shocked to learn that a favorite customer has died and left Mandy something—two trash bags packed with worthless old clothing. Full of questions, Mandy notices some antique buttons sewn onto the dresses and suspects the woman was trying to send her a message.

Convinced the button mystery is linked to her friend's sudden demise, Mandy starts nosing around the local button-collecting clubs…and stumbles onto another murder. And while removing bloodstains may be a cinch for an expert dry cleaner, Mandy hopes she won't have to try her luck against a cold-blooded killer.

"…entertaining, amusing amateur sleuth."
—Harriet Klausner

Available March 2004.

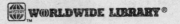 **WORLDWIDE LIBRARY**®

WDJ487